IF ONLY YOU KNEW

THEO BAXTER

INKUBATOR
BOOKS

Published by Inkubator Books
www.inkubatorbooks.com

Copyright © 2024 by Theo Baxter

Theo Baxter has asserted his right to be identified as the author of this work.

ISBN (eBook): 978-1-83756-422-4
ISBN (Paperback): 978-1-83756-423-1
ISBN (Hardback): 978-1-83756-424-8

1

"Teddy, I can't do this anymore. I feel like I'm walking on eggshells around you; you manipulate every word I say—"

"Every word you say? Please, Emily, you can barely string a sentence together."

Emily closed her eyes and took a deep breath. She knew this would happen. She knew he would contradict her every word and make her second-guess herself. "Teddy, listen to me."

"I'm driving, and it's raining. I have to focus."

"You always have some excuse not to listen to me. I'm done! I know how you knew that woman at the restaurant—"

"The server? I met her at the same time you did."

"I was talking about the woman at the table next to us. The two of you left at the same time...It's like you're trying to get caught, or make a fool out of me."

"Em, you're rambling. You had far too much to drink tonight."

"I had only one glass of wine," Emily recounted. "I'm always careful with my drinks around you."

Teddy jerked the steering wheel as he whipped his head around.

Emily jumped, but she knew the car was fine. He did things like this on purpose to throw her off, make her worry and forget herself.

"You had more than one; I remember refilling your glass," Teddy growled, staring back at the road. The rain was coming down harder, but he started driving faster.

"I didn't drink the wine. I switched to water. I know you're having an affair with that woman. I've seen you two together before. I am not doing this anymore, Teddy. I'm not going to sit in the corner and watch myself shrink as you gaslight me into believing I'm crazy and scare me so much I'm unable to walk around my own home without flinching. I'm leaving you, and I—"

Emily didn't get to finish her sentence. The car suddenly jerked off the road just as her seatbelt came loose.

The last thing she remembered was seeing Teddy's smiling face as the car wrapped itself around a tree.

EMILY GRAY STARED at the wall, watching a fly trying to get out of the office and back into the world. It buzzed in circles up toward the ceiling, then back down to the ancient clock on the wall, chasing a beam of light. Each time the fly thought he'd figured it out, he would bang his head against the plastered barrier. Its struggle mirrored her own. Every time she thought the divorce proceedings were finally over, she found herself banging her head against another wall.

This was supposed to be the final stretch in her divorce with Teddy Gaunt. It had been dragged out for three years thanks to Teddy's team of high-powered—and very expensive—lawyers. Emily had borrowed money from her father and sister and had completely depleted her savings trying to disentangle herself from her abusive husband. Yet no matter what she did, she still found herself tied to the man who'd tried to kill her.

"Emily," Sheldon Mason, her lawyer, asked, "are you listening to me?"

Technically, Sheldon was her father's lawyer, a general counsel he retained for business matters, not a divorce expert. It didn't take Sheldon long to learn the ropes of divorce proceedings, and Emily soon realized he was the courtroom bulldog she needed to stand up to Teddy's fancy lawyers. Sheldon was stubborn and protective, and, as the pair grew closer, he became more determined to protect Emily and get what she deserved, but sometimes Emily wondered whether this fight was even worth it.

Teddy lived in a gilded world, one where no one ever said no to him, and he could easily crush anyone who did. Emily's asking for a divorce was the ultimate betrayal in Teddy's eyes, and he was determined to systematically ruin her life. At first he'd succeeded, dragging out a mediation into a divorce trial, knowing full well that Emily couldn't afford a trial. He'd contested her small settlement from their prenuptial agreement, claiming that she'd petitioned for divorce in bad faith and had an affair, which nullified their agreement and left Emily with even less.

"Earth to Emily, come in, please," Sheldon said.

She turned back to the papers on the desk in front of her. Copies of email conversations; letters from her ex's former mistresses detailing their encounters and the money he'd paid to keep them silent; transcripts of text conversations;

hospital records—it was a small piece of the damning puzzle Teddy didn't know they were putting together. Sheldon had showed it to Emily at their last meeting and had asked for her permission to present it to the judge presiding over the divorce proceedings. It could damage Teddy's reputation, but it would also give the judge some context into the marriage and hopefully help him land on Emily's side.

For years Teddy had been manipulating everything Emily and Sheldon said to make her seem crazy. His alleged affairs became proof that Emily suffered from delusions of grandeur, and the car accident Teddy caused was painted as a suicide attempt from Emily. Emily had been trying to avoid this moment—she was sure Teddy would eventually see reason and stop this campaign of terror—but she was wrong. He wasn't going to let up.

"They have to know the truth about the accident," Sheldon said. "It was smart of you to record it. The fact you did means somewhere deep down you knew Teddy would try to weasel his way out of the blame."

Emily had resisted using the video of Teddy unlatching her seatbelt—which she hadn't known about until she'd watched the video—and driving the car into a ditch. She'd recorded the accident for her own protection, and out of sheer dumb luck, Teddy never found out. Occasionally she rewatched it when she was alone. Seeing video evidence that she wasn't crazy was the only thing that cured her insomnia.

"I just don't want to ruin his life," she admitted. "I know he's an asshole, and I don't want you to mistake me feeling guilty for second thoughts about the divorce. I can't help it. I did love him once."

"Emily," Sheldon said, extending his hand for her to hold, "Thaddeus Gaunt is a narcissist. He wanted to win your love to have power over you, and now that you have escaped, all he wants is to crush you. This is the only way we can prove everything he's been saying is a lie."

Emily blinked back the tears stinging her eyes. She knew Sheldon was right. Teddy was relentless, and he also had money and family connections. The recording was all she had. It was her ace card in the fight to extricate herself from their marriage. Still, entering the tape into the proceedings meant another day sitting in a stifling courtroom, feeling Teddy's eyes boring into her skull. The thought of having to go through with it made Emily want to puke. She still had nightmares.

Years on from the accident, her body had recovered, but her mind was stuck in that car. She could still hear the faint voice of her father begging the police to take the complaint seriously while she was lying in a hospital bed. There were tubes stuck down her throat and needles pumping her with painkillers, so she couldn't tell her father it was fruitless. Teddy's pockets were deep, and the police department often reached into them. There was no way anyone would believe he'd caused the accident.

A loud smack on the desk brought her back to the present moment.

"Sorry, there was a fly buzzing around in here," Sheldon said, wiping his hands on a handkerchief.

THE REST of their meeting went by in a blur. Emily tuned out as Sheldon talked through his strategy and what he was planning to present to the judge. He reviewed his counterarguments to the allegations Teddy's lawyers had made and the evidence he had to prove them. Sheldon told her how he would use the text message transcripts and the signed statements from Teddy's mistresses, but Emily didn't pay much attention. She trusted Sheldon now, and he could do whatever he wanted.

Emily left the office and walked to her car and got in, locking the door as she sat there. A small part of her wondered if she *was* crazy, maybe. It was what made Emily resist. She loved Teddy, and she remembered what he was like before they married. He had been charming and thoughtful, and it was hard to believe that he was the same person all these years later.

That's the gaslighting, depression, and post-abuse trauma talking, she said to herself. *Teddy made you give up your whole life, he took what little happiness you had left, and then he spent three years stripping away everything else.*

Then she burst into tears. Emily screamed, laid on the horn, made as much noise as she could, but nothing could match the bubble of anger and anxiety inside her. She wanted to go back in time and prevent herself from ever meeting Thaddeus Gaunt in the first place. She wanted to tear her hair out and start all over again from the beginning. She wanted to at least upgrade her old Corolla, but she couldn't afford to thanks to Teddy. It was a wonder he hadn't managed to get her driver's license taken away again, as he'd done after the accident. Not that it had mattered anyway, Emily had been so traumatized, it was over a year before she could get into a car again.

Emily punched the steering wheel, angry at everything, especially that she had to stoop as low as Teddy just to get back some semblance of a normal life.

If it even works.

There was a chance his lawyers could spin this in his favor. After all, they kept finding legal loopholes to keep the case going. But Sheldon felt the judge was ready to hear Emily's side of the story and finally end the proceedings. Emily wanted to believe Sheldon's theory, but she couldn't help but feel that this last-ditch effort at a fair settlement would crumble at the finish line.

She laid her head back and continued to sob until no more tears fell from her eyes. All the trust she had in Sheldon meant nothing. She'd once trusted Teddy with her whole life, and look where that had got her: driving a shitty car, living in a house that was basically her father's, in debt up to her eyeballs, and always looking over her shoulder, bracing herself for the next bomb coming her way.

Emily's life was exhausting. She had lost all sense of her own creativity and independence. There wasn't much to live for, really. Nothing but the tiny bead of hope that she could outlast Teddy's ire and rebuild her life, one step at a time.

Emily knew she was spiraling. The thought of that fly trying to escape Sheldon's office kept popping back into her head, causing her to start sobbing all over again. Was this a panic attack? Emily couldn't tell anymore. It was hard to differentiate between actual panic and despair.

Dr. Wright, her therapist, had armed her with mental exercises for moments just like this; the only problem was sometimes, when Emily felt this desperate, she couldn't remember a single one.

Just close your eyes and count to ten. Count every breath that goes in, every breath that comes out. Just keep counting to ten over again.

Emily started shakily counting her breath, in and out, until she got to ten, then started again from one. It took a little longer than usual, but her breathing started to regulate itself, and her heartbeat slowed down. Finally, her hands stopped shaking, and her mind stopped spinning out of control.

Just as Emily was ready to drive home, her phone started ringing.

She froze, fearing that it was Sheldon saying Teddy's lawyers had filed another motion or some other terrible thing.

She turned over her phone but saw a different number. It was someone who made her stomach turn over for different reasons. Someone who made her really happy and nervous at the same time, the way Teddy had done in the beginning.

William Summers.

William was Emily's comfort at a time when she needed it most. He was also, in part, the reason Teddy was so angry with Emily. In Teddy's eyes, William was responsible for their divorce. Teddy believed William had seduced Emily, who then cheated on Teddy, and now the two of them were dead set on stealing the Gaunt family fortune.

Even though none of that was true, Sheldon had recommended that Emily cut ties with William as soon as she filed for divorce, so Teddy's lawyers had less ammunition. Emily dutifully did as told and ignored all messages and calls from William. Eventually he got the hint. So she was surprised to hear from him now, even though she had texted him her new number. She hadn't wanted to sever their connection completely. And now, he was calling her, and she wasn't sure if it had been a wise thing to do.

"Hi," William said. "It's been a long time, and I wanted to see how you're doing."

I'm doing great. My ex-husband, who once tried to kill me, is ruining my life bit by bit, I barely have a job, I don't think I'll ever have a boyfriend again, the only man I see who isn't my own family is my lawyer, and I'm driving a car meant for teenagers.

Instead of blurting all that out, Emily said, "I'm doing alright, all things considered."

William didn't need to know what was actually going on. He could do without the gritty details.

"That's good."

Emily paused, unsure if she should hang up. "It's nice to hear from you."

"I'm glad I got to talk to you," William said. "I wanted to call sooner, but wasn't sure if it would be appropriate. I read about the divorce in the paper."

Emily knew that Teddy's mother had used her connections to put Teddy's "good" name out into the press. The local newspapers were filled with articles about Teddy's philanthropy, his business success, and now his long-suffering love life. It made Emily feel sick. Luckily for her, Sheldon had managed to get the judge to grant an order against mentioning Emily in any of these articles, which, she was sure, would have made her life worse. As it stood, Teddy came off as a prince who was in search of a princess, and all he'd found were nameless toads.

"I get it. Teddy and his mother are on the warpath, and it's best you haven't said anything. Teddy's still—" Emily cut herself off before she started crying again.

"We don't have to talk about that," he said gently. "Why don't we talk about you? What are you up to these days?"

Emily didn't know what to say. She was working as a virtual assistant to pay the bills, but she couldn't afford to go out much since most of her salary went toward her legal fees. It didn't really matter because Teddy had poisoned most of her friendships during their tumultuous eight-year marriage, and those friends had long since moved on with their lives. In her spare time Emily liked to read, but she hadn't been able to concentrate on anything, so her house was now filled with half-read novels and self-help books.

"My life has been taken over by the divorce. There's very little to report apart from that. I moved and live on my own. My dad and sister probably would say hi if they knew we were talking."

"Well, I'll say hi back." He paused. "There was another reason I called."

Emily hoped she knew what came next—her body was involuntarily trembling at the thought.

"I miss you, Emily."

She was touched. But she was afraid to start talking to William again, since the last time they were involved, it pretty much blew up her life.

"Would it be okay if I call you again?" he asked hopefully.

Emily took a deep breath. "Yes."

"Great. I'll talk to you soon." William hung up.

Emily sat in her car, thinking about when she'd first met William. He was a nurse in the hospital where Emily had recovered from her accident. Rather, from the accident that Teddy *caused*. William had attended her in the ICU when she was in a coma and for a while after she woke up.

Emily confessed to William the truth about the accident —that it wasn't a suicide attempt at all, but Teddy getting angry and running the car off the road. Emily also told him that her husband was charming in public, but a manipulative monster in private.

William encouraged her family to get Emily to a safe

place, and comforted her when she separated from Teddy. Their relationship grew into a friendship, which quickly turned into something more.

In the two months after she'd recovered from the accident, when she'd first separated from Teddy, William had brought Emily into his world. He was charismatic, creating friends out of strangers at a bus stop. He was always trying new restaurants or diving into a new hobby. It inspired Emily, who had given up most of her hobbies and her writing career when she married Teddy. William's energy was intoxicating, but not in the same way as Teddy's had been. William encouraged her to come out of her shell, trust in the kindness of strangers, and listen to what they had to say.

"Half of nursing is just listening," William had once explained. "Doctors are always so busy and self-absorbed they don't listen to what their patients are trying to say. I took that to heart and started listening to people. Once you *start* listening, you can't stop. I could listen to people talk forever and just keep asking them questions. But it gets weird after a while."

Emily always felt there was a side to William he kept hidden from other people. It didn't seem sinister—she had enough experience in that department to know William wasn't the same as Teddy—but the closer she had tried to get to him when they were together, the more he'd pulled away emotionally. She'd become convinced it was because there was something wrong with her. Maybe Teddy was right, and no other man could ever love her like he did.

Emily and William ended their relationship amicably, agreed to remain friends, and Emily reached out to her husband. Her father and sister didn't want her to, but Emily went back to Teddy, the only man she had ever loved. At first it seemed like he had finally changed, but she should have known better.

Unbeknownst to her at the time, Teddy's mother had kept tabs on Emily throughout her separation with Teddy. When Emily was back in Teddy's life, seemingly for good, his mother revealed everything to him—the affair, the fact that William was Emily's nurse when she was in the hospital, and William's hospital notes contradicting Teddy's assertion that Emily was suicidal.

She gripped the steering wheel and fought back tears as she remembered the night Teddy found out about William.

Emily had planned a romantic evening for the two of them. Homemade ravioli with a ricotta and butternut squash filling—Teddy's favorite—in a sage butter sauce. She was putting the raviolis into the pan to finish cooking when Teddy stormed into the kitchen. He slapped the pan away, splattering hot butter all over Emily, before pushing her into the wall.

The fight was a blur. She remembered she was crying, and Teddy was accusing her of taking him for a ride while she was secretly involved with William. She'd never told Teddy about the romantic tryst, knowing it would make him angry. But she never thought he would get this angry.

Emily tried to run, but Teddy tripped her, and she fell on the floor. As Emily crawled away, she realized Teddy was pointing a gun at her.

"If I can't have you," he said, his voice low and trembling, "no one can."

Emily braced herself for the bullet. Would it be hot? Would she even feel it? She felt tears stinging her eyes as the strength in her muscles drained away, and she lay on the floor in the fetal position. What else could she do but wait for the inevitable? She should have known that Teddy would never change. It was the same with her mother.

"You're pathetic," Teddy said, the gun clicking in his hand. "Get up." He kicked her onto her back. "It's not even loaded. Don't be such a weakling. Get up and face me."

Emily's whole body shook as she stood. She couldn't look Teddy in the eye. Her mind was spinning. She wasn't sure if she was alive or dead or in another coma, dreaming that Teddy was holding her by the shoulders and turning her chin to face him.

"I am your husband, you got that? I'm the only man you love. You came back to me because you love me, and no one else is going to love you like I do. If I hear about this William again, I'll load that gun, and you won't know if I'm going to use it on him or you until the bullet goes through someone's head." Teddy whipped her head away.

That was when she realized she couldn't stay with Teddy no matter how much she wanted to care for him. That was when she realized she would never survive her marriage.

Emily started and looked around, surprised to see the sun was starting to set. She had to get home. A good night's sleep would help clear the cobwebs, and she could save her worries for her next therapy session.

For now, all she could do was try to forget about the day for a little while.

3

Emily arrived at home in record time. The one good thing about crying in your car for hours was that you missed the rush-hour traffic out of downtown.

She lived in a small townhouse in the near suburbs, with no garage and a fenced-in yard surrounded by large hedges. She'd picked up a surveillance system from the 1980s, with zero connection to the internet, and installed it on her front and back doors. Her father had bought her this place, and Emily paid the mortgage as "rent" to him. When the divorce was finalized, he would transfer the deed to her name. This way she could keep living here, and there was no danger that Teddy would try to take it in the settlement, leaving Emily with no place to live.

Emily was ready to finally settle down for the night. Her day had been stressful, and she wanted to curl up with a book and fall asleep on her couch, maybe with a glass of wine on the table beside her.

Before she could do that, though, she had to go through her arrival ritual. It had started when she was living with her father, right after she'd left Teddy for good. She got into the habit of placing a small piece of tape above the door to make sure no one had entered while they were out. The tape was intact, so that meant Emily was free to go inside.

Next, Emily went around to each window to make sure they were still locked, and that the thin layer of baking soda on the windowsill was undisturbed. She checked the second-floor windows and then went back and checked all the windows for a second time. Then she checked inside every closet with a bright flashlight, just in case, before finally going around to each of the doors and windows a third time and ensuring that everything was locked.

Once Emily did all that, she could finally relax in her own home. Anyone watching would probably think she was crazy, but it was the best she could do to keep her mind at ease. Her therapist said it wasn't unreasonable—Emily had personal experience with abuse; she knew what lengths Teddy would go to if he was angry with her. Sure, he didn't know her current address, phone number, or email that she knew of, but that wasn't a reason to let her guard down. For all she knew, he could have hired someone to find her. She hoped not, but it wasn't outside the realm of possibilities.

Teddy wasn't the first abusive person she'd been around. Her mother was manipulative, and she'd kept Emily and her younger sister, Laurie, under her thumb for most of their childhood. Emily's father did very little to protect them; he was never able to see his wife for what she truly was: a narcissist.

Emily often beat herself up for not seeing Teddy's red flags sooner. There were subtle hints, vague manipulations about where she was going and whom she was going with. He needed to control what she wore and what she ate. It was all stuff her mother used to do, right down to the portion sizes at dinner, which would fluctuate based on whether or not Emily and Laurie had paid enough attention to their mother that day.

She knew, logically, that it wasn't her fault. Just as she knew, logically, that her father wasn't to blame for her mother's actions. Emotionally, Emily couldn't stop thinking that the victim was the one in control, and she and her father both could have done something to stop this abusive behavior. Maybe if she and Teddy had started therapy sooner, things would be different. Or if Emily's father had just moved Emily and Laurie out sooner than he did, then maybe Emily would have had a stronger resolve and wouldn't have ended up back where she started—helpless in the clutches of an emotionally abusive loved one.

Stop it. This line of thinking is catastrophic and not helpful. Instead, she closed her eyes and counted to ten.

When she calmed down, she checked the doors and windows again, then fell into bed.

"Wake up, sleepyhead," a gentle voice cooed in her ear.

Emily opened her eyes. Where was she? The luxurious sheets and bright natural light felt unfamiliar. Then she remembered— last night she'd stayed at Teddy's.

Teddy lay on his side, stroking her hair. He gently kissed her forehead. "You looked so peaceful. I didn't want to wake you."

"I'm glad you did. I could have slept all day in this bed. I can't remember the last time I was this comfortable."

"Sure beats that old spring mattress at your place." He chuckled before pulling away the covers.

Emily groaned.

Teddy tickled her side. "You can't go back to bed now. It's a beautiful day, and I've been slaving away in the kitchen, making you a gorgeous breakfast."

"Serves me right for dating a morning person." She yawned.

Suddenly Emily felt extremely sad, sadder than she could ever remember. It was like a cold hand was reaching through time and clutching her heart. She shivered.

Teddy gave her one of his sweatshirts, an old ratty thing that had seen better days, but still, Emily loved it. It smelled like Teddy, and it was soft even though the cotton had been washed hundreds of times.

She followed him into the kitchen, trying to dismiss the cold feeling deep in her gut. What was wrong with her? Teddy was the perfect man, every single one of her friends agreed, so what was this strange feeling?

"I made shakshuka," Teddy said, pulling out a chair for her. "I had it for the first time in Morocco. It sounds weird, but trust me, it's amazing."

"Did you make me fresh bread?" Emily asked.

Teddy blushed, his cheeks matching the tomato stew in front of him. "Well, it's really not as impressive as it sounds. I have a bread maker, and I started it last night."

"You were that sure I would stay?"

Darkness flashed across Teddy's eyes, gone just as fast as it had appeared. He didn't falter for a second, but the cold hand around Emily's insides tightened. He flushed harder, so Emily rubbed his arm to let him know she was only joking. They both knew she was going to stay, so there was no reason for him to feel embarrassed. That tight, cold feeling didn't let go until she felt Teddy's muscles relax beneath her touch.

Emily turned around, but everything around her had changed. It wasn't morning anymore. It was evening, and she was holding two wineglasses. They were weightless and heavy at the same time—*a fact that was only possible because they were made from expensive Czech crystal. She shivered when she touched them, terrified they would break.*

Teddy laughed. "They're stronger than you think. You don't have to handle them with kid gloves."

Teddy didn't really understand the value of his own glassware because he hadn't bought them. Everything had been purchased by his mother or was a family heirloom. Emily didn't come from the world of heirlooms that had more than sentimental value.

"I know, but I can't afford to replace them, so I'd rather be careful," *she responded.*

Her friends were waiting in the dining room, eager to open Teddy's wine. Heather had been Emily's roommate in college and had met Cal during freshman orientation—the ultimate fairy-tale romance.

Emily had been talking about Teddy nonstop for weeks, bragging about his skills in the kitchen—and elsewhere, but he'd been evasive when it came to actually meeting her friends. Finally, all four were able to get together, and Emily was desperate for the dinner to go well. So far everything was going perfectly.

Still, something loomed in the corners of Emily's mind. She felt confused and on edge, but there was no explanation why.

"You okay?" *Teddy asked, as if he were reading her mind.* "You look a little pale."

"I'm alright. Nerves, I guess. I don't know, something feels... Did you change the lightbulbs or something?" *Emily asked, her voice wavering. The cold feeling in her stomach was spreading throughout her body. Her arms and hands felt like they were filled with ice-cold water.*

"No, they're the same as they've always been," *Teddy said, taking the glasses from her.* "Maybe you should slow down and switch to water." *He strode back into the dining room, grinning from ear to ear.* "What's this that you guys brought, a merlot?" *His laughter rang out.*

Emily leaned over and clutched the kitchen counter. She wasn't quite sure what was going on, but suddenly the whole world felt off-center.

"Emily?" Heather called from the other room.

"She's just prepping a charcuterie board as a little surprise," Teddy told Heather. "But don't tell her I said so."

Emily silently thanked Teddy. That gave her a few minutes to collect herself and breathe through what must be a panic attack. She hated when people saw this side of her, the part of her that got overwhelmed easily, when she couldn't always control her emotions.

She breathed in, imagining the warmth from a fire filling her lungs, and tried to breathe out the freezing cold air trapped in her body. This sudden anxiety was so strange. Emily had never felt it before while with Teddy. He was a calming presence. Maybe it was the nerves, the fear of judgment she felt around her friends. She wanted so badly for them to like Teddy that it was starting to infiltrate her brain and body.

Once Emily had calmed down and prepared a surprisingly lovely and thoughtful charcuterie board, she called out to Teddy for help.

The voices in the dining room became hushed.

Teddy entered the kitchen. "You alright? Sorry if that made more work for you. I just thought—"

"It was perfect. You were perfect. It's like you were reading my mind."

Teddy smiled bashfully. "I know nights like this can be stressful. I hope you know I'll always be your partner. If you're feeling weird or nervous, just say so. I'll be there to help."

"Thank you. I feel—you have no idea how—"

He interrupted her with a kiss.

Emily let herself melt into Teddy's chest. Her whole body was buzzing with the desire to tell him that she loved him, and she wanted to be with him forever.

"I love you," he whispered. "I know it's probably too soon to—"

"I love you too." Emily beamed. It was perfect. Finally, she could see her life falling into place.

"What are you lovebirds doing in there?" Heather called out, breaking the spell between the couple.

The two laughed, their foreheads coming together.

"Be right there," Teddy said, smiling into Emily's eyes. He winked and pulled her in for another kiss.

Emily's heart felt so full she was about to burst. The cold, suffocating feeling was gone, and all that was left was Teddy's warm embrace.

The pair walked out to her friends.

But Emily walked out of his kitchen and into a boardroom. Heather and Cal were nowhere to be found. Instead, she was faced with Teddy, his mother, Belinda Gaunt, and a team of face-less lawyers.

"Teddy, what's going on?" Emily suddenly felt tired and sore, like her whole body had been beaten to a pulp. Her hands started shaking, and it was hard to hold the charcuterie board.

Belinda let out one of her signature snorts of derision.

"It's procedure, honey, for your protection as well as my own," Teddy replied. He held her by the elbow and led her to a chair.

His touch hurt. It felt like needles piercing her skin. Emily wanted to cry and throw up at the same time, but she was so tired she could hardly hold her head up. Teddy kept stroking her head, and every time his hand touched her, Emily winced in pain. Soon she realized she was dripping blood onto the cheese.

"Why am I bleeding?" Emily's voice was hoarse. "Can I have a glass of water and...and a bandage?" she stammered.

For some reason it was hard to think of the right words to say, and her head was pounding. Why was she feeling like this, and where were Heather and Cal? A moment ago, she had been kissing Teddy, and they'd said "I love you" for the first time, and now she was surrounded by angry, suspicious faces, feeling as though she'd been hit by a truck.

"You're bleeding because of the car you used to try to murder my son and steal all his money," Belinda droned. "We're going to be much more careful from here on out. Teddy has been far too kind with you. Emily Gray, you are weak, and I am going to make sure—"

"That's enough," Teddy said, cutting her off. "Can't you see that she's in a vulnerable state right now?"

He was coming to Emily's defense, so it was going to be okay. If she could just lie down and close her eyes, maybe she'd feel better.

"Thaddeus, don't you see? She's jealous of how much you love your mother, and she's trying to drive a wedge between us."

That wasn't true. Emily thought Belinda was overbearing and manipulative, but she was still impressed with the bond between mother and son. All she wanted was a mother of her own, someone who would hold her and protect her fiercely, the way Belinda did for Teddy. But Belinda didn't care about Emily. She saw her as a leech.

"Mother, you are talking about the woman I love. The woman I want to protect, whom I want to build a family with. I will not let you hurt her with this idiotic business of a prenup. Emily, we're getting out of here. Maybe we'll come back when my mother finally comes to her senses and decides to treat you like a human being." Teddy stormed out the door.

Emily couldn't get up. She was completely paralyzed, but whether it was fear or sadness she didn't know. She was still bleeding, and the bright red drops were forming a pool in the brie.

She could hear Belinda crying, but it felt far away. She was muttering something about it being "all her fault," and Emily could tell she was talking about her. She didn't know what was her fault, except that she'd walked in here expecting to find her friends and instead found a roomful of enemies that she couldn't escape from. All Emily could do was stare down at the blood dripping onto the charcuterie board. Her muscles started throbbing in time with her head. Nothing made sense. Teddy was gone, Emily was hurt, and there was no one to help her.

Emily was alone. She didn't know when it happened. A moment ago she had been surrounded by lawyers, and now she was surrounded by darkness. There were footsteps coming from somewhere, but they were still far away. She wanted to call out to Teddy, but she could barely manage a whisper. She felt sore, confused, and injured. Where were Heather and Cal? Where was her boyfriend? Nothing was right, and that clawing feeling in her stomach was back. It spread through her body again until she was so cold it was as if someone had dunked her in an ice bath.

She tried again to call out for Teddy, but her throat felt raw, and it was closing up. There was a hand around her throat, slowly closing itself around her. It was getting harder to breathe. Emily was dizzy from the lack of oxygen.

There was a beeping sound coming from somewhere in the darkness. It was getting louder and louder and louder—

4

Emily woke up to her alarm beeping maniacally. Her phone was under her pillow—strategic, but an annoying way to start the day. Her dream tickled the edges of her consciousness, causing her to feel a little faint. She reached her hand around her neck but found nothing there, and her body wasn't as cold as it had been in the dream. She looked around and found she was in her own bed, not Teddy's.

"It was just a dream," she said to test her voice. "It was nothing but a dream. You are here, in your own home, and you're safe."

She'd been having a lot of dreams lately. Or maybe she should define them as nightmares? They were definitely dreams at the beginning because they began with Teddy being the perfect boyfriend before suddenly turning dark and nightmarish as he turned into a monster.

When they had started dating, Teddy was charming, attentive, and chivalrous to a fault. He hadn't shown his true nature until they were married. Once he knew Emily was "locked in," he started to peel away the façade and reveal the real Teddy. In Emily's nightmare there was a persistent cold feeling in her gut; it could only be her subconscious self trying to warn her of what was to come.

"It was just a nightmare, Emily. You're safe, you're in your own home, and Teddy doesn't control you anymore."

She repeated this mantra to herself until her heart stopped racing.

THAT DAY EMILY had to keep taking breaks to meditate and get her heart under control. The dreams were taking over her life, and she was determined not to let them. Teddy had stolen enough of her time already. No, she had work to do and a life to live.

Emily kept busy in her job as virtual assistant to Horace DeVilliers—a renowned publisher in New York City. She'd never met him in person, but he was a good boss, and she felt oddly loyal to him. Emily scheduled his meetings and flights and organized his never-ending pile of books to be read and reviewed before sending them off to editors and printers. Her least favorite part of the job was having to send rejection after rejection. She'd never told Horace that she used to be a writer, worried that he would think she was just trying to break into publishing, but every time she sent out a rejection or acceptance email, her heart lurched into her throat. *That could be me.*

On Thursday evening, she was listening to Stravinsky when her phone rang.

Her whole body froze for a moment. Holding her breath,

she forced herself to check the caller ID. It was William, so she answered.

"It was so nice talking to you the other day," William began.

"I enjoyed it too," Emily said.

"I know this is a sensitive time, and I don't want to add to any drama in your life. But I miss you, Emily. I miss our long conversations, and I miss our friendship."

There it was, that classic William Summers charm, the kind that was almost too sweet and made her stomach do flip-flops.

"I wanted to see if you'd like to get together," he continued. "We could catch up over dinner."

"I-I'm not sure that's a good idea," Emily stammered. But she had to admit that deep down she wanted to see him again.

"Why not? I promise I haven't turned into a serial killer, if that's what you're afraid of."

Emily giggled. "I believe you. It's just..." She trailed off, trying to figure out how to explain. She couldn't tell William that their affair was the reason Teddy kept hammering at her in court. It wasn't William's fault, and it wasn't fair to drag him into all this.

"So what do you say?" William asked. "Can we meet for dinner?"

"I'm not sure," Emily hedged. She didn't want to say no. It would be a relief to see him and unwind for a few hours, but she knew it could look bad in court.

"Are you worried about Teddy?" William asked, as if reading Emily's mind. "What could the harm be? You're in the middle of a divorce, and who you see—in a friendly way

—isn't his business. Besides, how is he ever going to find out?"

William had a point, but Emily was still worried that somehow Teddy would find out and punish her for it. She forced herself to push away the paranoid thought.

"I promise to make it worth your while," he continued, "and if I don't, I give you permission to leave me by the side of the road with no way to get home."

"Wow, you'd do that for me?"

"I'd do anything for you."

Emily's heart leaped into her throat. How was it possible that William knew exactly what to say to completely disarm her? He was genuinely romantic, something Emily hadn't experienced in years. She was desperate to be swept off her feet.

"Yes, let's meet for dinner," she said, caving in to William's allure. "But I can't do this weekend. I'm having dinner at my sister's on Saturday."

"How about next Saturday?"

Emily closed her eyes and took a deep breath. "Sure. It'll be just a friendly dinner between long-lost friends."

"Casually catching up, because they haven't spoken in years." William's voice carried a smile beamed down the line. It warmed Emily's heart and relaxed her muscles. "It's a date."

It's a date.

"Is there anything you want to talk about today?" Dr. Wright asked.

Emily wanted to tell her that there was nothing she

needed to talk about. In fact, she might be finally cured. "I'm not sure."

"How has your sleep been?" she asked.

Emily flinched.

In true form, Dr. Wright made note. "Did I touch a nerve?"

Emily wanted to tell the truth, but she was always afraid Dr. Wright might commit her to an insane asylum. That fear made her hold back. "I've been having this nightmare. It starts as a memory. I'm with Teddy back at the beginning, long before he, um...changed..." Emily trailed off. She didn't want to talk about her nightmares again. Instead, she wanted to sit quietly in this cozy office until it was time to go home.

"It's pretty normal to have nightmares like that," Dr. Wright replied, smiling at Emily over her glasses. "You're breaking down the cycle of blame you've attached to yourself, and as part of that process, your subconscious is trying to find where it went wrong. It's okay to remember the good times. They were *good* times, after all."

Emily nodded. "How long—" She cut herself off, unsure if she wanted to continue.

Dr. Wright stared at her.

Emily sighed. "How long does someone have to wait before it's appropriate to start dating again? You know, after a divorce or something."

Dr. Wright's smile disappeared. She took off her glasses and rubbed her temples. "Are you talking about Teddy?"

"No. It's William," Emily said. "Remember?"

"Yes. I recall you saying you tried a relationship before you went back to Teddy." Dr. Wright put her glasses back on. "Let's talk about that first time you started getting involved with William. I believe you said that you had gotten to know each other fairly well while you were in the hospital after the accident?"

Emily hesitated. She hadn't been completely honest with Dr. Wright when she'd spoken of William before. She hadn't trusted her completely, and had to admit she had a hard time trusting her now. She was terrified that Teddy had compromised her therapist and would find a way to use this against her.

"I believe you actually had a bit of a crush on William while you were in the hospital, didn't you?" Dr. Wright smiled.

Emily's stomach turned from guilt. "I guess you could say that. We met up a few times after I was released. I thought maybe it was something more, but we never took it very far, then I went back to Teddy. Anyway, we recently...reconnected."

Emily felt bad, and it would probably send her years backwards in her therapy, but she just didn't want to admit that William was the one who'd reached out. She wanted the okay from her therapist to go on this date. So what if she fudged a little bit on the way there?

"How did you reconnect?" Dr. Wright asked, whipping out her notebook.

"I ran into him while going to my car, and we chatted a bit. He said he'd read about our divorce. That's the great thing about marrying someone from a rich family— everyone knows your dirty business. He asked me out and—"

"He asked you out? For a date or for a more platonic meeting?"

Emily bit her lip. Should she tell her doctor the truth? It was probably stupid to have brought him up in the first place. Emily doubted she could backpedal now. "A date, I think. He suggested dinner."

"It sounds to me like you aren't quite ready for this."

"What makes you say that?" Emily asked.

Dr. Wright took a deep breath. "I think you are still traumatized by your ex-husband, and you are constantly forced to retrigger yourself by having to face him in court. It would be better for you and your mental health if you were to take your time and heal yourself properly before getting romantically involved with someone new."

William isn't exactly new, Emily thought. "What about that old adage—the best way to get over someone is to get under someone else?"

Dr. Wright smiled. "If this were a normal breakup, I would kind of agree with that sentiment, though safely, of course. Sometimes exposing yourself to a new situation helps you realize what was lacking in the previous one. In this case, you're still rebuilding your sense of trust and of the world around you. You're still trying to figure out what's real and what's your ex's manipulation. I think any relationship right now, even a purely sexual one, would be confusing for you."

Emily wasn't really sure what she thought her therapist would say, but she never thought she'd be so...blunt.

A heavy silence descended over them.

"Why don't we end the appointment here?" Dr. Wright said, obviously picking up on the strange tension in the room. "You have a lot to process. Rather than hammer at your emotions, I think it would be best if you took a walk and allowed the nature around you to influence your emotions. See what happens when you feel the wind on your face and smell the strange city odors."

Emily left the appointment in a daze, not ready to drive home, but not willing to walk off her emotions. She knew her therapist was right—it wasn't safe or sane to jump into another relationship. At the same time, didn't Emily deserve to be happy? She deserved to have a purely sexual relationship if that was what she wanted, or at least a comforting friendship, after all that Teddy had put her through. That was really what she wanted out of her time with William—a few moments in the week where she didn't feel lonely.

***

"Please don't forget to bring wine," Laurie pleaded into the phone. "I don't think I can get through this dinner without it."

Emily had been standing by the door, holding her keys, when her sister called. Planning family dinners seemed to stress Laurie out much more than her. Emily felt she had been growing closer to her father than her sister lately. Perhaps it was their shared experience with abusive partners.

"I have wine," Emily said. "I'm bringing a red and a white, since you didn't tell me what you were making for dinner."

"Sorry. I hadn't really decided until today. I'm making pasta with a red sauce, so the red will be fine."

"And we can have white for dessert," Emily concluded. She started jingling her keys near the phone. "It's your last chance to ask for anything else. Unless you want me to arrive late, I have to leave now."

"Dad said he'd bring a salad, so if you could pick up

some bread, I'll make a little charcuterie board for after he leaves and it's just us."

"Sounds good." Emily hung up before Laurie could get a second wind.

She immediately texted William.

> My sister is still freaking out. I have to pick up a baguette now? But I know she won't eat it. She can't handle that many carbs in one meal.

> LOL. My sister is the same. She always wants to host, but every time she does, she stresses herself out so badly that by the end of the night she's always yelling—I'm never doing this again.

> LOL.

Against her therapist's advice, she hadn't broken off her date with William. In fact, they had been talking most of the day. William reminded her why she'd fallen for him all those years ago. They had a lot in common. He was funny, a good listener, and easy to talk to—all things Emily forgot were possible.

When she got home from Dr. Wright's office the night before, Emily had sat down and made a conscious decision to just trust William. Trust that he was still the kind man she knew. There came a point when one had to start rebuilding their trust in people, and Emily decided that time was now. She had to stop thinking that everyone was like Teddy, and there was no time like the present to just commit.

Maybe not for long, but for now.

"Excuse me?" Laurie screeched. "You are doing *what*?"

"I'm going on a date. It's next weekend with William—"

"Stop right there." Emily's sister closed her eyes and put her hand out. "Why do I know that name, and please tell me I am wrong about how I know that name."

"Emily, dear, are you talking about the nurse at the hospital?" her father asked.

Emily regretted every moment of this awkward dinner. Laurie was somehow under- and overprepared for company. She'd started making five different dishes and hadn't finished a single one. Emily's father was helping with the pasta while Emily turned on the oven so the frozen samosas would finally start baking. Laurie drank a glass of red wine to calm down. Emily nervously chatted with them, trying desperately to avoid talking about her divorce. That was the only reason she could explain why she'd decided to tell her family about William.

"You're already dating? Wow." Her father spoke barely above a whisper.

Emily wanted to disappear; she wanted to melt into the oven and turn herself into a samosa. "Listen, I know I shouldn't—"

"Your divorce isn't even final yet," Laurie reminded her. "Are you crazy? You're going to land yourself in another abusive relationship at this rate."

"Now, Laurie, we don't know that. We don't really know anything about this man apart from his job...if it's the person I remember."

Her father was soft-spoken. He didn't raise his voice and didn't like it when his daughters did either. Years of living with their mother and surviving her manipulations and emotional torture meant he did his best to avoid conflict, and reveled in his very quiet life. That being said, Emily often wondered if maybe her father was lonely, and she worried about ending up exactly like him someday.

"You're thinking of the right person," Emily told him. "It's William Summers. We met while I was in the hospital. We stayed in touch for a while." She cleared her throat and ignored Laurie's raised eyebrows. "But kind of lost our friendship. He read about our divorce in the newspaper and reached out. I said I'd go for dinner with him. It's a casual dinner, nothing special."

"I don't think this is a good idea," Laurie said, pouring herself another glass of wine.

"Why? It's just dinner."

Her father intervened. "What I think your sister is trying to say is that you may need a little more time with yourself before getting involved with anyone. Not because we want you to be alone or lonely—I know you are probably feeling a little bit of both right now—but because we want you to be your best self when you start a new relationship. You know how Teddy can be, and we don't want you worrying about him while you're out to dinner."

Emily bit her lip. "Sheldon thinks he has a plan that will put Teddy and me back on even ground, legally speaking, and there's no way Teddy could know. Besides, it's just dinner. I'm sure I could come up with a friendly excuse if I needed to."

"Emily, you know that doesn't matter," Laurie said. "Teddy *knows* you aren't together, but he doesn't care. Even if we take Teddy's insanity out of the picture, I still think this is a stupid idea."

"Why?"

"Because you barely know yourself. Before Teddy you

were a celebrated writer, and you had just graduated from one of the most prestigious schools in the country. You had a whole host of friends, and you were always talking about traveling. These days I have to twist your arm to get you to drive to my house, and you're working at home as a virtual assistant. You don't know what your hobbies are or what kind of movies you like—Teddy reprogrammed you to only care about *him*. If you go out with William, whether you realize it or not, you'll just turn into a reflection of what he wants you to be."

Her father bowed his head. He'd been nodding along with Laurie as she made her speech, and now he was fighting back tears.

Emily remembered what her father had been like when she was really little. He had been a vibrant, charming man who was always ready with a helping hand. Everyone loved him, and he had plenty of friends and a dynamic social life. After Laurie was born, her mother's narcissism sank to a new low. She hated how much more attention her husband dedicated to their two girls, and she started manipulating him more than ever before. By the time Laurie and Emily were grown, he had become a shell of his former self.

"I agree with your sister, dear," her dad mumbled. "As much as I want to see you happy, I think it would be best for you to get to know yourself again. I also think you can't be too careful when it comes to Teddy. We've learned from experience that he will use any shred of your life he can get his hands on to drag these court proceedings on longer than necessary. Until you get an official ruling from the judge, until that settlement is signed and sealed, I think it is best you stay single—both in name and appearance. William can wait. If he was willing to reach out after all this time, you can bet he'll still be there in a few weeks."

Emily felt frozen to the spot. She desperately wanted one person in her life to agree with her and give her the green light for this stupid date. So far, her dreams, her therapist, and her family were telling her it was a bad idea. It was only her heart that thought she should give William a chance.

Emily nodded. "I'm just feeling a little lonely right now, but you're right about waiting. I'm sure William will understand." She smiled, holding back tears.

Later that night, Emily would cry a little while having her wine. Maybe her father did understand, but there wasn't much he could do.

For now, and for the foreseeable future, Emily was alone.

5

E   mily sat in her car for a ten-minute meditation before going into the courtroom. The weekend hadn't been as relaxing as she'd hoped. She'd spent it debating if she should go on her date with William. One minute she was convinced she should cancel, and the next she decided it would be the perfect way to finally get over Teddy. It was enough to make her sick as she pictured the various paths her life could take.

In one, she got involved with William, and he turned out to be even worse than Teddy.

In another, she got involved with William, and he turned out to be the love of her life.

In yet another, she rejected both men and went to live in a commune in Arizona.

Why was it so impossible to make a decision these days? Even after therapy, Emily couldn't figure out her own life. She knew, eventually, there would come a day when she wasn't so filled with doubt and mistrust. She knew that with time and personal growth, she'd be able to trust another person's intentions and trust her own intuition again, but that day was always tantalizingly close and impossibly far away.

Now she wanted to turn around, drive back home, and go to sleep, but she knew that wasn't possible. There was only one path, and it led right to Teddy and his lawyers.

"ORDER IN THE COURT!" Judge Adisa tapped his gavel on the bench.

Teddy's lawyers had called the media to come down, and the bloodthirsty journalists and paparazzi answered. They were almost too excited.

"It's okay that they called all these people," Sheldon Mason whispered. "It'll be better for you. And clearly that means they have no idea what we've got."

Emily's palms were sweating. "Is it? I really don't want the whole city to know about my husband's infidelity."

Sheldon didn't respond. They both knew there was nothing left to do. Teddy's family always won in the papers. Even when they were the villains of the story, they managed to bring unwanted attention to everyone around them.

Carson Ciel, Teddy's lead lawyer and his old fraternity brother, got up to address the court. "Your Honor, today we're hoping to settle the matter of spousal support. According to the terms of the prenuptial agreement, my client is not required to pay *any* spousal support to his former partner due to her questionable relationship with Mr. William Summers—"

Sheldon stood up. "We've already discussed this matter, Your Honor. It was decided by this court that the relationship in question was platonic, and since the period of time in question was during a trial separation, it is exempt from consideration."

"Ah, except that it wasn't a trial separation," Ciel continued. "A *trial separation* is an agreement between the two married parties. It means *both* husband and wife decided to take time out and separate in their *own living arrangements.* But that wasn't the case here, was it? No, Ms. Gray was living in an apartment that was paid for by my client, and it was not a separation he agreed to."

"Ms. Gray was living in the condo *she* purchased prior to marrying Thaddeus Gaunt—"

"But the mortgage was paid for by Mr. Gaunt, and the deed to the condo was put in his name."

"It was understood—at least, until the beginning of these divorce proceedings—that the condo was still Ms. Gray's. She was unaware that the deed had been transferred to her husband's name only, and was under the impression that she was still on the deed."

"Well, she wasn't. Clearly her track record of deception and manipulation extends to her council, my condolences to Mr. Mason, but he is mistaken. Since this *affair* was carried out in a property that belonged to my client, the time spent in that apartment cannot be considered a true trial separation."

Judge Adisa looked at Sheldon and raised his eyebrows.

"Ms. Gray did not transfer nor gift that property to Mr. Gaunt," Sheldon responded. "Assuming you have paperwork saying otherwise, then it appears Mr. Gaunt has committed fraud. Is that what counsel is admitting in this court?"

Emily's eyes widened. She hadn't known that.

"Ms. Gray did indeed transfer the deed into Mr. Gaunt's

name. This is her signature." He handed the document to the bailiff to show the judge and Sheldon.

Sheldon looked at Emily. "One moment, Your Honor, while I confer with my client?"

"You have a minute," the judge replied.

"Emily, please tell me that he faked that signature."

"I don't know. He had me sign some things when we first got married...I didn't actually read them...he said they were for our bank account..." Emily's anxiety went through the roof.

Sheldon's eye twitched. "Your Honor, my client was unaware of signing the property over to Mr. Gaunt, as he asked her to sign without telling her what she was signing. I would classify that as fraud—"

"Your client signed of her own free will," Ciel replied. "We would like to petition the court to remove all spousal support, and will advise that Mr. Gaunt will be filing litigation for emotional damage in this situation. This is concurrent with the last motion, requiring that Ms. Gray pay the mortgage that was remaining on the condo she brought into the marriage, which was then transferred to Mr. Gaunt under the *guise* that he could pay off her debts."

Sheldon cleared his throat. "Does this mean that Mr. Gaunt's lawyers admit that the condo was and *is* Ms. Gray's property? And are they planning on transferring that *back* to its rightful owner?"

"The property in question has now been sold. Pursuant to the order of this court, while the actual property is now in the hands of someone else, the proceeds of the sale are being held in a trust until the matter of the divorce can be resolved."

"You're asking Ms. Gray to *pay back* the mortgage that Mr.

Gaunt paid on her property, however the property in question is now gone, and you're saying the assets to that property are now in a bank account held by Mr. Gaunt?" Sheldon asked, his face turning red.

Emily could feel the heat coming off her attorney. She knew she should be angry, but this was just another day in the life of being manipulated by Teddy. He took her condo, and now he was going to take her money and leave her with nothing.

Less than nothing, I'll be in debt.

"The proceeds are in trust," Ciel replied. "It's money that has been earned *by* Teddy Gaunt, during the divorce proceedings, which means Ms. Gray has no right to it. The deed to the condo had only my client's name on it and is therefore his property to do with as he saw fit. We've complied with the court's decision that the proceeds of the sale stay in a trust. I don't see what Mr. Mason's problem is, other than he's obviously starting to see the deceitful side of Ms. Gray." He smirked and looked down at his client.

Teddy wasn't even trying to hide the smug smile on his face.

"The discussion today," Ciel continued, "is to do with her infidelity during the period of their marriage after the accident in which she tried to cause physical harm to my client. We're aware of Ms. Gray's history and would like to advocate for other survivors of partners with narcissistic disorders. That is why Mr. Gaunt would like to donate one year's worth of the proceeds of what *would have* been his spousal support to the National Association for Domestic Violence." He paused for a roar of applause from the viewing gallery.

So that's why the media is here, Emily thought. *He's turning the narrative of our marriage on its head, making me the villain. I should have known.*

Ciel continued arguing against providing spousal support.

The room was a blur, and everything sounded like it was happening underwater. Emily couldn't believe this was happening. She wanted to run away, but she was glued to the chair.

This is it. My life is over. There's no point in fighting anymore. Teddy's won.

"Your Honor." Sheldon had waited until Carson Ciel was finished with his speech. He stood up with his hand on Emily's shoulder; it was their little signal. If she wanted him to go through with the evidence they had collected, Emily just had to leave it there. If Emily felt that she couldn't stoop so low, she would move his hand away.

She didn't move, staring at the wooden table in front of her. What good would it do anyway?

"Mr. Gaunt's lawyers have painted a picture of my client as the perpetrator of violence, manipulation, and deceit; however, I have documents that show all is not quite as it seems." Sheldon rifled through his briefcase, pulling out a file folder. "Here I have signed statements from multiple women describing the affairs they had with Mr. Gaunt during the period when he was married to my client, Ms. Gray. In these documents the women describe that Thaddeus pursued them and even used Ms. Gray's former condo as a love nest. One of the women describes Teddy outlining his plan to get the condo in his name and change the locks on it so that Ms. Gray wouldn't have access to it. We were unaware that he'd actually been successful in getting Ms. Gray to sign the papers required for that. My client was under the impression she was signing bank documents for the joint account."

"That's bullshit!" Teddy shouted from the other side of the court.

His lawyers pushed him back into his seat and whispered furiously.

Carson Ciel stood up. "Your Honor, my office wasn't given any notice about this."

"Actually, you were," Sheldon said. "I have the emails here. My secretary sent it to you and received a reply, and I quote, *'Doesn't matter anyway, since I have this in the bag. What could a pathetic old dude like you possibly have? I won't be wasting my time,'* end quote."

Teddy responded by banging his fist on the table. Even the judge jumped in his seat. There was a small commotion in the viewing gallery.

Ciel cleared his throat. "Clearly, whoever answered that email was having an off day. I still would like the chance to see these so-called letters. I would also ask that these women appear in person to confirm their statements and so we can cross-examine them."

"This isn't a criminal trial, Mr. Ciel," Judge Adisa said. "There's no cross-examination. Mr. Mason is free to present these statements to me as a recommendation for the settlement of the divorce. Though I do wonder why these women refused to appear in person, Mr. Mason."

"Your Honor, it was difficult to get them on record because they are afraid of Mr. Gaunt. They all describe Mr. Gaunt as controlling, manipulative, and dangerous. I only have their sworn statements because I promised each of them anonymity and helped them to secure themselves against Mr. Gaunt. That's why it's taken me so long to gather everything."

"So we don't actually *know* who is behind these letters? That sounds pretty convenient," Ciel said, his hand on Teddy's shoulder, holding his client down. "Your Honor, I'd like to move to dismiss these documents."

"I think I'll see them for myself," Judge Adisa deadpanned. He was watching Teddy's reaction with an unamused look on his face.

Emily knew that Judge Adisa was known for expecting proper courtroom behavior, and he didn't appreciate the temper tantrum.

Sheldon walked up to the bench and delivered the letters, each one handwritten and then typed out. "I also have video statements to submit, but my client and the 'girlfriends' have requested that this happen in private without the petitioners present. I have no objections to Mr. Gaunt's council being present, though. Their faces have been blurred to honor their anonymity."

The judge scanned the letters.

"I also have evidence pertaining to the car accident that Mr. Gaunt claims was caused by my client," Sheldon said. "According to the testimony presented by his lawyers, my client was suicidal, reached over, and turned the steering wheel, forcing Mr. Gaunt off the road. However, this isn't true. My client was worried Mr. Gaunt would react badly to her request for a divorce, so she recorded the conversation and in fact captured the entire incident. I have the phone recording to present to the court. In it we'll hear an argument between Mr. Gaunt and Ms. Gray, one in which we will hear evidence of Mr. Gaunt's emotional abuse and gaslighting of Ms. Gray."

"You fucking bitch," Teddy said, his voice low and angry.

The air was sucked out of the courtroom.

Sheldon cleared his throat. "I've provided a transcript for the court, and we have both audio and some video. In it you'll see that Ms. Gray at no point reaches across the driver's seat to the steering wheel, contradicting Mr. Gaunt's statement that Ms. Gray took control of the wheel. In addition, the video will show that Mr. Gaunt did in fact hit the release on Ms. Gray's seatbelt. I also have hospital records showing that she was given a clean bill of mental health and was not suicidal at the time of the accident."

Emily held her breath as Mason presented the transcript to Judge Adisa. She closed her eyes when he pressed play on the video recording, but from the angle of the phone you could only see Emily's side, the center console and the edge of Teddy in the driver's seat, as Emily had been partially sitting on the phone to keep Teddy from realizing she'd been recording.

"I didn't drink the wine. I switched to water. I know you're having an affair with that woman. I've seen you two together before. I am not doing this anymore, Teddy. I'm not going to sit in the corner and watch myself shrink as you gaslight me into believing I'm crazy and scare me so much I'm unable to walk around my own home without flinching. I'm leaving you, and I— Teddy, watch out!"

"What, this? This?"

Emily screamed, "Teddy, please stop, please. I'm sorry I brought it up now, okay? I'm sorry—"

"Sorry? You're sorry? I'll give you something to be sorry for."

Teddy's arm could be seen as he threw his fist into Emily's face, and you could hear the smack against her skin; she moaned and sputtered.

"Now are you sorry?"

"Teddy, I'm leaving you. This is—I can't do this anymore. I can't—"

"You can't do this anymore? Fine!"

The recording ended with the sound of metal crunching and tires screeching. The video clearly showed that Emily didn't reach over to the steering wheel. She was grateful for her past self throwing on the selfie camera at the last minute. The audio part of the recording was damning, but the video was incontrovertible proof that Teddy was the cause of the accident. The biggest takeaway was that it showed him reaching over and unfastening her seatbelt mere seconds before the crash.

"What the *hell* are you going to do about that?" Teddy yelled at his lawyer. "You told me we had everything we needed to bury that stupid bitch."

Carson Ciel was apparently used to this behavior, because it looked as though he barely flinched.

Teddy stood up to address the judge. "My family can put you away, so you have to dismiss that. Besides, it doesn't change the fact that she opened her legs to the first idiot she saw when she woke up. I will *not* allow this. I'll withdraw the petition. I'll tear the whole thing up before I give that bitch a cent."

Judge Adisa calmly signaled to the bailiff to remove Teddy from the courtroom.

"Don't you lay a dirty finger on me," he spat.

Ciel stood up and whispered something in his ear, and Teddy pushed him away. Ciel fell backward into his chair, blinking.

The bailiff pulled out his handcuffs.

But Teddy shrugged them away. "I'll go, but when I come

back, this whole mess had better be squared away. I will not let this be over like this. If she wants to divorce me, she's going to pay. No one says no to me."

The press was going to have a field day—that was, if their editors let them print the story and defame the city's most influential family.

"I think now is a good time for a short recess." The judge seemed to barely be hanging on to his temper. "Why don't we all tackle some lunch," Judge Adisa added, gathering the statements and transcripts from the bench before getting up to leave.

Sheldon smiled at Emily and patted her hand.

Emily just felt sick.

THE REST of the day passed quickly. Ciel had obviously spent his lunch working on a motion to squash the evidence Sheldon had presented. Sheldon had predicted as much and already had counterarguments prepared. Emily did her best to disappear into the wood. She felt shaky and afraid, especially since Teddy hadn't returned to court. He could be anywhere. He could even be waiting for her at home.

He doesn't know where you live anymore. He can't be waiting for you.

Still, Emily worried. She barely heard the judge adjourn for the day. Sheldon walked her to her car, but he had to run to a meeting and couldn't follow her home.

"Please, it's just to make sure Teddy isn't...waiting."

"I had security check the court parking lot earlier. They were instructed to let me know if they saw Teddy anywhere, and I haven't heard anything. It sounds like Teddy ran off."

Sheldon must have seen the fear in Emily's eyes because he softened. "I promise I wouldn't do this if I thought you were unsafe. Give me a call if you think someone's following you, and I'll get someone to chase him off." He patted her on the shoulder and ran back into the courthouse.

Emily blinked back tears and took a deep breath. It was true, there had been no sign of Teddy since his courtroom outburst, but Emily knew that didn't mean much. Teddy was a determined man, especially when he was angry.

She decided, just in case, to take the long way home. She drove around the city in circles until she was sure Teddy couldn't be following her anymore. Only then did she finally get on the freeway toward her house.

That night Emily checked the locks and security cameras twice. She decided to stay up late, and placed a hunting knife on the bedside table.

Sheldon called to remind her that exposing Teddy had been the right thing to do. His outburst in court would serve them well, in the long run, as it gave them a small window of opportunity to show the judge there was an angry side to Teddy they hadn't seen.

It's the right thing to do, Emily repeated to herself, *so why do I feel so scared?*

6

I need a flight for next Tuesday—unexpected meeting in London—can you schedule that? I'll need to arrive by 6 p.m. GMT. - H.DV

Emily stared at the airline booking website for a solid five minutes before remembering what she was doing and why. She had to get it together.

Horace DeVilliers wasn't an unreasonable or overly demanding boss. He needed meetings scheduled and his calendar organized, and someone to sort through the many emails he received. Overall, it was very little work for very good pay, and Emily wasn't sure how she managed to completely mess it all up. She'd sent a rejection email to a *New York Times* bestselling author and promised a lucrative publishing deal to a freshman college student. Horace was aware that Emily was in the middle of a very public divorce, so he cut her a lot of slack, but even Horace's patience was running thin.

Hi Emily,

Just checking in. I know you had a court date on Monday, and I'm guessing it didn't go well. Please know that if you need some time off for your mental health, I'm happy to oblige. You're no use to me when your mind is elsewhere. Let me know next time you have a court date, and maybe we can work something out so you have more time for mental rest. I can maybe book a few things in advance or have an assistant here in New York take over your duties for a few days.

H.DV

It was like a sucker punch to the gut. Emily hated doing poorly at her job. She didn't want to disappoint Horace and end up losing her job.

She couldn't help but worry. Sheldon hadn't said anything about the divorce trial this week, so she had no idea whether or not his "brilliant plan" had even worked. She was on edge about Teddy and was barely leaving the house, worried that her soon-to-be ex-husband was waiting for her around every corner. If she could at least get some reassurance that the bomb Sheldon had dropped on Monday wasn't for nothing, she could maybe go back to her normal life.

And then there was William. The guilt she felt over him was gone. Teddy's reaction on Monday reminded her why she had got out of that marriage, and why she didn't owe her almost ex-husband anything. That was replaced with anticipation and butterflies for her dinner with William. The pair were still texting consistently. They talked about their days, work, and the stupid TV shows they were watching.

> I know it's pointless, and the plot is completely insane, but I just love that doctor show Bloodletting. Have you seen it? All the nurses at the hospital are obsessed. It's so inaccurate.

Emily replied:

> Is it really? I read an interview that they have a medical consultant on the show.

> He might be a medical consultant, but I doubt he's worked in a hospital lately, lmao.

> We should have a viewing party. We can watch the show, and you can tell me how it's supposed to go IRL.

She knew it wasn't a good idea. Well, she knew her family and her therapist didn't think it was a good idea, but Emily wasn't sure she really cared. It felt good to talk to William again, and it reminded her why she liked him in the first place. He was the complete opposite of Teddy. Where Teddy was conceited, William was modest; he had a self-deprecating kind of humor that would have driven Teddy up the wall. William wasn't rich and didn't behave as though the world needed to bend to his every whim. William was the kind of guy who could admit to enjoying trashy TV that was written for suburban moms.

The people around her had the best of intentions. They could see what she was going through with Teddy and didn't want it to become a double feature. Were they right? Did

William really care about her, or was he another man thinking only of himself? There was only one way to find out. That Saturday, she could grill him about his intentions and his dating history. She could sit across from him and not drink a single drop of wine and see how he reacted. Would he be enraged that she refused to engage on their date, or would he ask how she was feeling?

Why go on a date when you could go to an inquisition instead?

No, Emily thought, *I'll just enjoy myself and see how it goes. It doesn't mean I have to continue seeing him. I can just go on one date and enjoy myself—that isn't a crime.*

The week dragged on.

Laurie called twice, desperate to get Emily to change her mind. "We *just* made progress with the settlement, and now you're going to throw it all away on some male nurse? At least wait until the judge has made a decision."

"The judge is taking his sweet time, and Teddy's lawyers have been drowning his office with paperwork to make sure he takes even longer. It's just dinner, and I don't have to keep dating him if I don't want to. I'm a grown woman. I can decide for myself what's a good idea or not."

"Given your track record, I think you should at least consider my advice, but if you're going to be stubborn, then fine. Give me the name of the restaurant so I know where to start asking questions when you suddenly go missing."

Underneath it all, her sister did care, but Emily wished she'd be a little more considerate with her wording.

"I'll keep my location turned on so you can keep tabs on

me, okay? If anything happens, I'll send you a text that says, 'the courts are full'—does that make you feel any better, Agent Gray?"

"You can laugh if you want, but when you've been taken advantage of by men repeatedly like I've been, you'll be asking the same kinds of questions."

Her father had said the same thing, but he was much more gentle. He softly suggested that she take measures to keep things casual. "Drive there yourself, and make sure to take the long way home so he can't follow you, okay? I know you dated him before, but remember, you're still trying to keep your address quiet from Teddy, so it's just a good idea all around to keep it private from everyone. Tell the waiter or waitress your name and be nice to them, that way they'll remember you...just in case."

Just in case I'm walking into my death, or I end up seated in front of Teddy at the restaurant—just in case this is another day where poor Emily Gray's luck gets even worse.

Emily was exasperated by her family. She wished she could turn off the phone and ignore them for a few days, to let herself be excited and anticipate the best outcome rather than the worst. She understood it all, but that didn't mean she had to like it.

It felt like a month had passed when, finally, it was Saturday. To Emily's surprise there was no Secret Service motorcade waiting at her door to protect her on her date. When she opened her door—because yes, she'd ignored her dad's advice about driving herself—William stood there with a gorgeous bouquet of flowers and a dashing smile. It was the first time they had seen one another in person for years. Somehow, William looked as though he hadn't aged a day. His dark wavy hair fell across his forehead, and his dark eyes pierced Emily's heart the same way they always had.

"You look great," he murmured into her hair as they held each other.

Emily breathed in deeply, luxuriating in the scent of his cologne. "So do you," she murmured back.

The advice her father and sister had given her slowly trickled out of her mind. She accepted the flowers and invited William into her home, giggling about the strange circumstances of their reunion as she found a vase to display them.

When he offered to drive, she didn't think twice about saying yes, and slid into the passenger seat of his car. He drove them to the hottest new restaurant in town, a place called Courts that had a tennis-court theme. All their cocktails were named after famous tennis stars, and William and Emily laughed while ordering the McEnroe Manhattan and the Billie vs Bobbie Bellini. After dinner, they moved to the bar. Emily couldn't remember the last time she'd had this much fun; she couldn't recall a night where she wasn't looking over her shoulder in fear. William made her fears about Teddy and the divorce go away.

She admired his movie-star good looks and basked in the light of his attention. She knew other women were jealous and allowed herself to delight in their envy. William only had eyes for her. He held her hand under the bar, but made no move to kiss her until she brought her face close to his.

"Shall we...move this elsewhere?" he breathed.

Emily felt intoxicated by the scent of his cologne mixing with the aroma of the cocktails they'd been drinking. She *wanted* to move this elsewhere. She wanted to wrap her arms around his neck and bathe in William's adoration. Her head was screaming at her, telling her this was enough. They should end the date while it was still going well, and Emily could get a cab home with the beautiful memory of William buying her cocktails and giggling about the cheesy themed restaurant.

"Yes, maybe there's a Wimbledon-themed bar down the street? Or should we switch it up and go to a basketball-themed place?" Emily laughed, feeling her cheeks getting red. She knew very well what William was proposing, but wanted to put it off, give herself a little more time before making a decision.

"Well, actually," he said, letting go of her hand and fiddling with her hair, "I was thinking somewhere a little more private."

Emily didn't know what to say. She blushed and stared down at her drink.

William cleared his throat. "I didn't want to—I'm sorry, I really didn't mean—I just figured you'd want to go somewhere less...exposed."

"You're not wrong," Emily said, stirring her cocktail. "I guess I didn't think about the possibility that we'd..." She trailed off as the waiter came near. The last thing she wanted was a stranger listening in to their conversation.

William waved the waiter away with charming ease. "We don't need to do anything. It doesn't need to be this...clandestine meeting. We're both single. Nothing is wrong with what we're doing."

"I know," Emily said, "but I'm not sure I'm ready to take this a step further. I don't think it's a great idea to get involved with anyone right now. I don't know how far Teddy's reach goes, and I'd hate myself if I got you involved."

William shifted in his seat. There was no good way to

respond when your date tells you they don't want to go home with you for your own safety. They were quiet for a while, each staring at the ice floating around in their glasses.

"We're grown-ups, and we can have a nightcap without it turning into something else," William said. "I think we both want to spend more time together. If there's a part of you that wants to keep talking in a place where we don't have to spend almost thirty dollars for a cocktail—then I'd love to show you my new apartment." He smiled and patted Emily's hand. "I'll be right back."

Emily watched him walk away. She caught the eye of their waiter, who gave her an encouraging wink. How could she possibly turn down an offer like that?

WILLIAM LIVED in an airy loft in a trendier part of town, and his place was modern but still cozy. He had artistic prints mixed in with photographs of family, a blend of cool and warm throughout the contemporary build.

"Wow," Emily exclaimed, "this really is a step up."

"I got lucky," William said. "A friend decided to move out of the city, but didn't want to give up their place. I've been renting from them ever since."

Emily tried not to let her jealousy take over. She wanted a cool home, but she didn't have the money or resources to decorate it.

"Do you want some wine?" William continued. "Or a cocktail? I make a mean martini."

"I remember, it's very mean the morning after you drink it. I'd love one."

William glided over to his bar, smoothly turning on the

stereo as he did. He was like an actor in an old movie, one of those stars with a megawatt smile and a mysterious glint in his eye.

Emily plopped down on the couch and pictured herself living in this apartment. She didn't have a care in the world, she was back to writing novels, and she had interesting artistic friends who brought her fascinating liquors from their worldly travels and argued over who had the best jazz collection. That world was far away from her now.

"Here you are," William said, breaking through Emily's daydream. "Vodka, with a twist of lemon rather than an olive. It's a little brighter that way."

"You can taste more of the vodka that way too. Cheers," Emily said.

William sat down close to her, so close she could feel his breath on her cheek. Emily flushed; she wasn't sure she could do this just yet.

"This view is incredible; how did your friend find this place?" She stood up and moved over to the window to look out.

"I'm not sure, to be honest. He's lived here for ages. I think he got in before the revitalization of the area hit. He was worried that this place would get turned into one of those glass high-rises with zero character, but the artsy neighborhood managed to save it."

Emily could hear William's footsteps as he followed her to the window. Would it be so bad if she gave in? She felt his hand on her arm.

"You've got goosebumps," he murmured.

Emily turned abruptly and stepped away from him. "I-I don't think—I want to—"

"Am I coming on too strong?" William asked, hanging his head. "I'm sorry. It's just—"

"No, it's—I get it. Believe me, I do, and I want to—y'know —I just...I worry."

"Worry about what?"

Emily bit her lip. She was still afraid to be vulnerable with William; she didn't want to break the illusion he had of her. "I worry about Teddy. He found out I was seeing you once before. He's using our past relationship against me in court even though we were separated at the time I was seeing you. I don't want that to happen again."

"How could it?" he questioned.

"You don't understand. He has a way of snaking into my life. I've changed my phone number and my address multiple times—I even have a PO box address that all my mail from him gets sent to, just in case he tries to find me again. I'm scared he'll snake his way into our relationship again and ruin it."

"Why? I have no connection to Teddy. He has no way of knowing where we are right now, or what you're doing. Even if he did, there's nothing he can do about it. You're divorcing him, so he doesn't have a say in what—or who—you see. Just like he didn't before. I don't understand how a judge could use that against you. You were separated."

"I know it seems that way, but when someone has that kind of control over your life and your emotions, it really messes with your perception of the world. I can't remember the last time I *wasn't* looking over my shoulder in fear."

William took a step toward her, then hesitated. "Do you feel like you're in danger when you're with me?"

Emily paused. She had to admit there was something about William that felt so safe, so protective. If anyone was going to make her forget about Teddy, it was him, but she wasn't sure she was ready to admit it.

"That's not really the point," Emily breathed. "It's about my perception of things. I know you're not going to hurt me. You would barely hurt a fly."

William smirked and took a sip of his drink.

Emily's stomach dropped as she caught a glimpse of his muscles flexing under his shirt. She wanted to be wrapped up in his strong arms, falling asleep after having made love. Emily had thought about it a lot—especially over the past week. Their nights together had been long and passionate and had reminded her of the femininity she thought she'd lost in her marriage. Teddy had desexualized her and saved his passion for his mistresses. He'd expected Emily to be the perfect wife, to submit to his control, and to have no desires or needs at all. It interfered with his narcissism to think of other people.

Emily smiled. "I know you're trying to seduce me, and you're not being very subtle about it."

"I'm not being creepy, am I?"

"No, I just know you well enough that what you're doing won't get past my defenses."

"Oh?" he asked, raising an eyebrow. "So I'm going to get caught up in your arms, is that what you're saying?"

Emily gave in. She allowed William to wrap his arms around her, to play with her hair and nuzzle her neck. She melted as William kissed her gently from her ear down to her shoulder and across her collarbone. She shivered with pleasure, and William looked up at her, smiling.

"Like I said, you weren't very subtle about it," Emily said, sinking down to the floor with William.

EMILY LAY enveloped in William's arms after they made love. Her body felt right within his curves. William was asleep, and she could feel his chest rising and falling against her back.

For the first time in years, she felt truly relaxed. But something wouldn't let her sleep. Emily felt energized; her body was buzzing with anticipation. Was this the aftermath of good sex, or was something else nagging at her? She felt compelled to wake up, pulling on one of William's shirts.

Someone or something was moving around downstairs. They'd probably left a window open. Emily heard a glass crash to the floor and jumped.

Behind her, William remained fast asleep.

She knew it was a bad idea, but she had to know what or who was downstairs, so she could get to her phone and call the police.

Emily crept out of the bedroom and went downstairs, trying to get a glimpse of what was going on in the kitchen. William's kitchen was familiar—it almost looked like her old place, the one she'd shared with Teddy. Emily padded over to the couch to get her phone, but her bag and all its contents were gone.

"Looking for this?"

Emily froze—it couldn't be, it wasn't possible. She whipped around and came face-to-face with Teddy, his face contorted with anger, one fist over his head, holding the martini glass she'd been drinking from earlier.

"You thought I wouldn't find out? I always find out. I know everything. How dare you embarrass me like this, you pathetic little—"

"Don't!" Emily screeched, her body lurching forward. Her breath was ragged as her eyes focused on the world around her.

"Emily? Emily, it's okay. It's just a dream," William said, holding her arms by her sides.

Emily realized she'd been kicking her legs and flailing around. The pair were lying on the carpet, using their discarded clothes as pillows. Emily pulled the throw blanket from the back of the couch around her exposed body as she tried to catch her breath.

"You were having a nightmare," William said. He left the room and returned with a glass of water filled with ice. "Here, drink this."

Emily felt too panicked to drink. He sat down next to her and tilted the glass to her lips. Slowly, Emily's tears subsided, and her breath returned to normal.

"What was your dream about?" William asked, gently touching her shoulder.

Emily flinched and muttered her apologies, ignoring his question. "I have to go. It's late, and I, uh—" She cut herself off as she scrambled to put her clothes on.

She had been wearing a bra. Where the hell did it go? William handed it to her without a word, but Emily couldn't look him in the eye. Now she realized it was just a nightmare. She'd been reliving the day Teddy had found out about her relationship with William mixed with her evening with William. In this nightmare, Teddy knew they'd been intimate. It dawned on her she'd never seen him as angry as he was that night they'd fought, and it was no wonder her subconscious mind had conjured him up and what he would have done if he'd discovered she'd been with William like this.

Emily collected her things and muttered goodbye, still pulling on a shoe as she hopped out the door.

"Can I see you again?" William called down the hall.

Emily looked back and opened her mouth to say something, but the elevator came, and she surged forward, begging for the claustrophobic space to herself. She could answer him later when she wasn't embarrassed and scrambling to get out of his apartment.

This was stupid, so fucking stupid, Emily. What the hell were you thinking?

She held herself together long enough to hail a taxi, but the ride home was a blur.

The whole night had been a mistake. How could Emily think she could go back to normal without Teddy haunting her dreams?

7

E mily woke up the next morning to a text from William.

> Hey, just checking in. You left so quickly I didn't get a chance to say goodbye. Was I that bad? LOL.

Her hands shaking, she replied:

> No, of course not. I was just a bit overwhelmed.

> Do you want to talk about it on the phone?

When Emily agreed, William called. "What made you overwhelmed last night?" he asked gently.

"I had a nightmare that Teddy found us in bed together. I have insomnia because I'm frightened I'll have another nightmare about Teddy. I've been paranoid for three years, waiting for him to appear at my door. I want to see you and rebuild our relationship, but I'm afraid." She braced herself, waiting for William to unleash his frustration.

He took a deep breath. "I'm so sorry. I don't want you to feel pressured or anything. We don't have to be intimate right now. I just want to be your rock, Emily. Anything you need, please tell me. I'll be here."

"I appreciate that. I have to say, I really like you. It's easy to talk with you, and I'm glad we're back in touch."

"I feel the same. Do you want to get together Friday? We can go someplace a little quieter."

Emily drew in a single ragged breath. She'd had a panic attack when she got home, and it had taken her ages to calm down and get to sleep. She'd had a good time on their date, but as soon as she closed her eyes, her nightmares took over completely. It was the fear of Teddy, the terrifying potential that he could rear his ugly head and attack her again, that held her back from seeing William again.

"Can I think about it? I have a really busy week."

"Sure. I'll check in later," he said, then hung up.

Now she had some time to figure out how to keep herself from having a nightmarish panic attack every time she had sex.

OVER THE NEXT couple of days as Emily worked, writing rejection letters and scheduling meetings for Horace, she thought about William. She'd had a good time with him, and she wanted to see him again. So she pushed away her fears and accepted his invitation for Friday night.

Emily got excited for their date and reminded herself that not every relationship needed to be an intense emotional connection. She knew she could get there with William, she'd done it once before, but there was no need to go that far right now. Not while she was still painstakingly extracting herself from Teddy.

Their second date was practically a carbon copy of their first. Dinner at a trendy restaurant, cocktails at a stylish cocktail bar, well, one cocktail for her and then a mocktail after that, followed by an invitation for a nightcap at William's loft.

This time, Emily settled for making out next to her car rather than return to his apartment. She didn't want to fall asleep in William's arms if it meant she'd have a nightmare about Teddy.

"I'm sorry, but I don't think I'd be very much fun tonight," she said, feigning a yawn. Before William could protest, she kissed him goodbye and slid into her car.

The guilt she felt took over as she drove away. Emily questioned whether it had been the right move, if William would be offended and never want to see her again, and if it was what she really wanted. She craved the feeling of William's muscular arms around her waist again, wanted so badly to nuzzle into his neck and bury her fingers in his hair as they made love.

She knew leaving for home was a rational call, but it went against her emotional desire to be enveloped by William.

———

"You went on a date with William?"

"Two dates, actually. And we slept together." Emily grimaced, waiting for her therapist's reaction.

Dr. Wright sighed and rubbed her temples. "Emily, what happened to focusing on yourself? Putting dating aside for the time being?"

Emily shrugged. She didn't see the problem with going out on a few dates. "I'm lonely. William was comforting at a time when I needed it the most. It's nice to reconnect with him and feel *wanted* for once. Is that so bad?"

"Of course not," Dr. Wright said, "but I can't help but be concerned. I think it is too soon for you to be in any kind of romantic relationship. You aren't even properly divorced from your husband, a man who is controlling and abusive, who will likely use this information as leverage against you during your divorce."

Emily noticed how her therapist's voice deepened and her eye contact became more intense. It had Emily feeling that she was mad at her. It also reminded her of Teddy and her mother: the uncontrollable anger they had when someone disappointed them. She wanted to leave, call William, and cry about her session.

"I don't—I'm not—I'm sorry," Emily muttered.

"Why are you apologizing?" Dr. Wright asked.

"Because you're angry that I didn't take your advice to avoid William."

"I'm not angry at you, Emily," Dr. Wright said, her voice softening. "I am concerned for you as a mental health professional dedicated to your care. I'm sorry if my tone made you think I was angry. I promise that isn't the case."

Emily took a deep breath. "I want to feel loved. I want to feel wanted. I don't really have any friends. And I want to talk to someone who isn't going to give me advice or treat me like I'm about to fall to pieces, and that's practically impossible with my dad and my sister."

"Do you feel you can get that sort of relationship from William?" Dr. Wright asked, pulling out her notebook.

"No. What I can get from William is a little bit of fun, lust, the feeling of being wanted, and someone to listen when I talk without thinking that I am in danger. I know I'm not the best at making boundaries, but I have made them with William. I know the risks, and I know how to watch for any red flags." What she really needed from others was understanding and acceptance of the fact that she could make her own choices.

"I don't think you need my approval to go about your life and tend to your needs as you see fit. As your therapist I can only say that, in my experience, it's best to deal with your traumatic experiences before committing to another relationship. That being said, you are acutely aware of what to look out for in a partner, and you're setting boundaries."

Emily nodded.

"As long as you put yourself first while you're still figuring out how to deal with the trauma of your past, I think you're on the right path," Dr. Wright continued. "If William really does care about you, he'll understand why he doesn't come first right now."

Emily felt a weight of anxiety lift from her shoulders. "I will—and I have been. I like his calls, but if I'm not in the mood to talk...well, maybe I don't have to answer." It was as though that thought had just occurred to her. The idea that she could send his call to voicemail was shocking and had her anxiety building again, but she knew it was coming from her past. If she'd done that to Teddy, he'd have gone ballistic.

"You absolutely can do that. You do not have to do anything you don't want to, including answering his calls. I can see by your face that you're in uncharted territory right now. It will be okay. Keep things casual, and keep putting yourself first. Just take it one day at a time."

Emily nodded, grateful Dr. Wright understood where she was coming from and what she was feeling.

With that off her chest, she changed the subject back to Teddy, but her mind continued to play over Dr. Wright's words of advice. If William was the kind of man Emily thought he was, he'd understand why she was keeping him at arm's length and that she couldn't put him first right now. If he didn't, then she'd have to say goodbye.

The question was, would it really be that easy to walk away from him?

WILLIAM CALLED Emily every night before she went to bed. It proved to be somewhat cathartic to have someone to complain to. Emily ranted about work the way she used to do with her girlfriends, and William laughed, gasped, and commiserated exactly when she needed him to without offering to fix the problem for her, which she appreciated.

William, in return, respected her boundaries. They went on a date once a week, and they weren't followed by anything more intimate. She knew he'd call every night around nine, and she felt free to ignore the call if she wanted to, though she rarely did. Emily knew that William wasn't angry or upset about the arrangement because he'd agreed to her terms with no hesitation at all.

"I don't want to add stress to your life," William told her. "I just want to be around you."

They were out again on their weekly date. This time

William took her to a romantic comedy from the 1980s that was playing at an indie cinema downtown.

They were waiting in line to be let into the tiny theater, and Emily worriedly brought up their talk about *boundaries*. "I don't want you to feel it's a rejection. I just want to pump the brakes a bit."

"I totally understand," William said. "It's smart of you to lay it out like that. I feel like most women would feel awkward doing so, but it's nice to know where your head is at and what you're comfortable doing." He leaned in to kiss her on the forehead, but pulled back at the last moment. "May I kiss you?"

Emily nodded and smiled. She appreciated that William's ego wasn't bruised.

They were knocked aside by someone going past on the sidewalk, and Emily's radar for danger suddenly spiked.

Tonight was the first time in a long time that Emily had gone out to a movie. The idea of being trapped in a theater for hours on end made her feel like a sitting duck, but William promised to hold her hand and that they could leave if she felt uncomfortable. Getting shoved on the sidewalk broke her bubble of comfort all of a sudden. Her muscles tightened as she remembered that she was open game for Teddy.

"It's okay," William told her, rubbing her arm. "It's a squished sidewalk, that's all."

"Thanks." She opened her mouth to say something but was unsure of how to explain. She didn't want to paint herself as the victim again, but she also didn't know how else to tell William that this night was far out of her comfort zone. At least they could see everyone around them at a restaurant.

At a movie theater, Teddy could be hiding in the back row, and she wouldn't know until it was too late. She knew it was unreasonable to live like an agoraphobic grandmother for the rest of her life, but that didn't mean there wouldn't be growing pains as she started to step into *real* life again.

She glanced at the marquee to see what movie was playing. *Pretty in Pink.* "So have you seen this one before?" she asked, nodding to the picture of Molly Ringwald.

He flushed. "Yeah. I used to watch it a lot as a kid. Something about it just struck home. You know?"

She smiled but admitted, "I've never seen it."

"Never? Then you're in for a lot of teenage angst and drama and fun," he replied.

She stood on her tiptoes and gave William a kiss on the cheek. As she did, she saw a man staring at her from behind a car. A chill ran down her spine, and Emily tried to brush it away. They were almost inside the theater, and she'd ask William to sit at the back just in case. It wasn't weird—she'd just caught the eye of a stranger for a moment. *It's completely normal, Em; you're letting your imagination get away from you again.*

The line started moving, and Emily and William shuffled ahead. When Emily looked back, the man was gone.

***

"I can't believe she went after Blane. Duckie was right there," Emily huffed, irritated with Andie for not realizing that her best friend was in love with her and choosing Blane.

"I know, right?" William shook his head. "Did you like it though?"

"I did. Still think she chose wrong, but Blane sort of

redeemed himself at the end by rebuffing Steff and cutting off that friendship. Maybe it will work out, but—" There was just too much of a resemblance to Teddy in Blane for her to want to see the main character end up with him instead of a good guy like Duckie.

"As a kid I always kind of felt like Duckie. The best friend, never the boyfriend." He smiled.

"Maybe this time will turn out different," Emily offered, looking at him shyly.

His face brightened. "Such a good movie; thank you for seeing it with me."

"Thank you for inviting me," Emily said, kissing William deeply on the lips. "I'm only sorry we didn't get to make out in the back row like teenagers."

"I guess we'll just have to make out in the corner booth at the cocktail bar, like adults." William winked.

The night air was crisp, and Emily shivered. William wrapped his jacket around her arms. They walked in silence for a little while in the direction of the bar, each lost in thought.

Emily suddenly stopped in her tracks.

The man was back.

8

The same man she'd seen earlier, wearing a leather jacket, the man she'd made eye contact with before the movie started. The same guy who'd bumped into them when they were standing in line. He was standing at the end of the street, smoking a cigarette.

"Emily, what's wrong?" William asked.

Emily didn't know how to answer him. She was sure the man was following them, waiting until they were out of the movie theater. Could it be Teddy in disguise? The man was the same height as her ex, but had a bigger build. She wanted to run in the opposite direction but worried he would follow her.

"Nothing, just a little cold, that's all. Why don't we grab a cab to the bar?"

"It's only two blocks away. Are you sure you're okay?" William asked.

Emily gestured behind him with her eyes. He tried to turn around, but Emily stopped him. "No, it's better you don't look right at him. We should cross the street." She tugged on his arm.

William followed her, allowing Emily to guide them across the street.

She tried to subtly glance behind her, but she didn't see the man again. Was Emily's mind playing tricks on her?

"Emily, what's going on? Did you see Teddy?" William asked, his head roving around the street.

"I thought I saw someone following us, but he's gone now. I must be imagining things."

William stroked her arm and quickened his pace. "Let's get you inside."

EMILY COULDN'T FOCUS for the rest of the night. William kept trying to engage her in conversation, but she couldn't remember what they were talking about. She could only think about the man.

"You don't think Teddy knows about us, do you?" she asked.

"No, of course not," William said, putting his hand on hers. "It's just a coincidence. The guy was just having a smoke outside a dive bar by the movie theater."

She knew he was right and started to calm down. But then she saw the same man in the leather jacket, walking past the bar on the opposite side of the street. He must be following them; this kind of coincidence didn't just happen.

"Do you want me to take you home?" William asked, sounding concerned.

"I-I don't know," Emily said. She could feel the walls of her paranoia rising up around her. She wanted to crawl under the table and hide. Why had that man followed them here? How long had he been standing there, waiting for them?

"Emily, I'm here, and I'm listening," William whispered. "You're okay with me. Please tell me what's wrong." He held her shoulder.

It wasn't aggressive, the way Teddy used to grab her shoulder and direct her where to go. It was solid and comforting, the practiced grasp of a nurse who was used to panicking patients.

"The guy is outside. I can see him across the street. He's looking right at us." Emily stared at her drink. "I know I'm probably being irrational, but I think it's Teddy or someone who works for him."

William shuffled around in the booth to get a good look at the man. "It doesn't look like Teddy. From what I remember, Teddy is slimmer."

"But you agree that he's following us, don't you? He's watching us from across the street, and definitely waited for us outside the theater."

"He's waiting by my car. I'm guessing he knows we're on a date and thinks you probably brought a nice bag and maybe some nice jewelry..."

"What does that mean?" Emily breathed. She was trying to calm herself down, follow the directions her therapist gave her: take deep breaths, hold your breath, and let it out slowly.

"I think he's going to try to mug us. That's the only explanation I can think of. There's no way Teddy would risk his part of the settlement by having someone follow you. No, I think this guy is just a regular lowlife." William looked back at the man in the leather jacket. His grip tightened slightly on Emily's shoulder. "I'll go out there and get him away from my car."

"No, William, it's dangerous. Let's call the police, or maybe we'll walk around the block a few times and lose him."

"Emily, it's okay," William said. "I've dealt with creeps like him before. They want an easy target, someone who won't fight back or cause a scene. These guys slip through the shadows, and as soon as you shine a light on them, they run off. Just stay here and finish your drink. I'll be right back." He pulled on his jacket and hurried out of the bar before Emily could protest further.

From her seat she watched him cross the street and go over to his car. The man in the leather jacket tried to hurry off, but William caught up to him and blocked his path.

Emily braced herself for a fistfight, but it didn't happen. As soon as William confronted the man, he scurried away, as if he was embarrassed that he'd got caught, his arms crossed over his chest like he was hiding the rest of his loot.

Soon, William jogged back across the street, his dark hair billowing in the wind, dimples visible from miles away. She couldn't help but swoon a little.

"It's just as I thought," he said as he returned to his seat. "Little creep was so busy scoping out my car that he didn't see me coming up to him. As soon as I told him we could see what he was doing, he ran off. I wouldn't really recommend going after a stalker, but I knew I could take him."

"Wow, my hero." Emily smiled. "Thanks for keeping a cool head."

"Don't worry about it," William said, squeezing her tight. "You're safe with me, I promise."

Despite his words, Emily had an unsettling feeling wash over her.

EMILY and her therapist sat across from each other in silence. Emily wasn't sure how to bring up the subject of her date with William. She knew that Dr. Wright was there to help her, and she had been very helpful in the three years leading up to this point. Emily's insecurity didn't change that.

"What's going through your mind?" Dr. Wright asked, interrupting Emily's thoughts.

"I was thinking about my date with William," Emily replied. "Something happened that felt really messed up."

"Are you okay?" Dr. Wright asked, leaning forward in her chair. "Did he harm you?"

"Yes, I'm okay. He didn't hurt me. That's—no, it wasn't him. I just..."

"Why don't you start from the beginning?"

Emily paused, trying to figure out how to tell the story. "I'm not sure how to explain it without sounding like I'm being paranoid."

"Tell me what happened, and we'll go from there."

Emily told Dr. Wright about the man in the leather jacket who'd followed them from the movie theater to the bar. "He was about as tall as Teddy but with darker hair and a larger build. I know it's going to make me sound crazy but—"

"You thought it might be Teddy?"

Emily nodded, tears stinging her eyes. She felt so silly repeating the story, but it was a moment of intense anxiety for her. "It wasn't him though. William said the man was probably having a smoke break at the bar, and that's why we saw him earlier too. It made sense. Also, I think a lot of people who were leaving the theater were headed to the same bar we were going to, so maybe it was just a coincidence."

"That's pretty rational reasoning. You were afraid that he was threatening you personally and then realized he wasn't. I think you can be forgiven for that."

"Oh, there's more," Emily countered. "While we were having drinks at the bar, I saw the man again. He was staring right at us. I became convinced that it was Teddy in disguise or someone he'd sent to spy on us. I shared what was going on with William, but he thought the man was just a mugger because he was hovering around William's car. So he confronted him."

"That seems a bit reckless, don't you think?"

"I do, actually. I told him not to, that we should just call the cops, but he insisted on taking care of it. He said all you have to do with these muggers is show a little force."

Dr. Wright's eyebrows shot up. "I have to say I disagree with that, but go on."

"William scared him off, then came back and told me he was right—the man was just a mugger who was scoping out his car. I felt so stupid to be as anxious as I was."

"You don't have to feel stupid for that. It's your anxiety talking, that fight-or-flight response. You know how Teddy would react to the knowledge that you're dating again, so your guard is up a little higher than usual. You were right in that the man was following the two of you, and given your history, it's logical that you jumped to the conclusion that the man was somehow related to Teddy. Tell me, was

William feeding into this fantasy, or was he more occupied with the face value of the situation?"

"I would say he was more occupied with it at face value. He agreed the guy was watching us, and went with a more logical outcome. He tried to talk me down, pointed out how my perspective was wrong, but didn't make me feel like an idiot for thinking the way I did."

"That's good, healthy. Had he told you that you were imagining things, or tried to dismiss your fears, we'd be having a different discussion. While I disagree with how he handled it—in my opinion, it's better to keep your distance from a mugger than confront him—I think it's great that he knew exactly how to talk you down from a ledge."

Emily nodded. She was relieved that it wasn't just her being crazy. There was a legitimate worry that Teddy would stalk her. This time it was just a mugger, but anxiety made her think next time could be worse. "So you don't think I was being paranoid for no reason?"

"Absolutely not. It tells me you're aware of your surroundings and you're paying attention. And while your anxiety had you jumping to conclusions, you allowed your-self to accept the reality of the situation and let it go. That is a great breakthrough," Dr. Wright replied with a smile.

THAT NIGHT WHEN WILLIAM CALLED, he wasn't his usual self. He seemed upset.

"Is something wrong?" Emily asked.

He sighed. "I've had a very stressful day."

"Do you want to talk about it?"

"I appreciate that, but I don't think so," he said.

"I'm sorry. If you change your mind, I'm here..." Emily trailed off. She didn't know what to say, so she started babbling. "I was wondering if you'd like to come over and have a homemade dinner instead of going to a restaurant. I've become a pretty good cook lately, and there's a couple of recipes I want to try."

"I don't think I can get together this week. I need some time for myself. Sorry, Em, I have to go. Have a good night, okay?" William hung up.

Emily tried not to cry, but she couldn't help herself. She'd experienced a brief moment where her whole life wasn't falling apart, where she could be herself and actually have a little bit of uncomplicated fun. But just as quickly as it began, it all ended again.

———

EMILY HAD a night of fitful sleep, followed by a stressful morning. It started off with a call from her lawyer, which was never a good thing.

"Turns out there was a filing error," Sheldon said. "Teddy's counsel filed a motion that had already *been* filed months ago, for a media embargo, but they forgot to change the date. I already filed a petition against it since *they* were the ones who invited the media into the courtroom in the first place, but you know how this all goes. The courts won't get to it in time for our next scheduled appearance."

"How many weeks will it be delayed this time?" Emily asked.

"About three? Possibly four?" Sheldon answered. "I know this is frustrating, but the silver lining is this gives me more time to dig up the rest of the dirt on Teddy's infidelities and create a stronger case for you when it comes to the spousal abuse you suffered. It's been tough getting some of the hospital records, especially the ones where you and Teddy gave a fake name for registration and he paid the bill in cash. Sit tight. No good deed goes unpunished, as they say. Listen, I have to go," he said before hanging up.

Emily could picture him in his office, a blur of action as he called to his secretary to type another petition, or started dialing the phone to contact another hospital. She wanted to feel relieved that she could go another month without seeing Teddy, but Emily just felt drained. She was still waiting on a divorce, and still waiting by the phone for another man.

Her life was in limbo once again.

9

Emily didn't hear from William the next day. Or the day after that.

After two weeks of staying by the phone, waiting for it to ring, Emily gave up. She figured William realized she was probably more trouble than she was worth, and he ghosted her.

"You can't blame yourself," Dr. Wright said to her. "He was not prepared to enter into a relationship with you, but that doesn't make either of you a *bad* person. Just two people who might be right for each other at a different time in their lives."

Emily wasn't comforted by that. It only made her feel worse that somehow the universe was dangling a normal life in front of her, only to snatch it away.

Her sister and father weren't much help either. Both echoed Dr. Wright and said it wasn't her fault.

No matter what anyone said or whom they blamed, Emily couldn't ignore that she was alone again, and that she would be alone for some time. Even Sheldon was too busy for her, with Ciel and Associates trying their best to drown him in paperwork before the next court date. Sheldon hired an extra paralegal just to deal with the number of arbitrary motions Teddy's lawyers were sending his way, so he didn't have to dedicate an extra minute to the more facetious ones.

Emily gave up hope that William would change his mind. It didn't take much for Emily to resign herself to a lonely life again. She went back to her regular routine, checking the doors and windows before settling down with a glass of wine and a book, then falling asleep on the couch. She stopped looking up cute restaurants to check out and searching for fun date activities. She stopped waiting, so easily sure that there was no point. Her life was on hold until Teddy finally released her, and there was nothing she could do about it.

"Hey, um...I know I've been MIA, but, um...if you want to talk, please call me back. It's um...it's me...William."

Emily replayed the voicemail over again. Yes, it was the same—it was William's voice on the message. William had finally called her. After a solid three weeks, Emily had mentally prepared to never hear from him again, and she was *almost* fine with it.

Emily called Laurie and told her sister about the voicemail.

"But what does that mean?" Laurie squealed. "Is he trying to apologize for ghosting you?"

"I don't know. I was hoping you could tell me," Emily replied, chewing her fingernails.

"You should just leave him hanging. Give him a taste of his own medicine."

"I can't do that, Laurie. I'd rather call him back and say to his face that he really hurt my feelings, or never speak to him again."

"Ugh, fine, then you should do that. Just ask him why he tried ghosting you and then came crawling back later. If he's offended, then you'll know for sure that you are better off without him. If he answers, then good, you can decide whether or not you're going to accept him back. Either way, I'm not going to be able to help you unless you help yourself."

Emily hung up more confused than she had been before. Should she take her sister's advice and let William squirm a little bit? She had a ton of work to do for Horace, so it wasn't like she had a bad excuse. She could leave it until the end of her workday, and if William asked, she'd tell him as much.

No one expects a callback in the middle of a workday unless it's some kind of family emergency, she thought. Emily scrolled back through her work meeting notes from her last conversation with her boss, trying to decipher her erratic shorthand. That would take a few hours itself; might as well dive into her work and try to forget the voicemail until later that evening. Maybe she'd answer at the end of the day, after she had calmed down with a glass of wine. William could wait.

After all, she'd been waiting for the past three weeks.

When her workday was done, Emily settled into her favorite chair with a glass of wine and her phone. She'd made a list of questions for William, but left them in her office, hoping to make this a normal conversation rather than an inquisition.

William answered after the first ring. "I was hoping you'd call back. I was afraid you might not want anything to do with me."

"I'm curious, I guess. You were so invested in our relationship, and then suddenly you were gone. I can't help but think I drove you away."

"Nonsense," William replied. "You didn't drive me away at all. I just..." He trailed off and sighed. "I was having a little trouble with an ex."

"You were having a little trouble with an ex, so you ghosted me? William, I have the *ultimate* troublesome ex, and I still started dating you. What could possibly be so bad that your solution was to check out altogether?"

"I know. I know, it's not a very good answer, but it's what I can give you without having to explain...everything else. It's complicated, but maybe we can meet for dinner and I can explain it to you? I have a reservation for us."

"Why should I give you another chance? How can I be sure you won't ghost me again?"

"Well, at least this time you'll have the reservation. I'd never give that up; my reputation in this town would be ruined," William exaggerated.

This time Emily didn't find his antics very funny. It had taken a lot for her to trust him, and it had all been ruined so easily. How could she trust him again so soon?

"William, please don't joke. I really felt abandoned when you did that. Like I wasn't worth your time, like my emotions were too bewildering for you to understand. Why should I wait for you to say this in person? Why can't you say it over the phone?"

"It's the kind of thing that is so much more complicated when I can't look into your beautiful eyes, you know? Please, I know you've been loving all the restaurant-hopping; you can't honestly tell me you want to give up with Maison Maguro on the line?"

Emily had seen Maison Maguro when she was

researching trendy date-night restaurants. It was French-Japanese fusion with an emphasis on sushi. The chef had been born in the south of France and spent ten years cooking in Japan as a private chef. There was nothing like it for miles around, and reservations had to be made a month in advance. Emily couldn't believe William even had this planned; he must have booked it when they first went out. Emily wanted to go, and William knew it. She wanted to resist, but she also wanted answers, and William was dangling them in front of her like a carrot.

"If I go, and you aren't there, I'm deleting your number and taking the reservation for myself. I'll even invite Laurie, so she can hop into your place if you're so much as a minute late. I'm not kidding, William. I don't want to play games. I'm sick of it. And on top of that, I want answers as to why you ghosted me."

"Aye, aye. If I'm not there Friday at 7 p.m., I'll consider myself out of the running as a suitor, and I'll kick myself for all of eternity. Can I call you tomorrow night? Maybe we can talk about our day, and I can apologize profusely again?"

"I think it would be best if we keep some distance between us until Friday. I don't want you to show up just out of guilt or something," Emily said. "Goodbye, William. I hope I see you at the restaurant." With that, she hung up.

She felt the way she did before she started dating Teddy —a strong woman who had men in the palm of her hand. Her terms were clear, and they were final—if William wasn't there on Friday, she would forget about him and focus on getting over her divorce, once and for all.

MUCH TO EMILY'S SURPRISE, William was true to his word. At 7 p.m. on the dot, Emily showed up to the restaurant and was met with William holding a large bouquet of pink peonies and a small teddy bear.

"Figures, the first time a man doesn't disappoint my sister and I'm missing out on dinner. Have fun; try not to break her heart again," Laurie said before waving them off and leaving.

William raised his eyebrows at Emily, then whisked them into the restaurant. "Glad I showed up. I think your sister would have tracked me down."

"Not before we ate; she's been dying to go to this restaurant."

Maison Maguro was just as Emily had expected. Fine dining with an exotic twist and a delicious cocktail menu. She couldn't decide, so she ordered their Tokyo Martini and a Kyoto Kite and took tiny sips of each. The meal was magical, but Emily felt she couldn't completely enjoy it. She kept wondering about William's mysterious disappearance, but she was hesitant to bring it up. It wasn't until dessert came around that Emily finally asked him about it.

"I really am sorry, Em, and I'm sorry for being so vague about it. Like you, I have an ex who...likes to hold our relationship over my head. I didn't want to bring you into it, especially with the divorce, so instead I just pivoted, and in the process I ignored you—"

"Ghosted me," Emily interrupted. "You should have said something. I would have understood. Sometimes it's easier to focus on one piece of drama in your life at a time, and you don't need to tell me every little thing. If you had said you needed some space—hell, you could have lied and said you were going out of town for all I cared—then I would have understood, and it wouldn't have made me feel quite so shitty. I really thought I did something wrong—"

William put his hand over hers and quieted her with a kiss. "You're right. I'm sorry for treating you so carelessly, to almost lose what we've been building together." He chuckled. "And for the record, I doubt it's possible for you to do something *wrong*."

"You'd be surprised."

"Hey, I meant what I said. You didn't do anything wrong. I just have a slightly haunted past that managed to rear its ugly head at a very bad moment. You really didn't deserve that, and I'm sorry." He kissed her again, a little longer and deeper this time.

Emily wondered what his haunted past was. She assumed that William had a pretty cookie-cutter life.

"Why don't you drive me home?" she whispered. "My sister was so convinced you wouldn't show up that she drove us both here. I don't have my car for once."

"Haha, I figured you didn't since you made a meal out of the wine pairings themselves. But yeah, I'd be honored to drive you home."

During the drive, they chatted about the restaurant, and William asked about her plans for the rest of the weekend.

"I'm going to stay home. I have a pile of books to catch up on."

When they got to her house, Emily played with his hair and tried to disarm him. "Wanna come inside? We can share our little secrets over some tea," she breathed.

William kissed her, sliding his tongue between her lips. "Sure, maybe we can play a little truth or dare, make it a real sleepover." He winked. William's hand found her waist, and the two made out in his car like a pair of teenagers.

"Is your dad home? I don't want him to get the wrong idea," William joked.

Emily giggled and led him into her house. She forgot about his haunted past. She forgot about everything except the handsome man in front of her who was slowly undressing as she led him to her bed.

10

Emily tried to be indulgent on Saturday. William had left after breakfast, and she spent the day catching up on the latest book releases. Her career as a writer haunted her in weird ways; she felt like she was always reading and editing at the same time. She couldn't get enough of stories, but couldn't help but think of the ways she would change them. Taking someone else's raw draft and crafting it into something more was the only creative output that stuck. That was all she could do when she was married to Teddy, and even now with all her free time, she preferred improving the stories of others to sitting down and writing something herself.

It's the benefit of living in hindsight, I guess.

Rather than drown herself in wine that night, Emily drew a bath. She read something new for her—a self-help book about tapping into your latent creativity, and journaled the night away.

At 9 p.m. on the dot, William called. "How was your Saturday?"

"Good." She told him about the books she was reading.

"I think your weekend will get more exciting soon," he said with a bright tone.

Emily wanted to ask what he had planned, but she figured he wouldn't tell her. William's secrets were under lock and key.

Their conversation went the same as they all had. Gentle ribbing and general flirting.

She spent her Sunday selfishly too. She was about to call her sister when the doorbell rang. *Weird, Laurie never shows up unannounced,* she thought. It could be her dad; he sometimes came by to "borrow" something and check up on Emily and the house.

Emily tiptoed toward the door, and to her surprise it was neither of her family members standing on her porch.

It was William.

William patiently waiting, holding a large bouquet of flowers and a paper bag.

"William?" Emily called through the door. She could see him on the little home security camera and then through the window. She knew it was him, yet there was still part of her that thought it was too good to be true.

"One and the same. I was wondering if you wanted to have an early dinner. Or maybe a late lunch?"

Emily slowly opened the door. William stood in front of her with a big goofy smile on his face, holding takeout and a bouquet. She didn't quite know how to feel. It felt presumptuous, like an invasion of her private space—but it was also so kind, so chivalrous and sweet that she couldn't help but blush.

"It's sushi. I hope that's okay."

"French sushi or regular sushi?"

William laughed as he came in. "Regular. I have California rolls, spicy salmon, some tempura. I got a platter for the two of us."

Emily gestured for him to come into the living room while she went to the kitchen to gather plates. "It's like you read my mind. Ever since going to Maison Maguro, I've been thinking about how I'd rather have a plain ol' California roll than deal with an aubergine aburi again."

"I thought the restaurant was good. You didn't like it?"

"Don't get me wrong—I absolutely loved that place and would go back in a second, but it will never, *ever* take the place of a Maki Special number three in my heart," Emily said as she came back into the living room.

William had set their food on her little coffee table and was waiting for her with the flowers. They embraced, her senses engulfed by the perfume from the flowers and William's naturally musky scent. He took the vase and cutlery from her, making a meal out of arranging their tablescape.

"What do you feel like watching?" Emily asked.

"You," William said, "but if that's weird, I'd settle for a romantic comedy or a political thriller. Nothing too good. I want to be able to talk over the movie."

She laughed.

He plopped himself onto the couch beside her and turned to the TV. "We should get started. I realize *I'm* the one who showed up unexpectedly and interrupted your lazy Sunday, but I can't stay late. I told one of the other nurses I'd cover her early shift tomorrow, so I have to be at the hospital at 6 a.m."

Emily put on the latest true-crime documentary on Prime. "This isn't too long, and who doesn't love an in-depth look at a serial killer who captured the nation's attention?"

"Ahh, not gory but unbelievable," William said. "Sounds like the perfect pairing for raw fish."

WHEN THE DOCUMENTARY WAS DONE, William helped Emily with the dishes. Then she walked him to the door, and they made out for a bit on her front step before he got in his car to leave.

Exactly thirty minutes after William had left, her phone started ringing. The caller ID came up as unknown caller. Each time she answered, the caller hung up.

Was someone watching her?

11

"**W**hen did the calls start?" Sheldon asked.

"Last night, maybe around six," Emily replied. "It was exactly half an hour after William left."

"Right. Maybe make note of it; if it was William feeling guilty—"

"But that's the thing, the calls weren't coming from his number, and I know he doesn't have a landline at his apartment. It was from an unknown caller."

Emily thought the calls could only be linked to one person: Teddy. He was always on the table when it came to any abusive behavior. It was possible this was another of Teddy's attempts to intimidate Emily into settling their divorce on unfavorable terms.

Sheldon leaned back in his chair and stared up at the ceiling. "I have a friend on the police force. I can see if he'll do me a favor and figure out where the calls are coming from. Your phone service should have records of the calls, and they can triangulate it with the cell towers to see where the call originated from, but it might be a moot point, as it could be a burner phone; still, I'll see if they can try. In the meantime, do you still have the recording app on your phone?"

"I do."

"Good, make sure to use it every time you get a phone call from an unknown number. That way we have a record of how often this person calls, and if they say anything, we'll have it recorded."

Emily nodded, grateful that she had a court date today. Sheldon was never the shoulder she had wanted to lean on, but he was often the person who gave the best advice. She had met Sheldon at the courthouse so he could brief Emily on the evidence he had collected on Teddy.

"I've found a local nonprofit that works with victims of domestic abuse. They've been a valuable resource," he said. "I wish I had known about them sooner. They have a whole network of lawyers and social workers who do everything they can to protect abuse victims. Talking to some of them...it's crazy what abusers have access to these days. They can attack from all sides; it's not just about showing up at your house and intimidating you in person anymore."

Emily understood what he'd discovered. She'd tried to tell him, but since he wasn't typically a divorce lawyer, this was really all new to him. She was just glad he was doing the research needed to help her.

"MR. CIEL, SIT DOWN."

"I will *not* sit down!" Ciel exclaimed, his face bright red.

"Not while my client is being *slandered* by this conman disguising himself as a lawyer."

Sheldon had just finished a long presentation describing all of Emily's hospital visits and how they coincided with Teddy's absences from work and small injuries of his own. Bruised knuckles that matched patterns of bruising on Emily's face; a sprained ankle that happened just after Emily was thrown down the stairs. Sheldon had even had a crime scene investigator write a report on each and every incident of domestic violence and how it was not possible for Emily to be the perpetrator of abuse while suffering the injuries that she did. It all started with the car crash, and since then Sheldon had made it his mission to comb through every minute of their marriage and expose what had happened behind closed doors.

Emily felt sick to her stomach, but she was impressed that he'd been able to piece it all together.

"All this is evidence of how far Ms. Gray will go to emotionally abuse my client. She knows that the work she put in years ago to hurt herself and take herself to a hospital is finally starting to pay off. The narrative of an abused wife is one that tugs at the heartstrings of many, which is why Ms. Gray had a years-long plan to destroy my client's reputation. Even in the so-called recording of the drive in which Ms. Gray attempted to kill herself and my client."

"Your Honor, we've determined that—"

Judge Adisa raised his hand at Sheldon and turned to Mr. Ciel. "I believe it was agreed by *both* parties not to reference that incident as an attempted suicide."

"This is a complete waste of time, and I think we need to start over with a new judge who hasn't been tainted by this two-bit opportunist," Ciel replied.

"Perhaps giving your fellow bar member some grace is what is needed in this situation, Mr. Ciel," Judge Adisa said. "I must point out that when you have the floor, Mr. Mason is very patient with your client's many accusations against Ms. Gray—accusations that I still have in front of me, that I will consider just as seriously as these."

"While we're on the subject of a waste of time," Sheldon interjected, "I would like to bring to this court's attention the many wasteful 'motions' being put forward by my opposing counsel. I've had to hire an associate just to sift through his correspondence to find what is actually relevant and needs to be addressed. I would also like to note the many errors that were made in recent court filings by Mr. Ciel's team— errors that were easily corrected by things like *spell check*, which caused weeks of delay in this settlement."

"Trust me, Mr. Mason, those have been noted," Judge Adisa said, staring at Carson Ciel over his half-rimmed glasses.

"We've already addressed the errors of my office," Ciel responded. "Mrs. Belinda Gaunt has made an extremely generous donation to the restoration of this courtroom as an unofficial apology. However, I resent the idea that all of our motions are a waste of time. I'm trying to protect my client from slander. Ms. Gray is obviously trying to ruin his reputation, and we are doing our duty to shield Mr. Gaunt from her vicious mistreatment."

From the back of the viewing gallery, Emily heard her sister scoff.

"I'm just saying," Ciel continued, "that all this 'evidence' needs to be examined, along with Ms. Gray's mental state. She is obviously delusional and is bringing her lawyer down with her. If we allow this to affect the settlement, then what will be next? Will Ms. Gray claim that my client tried to poison her every time she had the flu?"

Emily's stomach started to turn. She was doing everything she could to keep it together, to tune out what Mr. Ciel was saying, but it was becoming impossible.

"There is a huge difference in *correlation* between the flu and a broken nose," Sheldon argued. "I'm not bringing these out facetiously; this is to prove to you, Your Honor, that certain statements made by Mr. Ciel and company, especially where it concerns this settlement and what my client has the right to, are false and hypocritical. How can he say she doesn't have the right to any money due to an alleged affair, when I have evidence that his client had multiple affairs throughout their marriage?"

"She is clearly a gold digger who got too far over her head," Ciel said, "and now is grasping at straws, trying to take what is *not* rightfully hers."

Teddy stared at Emily with a self-satisfied smile.

He knew what this was doing to her—Emily had never wanted to stop working when they got married. She had wanted to continue writing, but Teddy and Belinda cajoled her until she broke down and gave in to what they wanted. Throughout their marriage, Belinda had perpetuated the idea that Emily had married Teddy for his money, but Emily didn't know how deep the Gaunt pockets were until *after* they were married—Belinda made sure of it, because she didn't want Teddy to get trapped by a gold digger. Their whole life was a contradiction, a long journey in hypocrisy. Emily wanted so badly to cry, but she knew Teddy's lawyers would turn it against her if she did—they would say she was lying, just as they said she was lying about the car accident, and she had that on video.

"One can argue that Ms. Gray shouldn't be relying on my client as a gravy train any longer because she willingly gave up her career, and it was her decision to get divorced. It seems that the moment Ms. Gray faces the grim consequences of a poor decision, she shifts blame elsewhere so that she can avoid facing the negative outcome. Now she's resorting to sordid tactics in order to get what she wants. Digging in to Mr. Gaunt's life, dragging his name through the mud, provoking him to the point where he has a panic attack, and even going so far as to claim an 'expert' has examined these hospital photographs and cleared his client of any wrongdoing. Ms. Gray is an opportunistic vulture, and in my opinion, we shouldn't reward her by entertaining her delusions."

Did he even take a breath during that whole speech? Emily thought. She was fighting her instinct to get up and run away, or scream back at Carson Ciel. Sheldon was calm; he listened to Mr. Ciel's speech like it was a bedtime story. Was her lawyer even going to get up and defend her? Or was all this work, all this debt, for nothing?

"Your Honor," Sheldon said, standing up, "I—"

Once again Judge Adisa put up his hand. "Mr. Mason, you don't have to waste your breath. Mr. Ciel, while I appreciate the passion you have for defending your client, I'm afraid you've lost the plot when it comes to this case. This is a divorce settlement, not the latest episode of a legal drama. There will be no tirades here, and if I hear a speech coming out of your mouth again, I will not hesitate to hold you in contempt of court—understand?"

The case continued, with Sheldon presenting more evidence of Teddy's infidelities and abuse, as well as proof he more or less forced Emily out of her career by faking rejection letters from various famous publishing houses.

When Emily heard that part, she felt sick to her stomach. She hadn't known the rejections were fake. How had Sheldon discovered that? She wanted to ask, but the second court adjourned for the day, Emily scurried off, ignoring her sister and father, who were trying to get her attention. She spent a good twenty minutes emptying the contents of her stomach and crying so hard a woman in the next stall thought she was choking. Eventually she was rescued by her sister.

"Dad got your purse from Sheldon. He's driving your car back to the house," Laurie said. "I've cancelled my plans for the rest of the day so I can make you dinner, draw you a bath, and make sure you don't throw yourself out the window tonight."

"Thank you," Emily choked out. "I really appreciate it."

They were mostly silent on the drive home. Tears continued to stream down Emily's face as she tried to let go of the day, but it felt impossible.

"Laurie," Emily asked, "how am I supposed to trust a man after all this?"

"What are you talking about? You trust William, don't you?"

Emily shifted in her seat. "I just mean—I thought Teddy was perfect when I first met him. He was so kind and charismatic. He was so understanding when I talked about Mom. Then as soon as we were married, he turned into this narcissistic monster. How can I know that a guy isn't going to turn out...toxic? How can I know their real personality?"

Laurie took a deep breath. "Honestly, there's no way of knowing. Dating is a gamble; it's a weird luck of the draw where the more experience you have, the better you get at figuring out when to bet. Let me ask you—other than the ghosting thing, has William given you any reason to doubt him?"

"No." Emily sniffed. "He's been kind and considerate. And he apologized for ghosting me. If anyone can understand what it's like to deal with an ex, it's me."

"I have to say it sounds like you're *trying* to find something wrong with the guy. You should trust him, but trust yourself more. If you feel uncomfortable, or if you aren't excited to see him anymore, break it off."

It seemed so simple when Laurie said it, but Emily had been burned so badly in the past it was hard to take her sister's advice. She wanted to restart, but worried that no matter what she did, Teddy would drag her back into his orbit.

12

Emily made lists, talked to her therapist, and even considered consulting a psychic, but by the end of the week she was no closer to figuring out a foolproof method for sniffing out a toxic man. It was just as her sister said: you had to trust your instincts even when they had failed you in the past.

In the meantime, William continued to do nothing that supported the idea he was a toxic or suspicious suitor. He called Emily on Tuesday, to give her a little breathing room after the court date. He sent flowers when she told him about all the horrible things Teddy's lawyers were saying, with a card that listed all her good qualities. William continued to be perfect, but Emily continued to be suspicious. It was as though she was just waiting to see what happened next, and there was nothing to solve this stalemate of her emotions in her mind.

"Just relax," Laurie said. "At this point you're looking for a reason to fear him. He's done nothing wrong."

She knew her sister was right. Still, Emily felt nervous.

She just didn't trust her own instincts and hated that she had to put her own romantic life through that.

————

WHEN FRIDAY CAME AROUND, Emily was ready for another date with William. The unhealthy thoughts aside, she did enjoy these weekly excursions into the world. They had made her start thinking about how to begin her life again. Going out with William made Emily crave a social life again —maybe a supper club or a book club. Something that would get her out of the house and into a less romantic relationship.

"I think it's a great idea," William told her. "You've grown as a person in the past few years. Might be nice to get reacquainted with yourself."

They were about three drinks into a tasting at a mezcal-tequila bar. All the cocktails were made with one of the two spirits, and the bar had flights you could buy to try the rest. It was Emily's idea—though now she couldn't remember why. She wanted something like a whiskey bar, but with less whiskey, and somehow came to the conclusion that a mezcal-tequila bar was the solution.

"I could start a tequila club." She giggled. "Every week we talk about a new tequila until someone admits that they've been cheating on their spouse with the pool boy."

"Does it have to be a pool *boy*? Can it be a pool *girl* as well? Who is invited to this club? I need details, Em," William said, his head bent down.

"It can be either gender; members can be either gender. There are only two rules. Rule number one: you have to drink tequila. Rule number two: you have to keep drinking tequila until someone admits to having an affair with the pool staff."

"But what if people don't have pools?"

"It can be an inflatable pool."

"What if they don't have staff?"

"Then they can't come. Only people with staff, that's what makes it so juicy. Rich people would rather drink themselves silly than admit to an affair."

"It's brilliant. You should make this a TV show."

"Yes! It's the next reality franchise—Real Poolies of Tequila!"

The two burst into giggles and fell into each other. Emily was drunk. William was drunk. Neither could tell who was more drunk. The waiter was starting to get annoyed; pretty soon they'd get cut off. When Emily pointed this out, William's face went white.

He took a deep breath and steadied himself. "We can't get cut off, it's too early."

"Neither of us has admitted to sleeping with the pool boy!"

That made them burst out laughing all over again. It didn't even feel like a date. Emily felt like she was out with one of her oldest friends, giggling about ridiculous scenarios that might never happen, but *could*.

"I miss this. I miss feeling so carefree," Emily said, almost knocking over her glass. It was the first time she'd let herself go like this since college. She could hardly remember what they drank, and at this point it kind of felt like it didn't even matter. She wanted to keep drinking, to drink until she had to throw up, like she had done in college. She said as much to William, who laughed alongside her.

"If you think I'm going to hold your hair back—"

"No one needs to hold my hair back," Emily slurred. "I'm an expert."

That was when the waiter came over and finally kicked them out.

The second they stood up, Emily realized—she was *wasted.*

"I can't go home like this," she muttered as they walked out of the bar. "I can't drive like this. I-I can*not* be beehive—behind the wheel of a car."

"What are we gonna do?" William asked, his tequila-laced breath wafting around her hair. "Man, I did *not* know we would get this drunk."

"We need food. Good food. We need to sleep. We—I need to sit down." Emily plopped herself down on a nearby bench and crumpled like a rag doll.

William pulled her up, and together they stumbled down the street toward a small hotel. Luckily for them, it was only a block away from the bar—a benefit of being on the trendy side of town. Somehow William managed to communicate that they needed a room for the night. Throughout all this Emily tried her best to keep the room from spinning too fast around her.

The last thing she remembered was the strangely patterned wallpaper of their hotel room and the sound of William ordering room service.

"I HAVEN'T HAD a night like that since college," Emily said the next morning.

"Neither have I, and now I understand why."

Emily and William were lying in bed, each holding their head.

Emily felt embarrassed as the night came back to her. She cringed at the thought of them getting kicked out of the bar. Emily wanted an Advil, and she wanted to get home. "William, I have to—"

"Say no more. I have to get my car and get home to my own bed before I puke."

They quickly checked out of the hotel and went to find their cars. William brought up the question of brunch, but she figured it was more of a courtesy than a real suggestion —at least she hoped that was the case because Emily didn't want to think about food just yet.

"Even though I drank to the point of not remembering much," Emily said as they parted ways, "I do know I had fun. It felt good to let loose a bit."

William kissed her on the forehead. "Maybe next time we'll get a little less loose."

Emily cringed and got into her car, determined to get home. She headed for a local Mexican take-out place, ordered a burrito, then drove the rest of the way home.

She arrived less than an hour later, burrito in hand, ready to spend the day tackling her pile of freshly bought books. She threw her keys into the bowl, but missed, and they went tumbling down the back of her console table.

Weird, I usually have much better aim, Emily thought as she went digging for her keys. The console table seemed oddly out of place. Like it had been moved about an inch away from the wall. Emily dismissed it as a symptom of her hangover and went into the living room.

But the feeling of her house being off-kilter didn't go away.

The TV felt like it was at a different angle and was receiving more glare from the windows. Her couches felt like they had been moved in the opposite direction than the TV, so the angle from where she was seated was wrong too, but only slightly. There was no logical explanation for how she felt— everything in her house was slightly off-kilter. Just enough for Emily, who spent almost all of her time at home, to notice.

It's just the hangover, Emily. You're not twenty-one anymore; it takes longer to recover.

She moved over to get a glare-free view of the TV before digging in to her burrito. She noticed the TV screen was a little darker than usual when she turned it on. It felt as though Emily had stepped into her house in a different dimension, just one league over from normal. Whether it was the hangover or something more sinister, the effect had Emily feeling like she was suffering from motion sickness.

She pledged never to drink again as she adjusted the brightness on her TV and struggled to get comfortable on her couch. The air in her house felt off too; it was stuffy and felt familiar in a weirdly alien kind of way. This was the smell of a different home, of a different time in her life. She was about to light a candle when she realized what the smell was—tobacco and musk. Teddy's cologne and the tobacco from his cigars; the smell had hung in the air in her old home. Teddy always refused to let her light the powdery floral candles that she loved.

I must be going crazy, she thought. *I haven't been this hungover in years; my brain is short-circuiting or something.* The hangover anxiety was taking its toll; this recovery process needed more than just a burrito. She needed to sleep some more, take a long afternoon nap, and wake up cured of this strange unsteadiness of her perception.

Emily took a tranquilizer and put herself to bed. She would write off the day and start fresh tomorrow morning.

EMILY WOKE UP HOURS LATER, the house blanketed in an inky darkness. She shuffled to the bathroom to throw some water on her face. She was hungry; she needed dinner and a large glass of water—the tranquilizers always made her thirsty.

The house was quiet except for the sound of water dripping. It must be the kitchen faucet; that thing desperately needed to be replaced. As Emily turned to go downstairs, she heard footsteps heading to her kitchen, and then the dripping stopped.

Emily froze. Who could be in her house? Didn't she lock the door behind her? She was so hungover and tired; she didn't check the locks on her windows. It could be anybody.

The footsteps continued; they were headed to the living room now.

Emily crept downstairs, grabbing an old vase from the hallway. It could be nothing. It could be her imagination— but it could be an intruder. It could be Teddy; the house was filled with his scent.

As soon as she got downstairs, the footsteps stopped. She went into the kitchen, but there was no sign of anyone there. The sink was completely dry, with no evidence of a dripping faucet.

Suddenly the footsteps started again. Upstairs this time, nearing her bedroom—how did they get upstairs without Emily seeing them?

She held her breath and tiptoed across the kitchen to the

stairs, hoping to catch a glimpse of the intruder. She saw nothing, even when she leaned into the stairwell.

The intruder moved again. This time they were closer, and it sounded like they were coming from the living room.

Emily ran into the room, but there was no one there. The window was open, and a breeze was rustling her curtains. Emily ran over, but there was no sign of anyone running away from the house. There was no one hiding under the window.

When Emily whipped around, she was still alone. There was no one in her house.

But there were footsteps in her entryway; then she heard the front door open and slam shut.

13

"It was just a dream."

Emily sat up in bed, trembling as she remembered her nightmare. "There's no one in the house; you're safe. It was only a dream," she repeated into the darkness of her room.

The tranquilizers always gave her strange dreams; that was part of the reason she'd stopped taking them. The paranoia she felt in her waking life seeped into her dream life, leaving her with an unsettling nightmare.

"It was just a dream. There's no one in the house; you're safe. It was only a dream."

Emily repeated her mantra over and over until finally her heart stopped racing.

Eventually she fell back asleep, this time dreaming about nothing, as if her body was waiting for sunrise.

LATER THAT SUNDAY MORNING, Emily woke up dazed and confused. Her weekend was practically over; she'd spent half of it in bed. Her house was still off-kilter, so she spent the morning readjusting her furniture and checking her doors and windows. Someone must have broken in and played a sick joke on her. It was probably Laurie, the only person with a spare key. And there was the fact that Emily had ignored her sister's call on Friday night when she was out with William, so this was likely Laurie's silly idea of a prank.

Emily knew Laurie had a mischievous streak. Her baby sister could take pranks too far, usually when she felt no one was paying enough attention to her. Dr. Wright attributed this to being the younger child in a family dealing with narcissism. Their father had been busy attending to their mother's many needs, Emily was always busy taking care of her father and mother and mothering Laurie, and this left Laurie feeling unloved by their parents, unable to draw attention unless she acted out. It was the logical progression of how abuse affected a family; no matter what Emily did to protect Laurie, there was no way she could shelter anyone from their mother's emotional abuse.

No, instead of calling and yelling at Laurie, Emily would just invite her sister over for dinner tonight. She would see that Emily had dismantled her little prank—that would be enough manipulation between sisters for one weekend. Emily tried calling, but Laurie didn't answer. Emily tried a few more times, but her calls kept going straight to voice-mail, and she left messages each time.

After the last voicemail, Emily rolled her eyes. *Fine, if you're really that angry, I'll just leave you be.* Laurie could be astoundingly immature, and it drove her up the wall. She poured herself a glass of wine and started preparing dinner. Laurie could order takeout for all she cared. Just as the pasta started to boil, Emily's phone rang.

"Finally, you know if you weren't my sister, I'd—" Emily cut herself off—Laurie wasn't on the other end of the line. No one was. There was something going on—whoever called was in a café or a bar, Emily could hear the din in the background, but they weren't saying anything.

"Hello?" she asked.

There was no answer, and the person hung up.

Emily checked her call log; it was from a private number. The call sent chills down her spine, especially after that strange nightmare. The feeling of being watched, of someone in her private space, filled Emily with anxiety.

"Emily, you're safe. You're in your own home. The doors are locked, so are the windows. You're safe; it was only a dream."

She had to repeat the mantra over and over again, muttering it under her breath while she cooked. The phone call was unsettling, and Emily was still too sensitive to brush it off. She wished she had recorded it, and then wished her sister were here; even if she didn't apologize for the prank, it would have been nice to have had some company.

———

THAT NIGHT, Emily settled into her couch for her favorite activity—watching a movie until she fell asleep on the couch. She chose the lightest, most inane comedy to calm her nerves. All she wanted was to forget her nightmare and the strange prank pulled on her. Nothing was working. She chose her favorite romantic comedy, but the will-they-won't-they chase felt more like a man stalking the object of his desire. She chose another buddy comedy but couldn't handle the crude humor. She went for an old sitcom, but was disturbed by how the main characters spied on their neighbor.

To top it off, since the weird hang-up call, Emily had felt like someone was watching her. There was a presence in her home—the same presence that was in her nightmare—waiting for the next moment she could be caught off guard. The presence was waiting to ring her doorbell and run away, or call her and hang up again. The presence wanted her to leave so it could cause strange havoc in her home again.

This was a completely illogical thought, and Emily knew it, but there was a time she would have said divorcing Teddy was completely illogical—how else was she supposed to learn how to trust her instincts if she didn't listen when her instincts were telling her something was wrong?

Emily did her security routine. She made sure her car didn't have anything on it—no tracking devices or tiny cameras, then went back inside and checked her cameras and the doors and windows twice. The time she could have spent watching a movie was spent making sure she wasn't being watched.

When Emily was finally satisfied that she was well and truly alone, she dragged herself to bed and went to sleep.

―――――――――

THE FEELING of being watched didn't go away. The next day Emily worked from a nearby café, just to avoid the feeling that her home was compromised. She was supposed to have two calls with Horace, but he abruptly cancelled both, leaving Emily with a mostly empty schedule. She waited by her computer for Horace to reach out randomly as he sometimes liked to do, but he never did.

"Do you need the Wi-Fi password or something?"

"Sorry?" Emily looked up at the handsome college student awkwardly standing over her.

"Do you need the Wi-Fi password? You have your computer open, but you're just reading."

"Oh! No, I'm good. Just waiting for my boss to email me." Emily smiled, waiting for the barista to awkwardly back away. There wasn't much for her to do, but it felt easier to do it in public.

Just then, as if her computer heard her, a notification lit up her screen.

A request has been made to reset the password associated with the following email address: gray.emilyamelia@flamingopress.com. If this is you, reset your password at the link below. If you do not need a password reset, feel free to ignore this email.

Weird. How could Emily have requested a password reset when she was already signed in to her email account? She sat there staring at her inbox. It wasn't possible that she—

Don't start panicking, Emily. You went through the Flamingo Press security course, so you know exactly what to do.

It wasn't personal. It was just another hacker trying to get into the publisher's server. Emily ignored the email, bypassing the link and changing her password through her account settings. She set a reminder to change it again in a few hours, just in case. She then made sure to sign out of all her accounts, getting back into her email right away before someone could change the password again. Then she sent the email to the Flamingo Press security account, detailing the phishing attempt.

Hopefully, that was enough. It was probably why Horace had cancelled their meetings—if they were going after her, they probably tried going after him first. If that was the case, she ought to have been the one he contacted. She would have to get his new passwords so she could sign into his calendars. Emily was halfway into writing an email to Horace when she realized there was a half-finished reply in her drafts.

Dear Mr. DeVilliers,

I, your assistant, have decided to quit. Frankly, I don't think I can continue working for you. Not only do I think you are a fat asshole who can't read to save his own life, but I also think you are a misogynist and probably a pedophile. Everyone knows that at the top of the publishing world is a cabal of men who take advantage of children and perpetuate ideas of witchcraft, and I cannot work for that industry any more. I have finally come to my senses, and I only hope you are able to do the same.

Seek God, Horace! Seek the Lord as I have! You don't have to keep doing this, you can save yourself if you just leave your position and come meet me. I will be in Los Angeles on the 26th of November of this year for my baptism, I hope you can come. If you do, a pastor will explain to you why the upper echelon of this country is filled with witches and bitches who want nothing more than to turn men into cuckolds. I hope you are not yet a cuckold because I am obviously in love with you, that's the only reason I could ever keep working for a fat, ugly man like you.

I quit, and you should come to my baptism. If you were baptized, you could finally be filled with light and we could have sex.

Signed,
Emily Gray

Emily's blood ran cold. This was obviously the reason why Horace had cancelled their meetings. He knew Emily had struggled with her mental health and probably saw this email as some kind of relapse. She felt herself deflating like a balloon, and struggled to read the next message in their email chain.

Dear Sir or Madam,

I am writing to inform you that this email has been sent to our security team at Flamingo Press.

Best,
Horace DeVilliers

There was still a chance. Emily might not completely lose her job and livelihood yet.

Dear Mr. DeVilliers,

*I'm sorry for the erratic and emotional email. As you are
aware, I have been struggling with my mental health for
quite some time. Because of that, I think you should fire
me. I want to quit, but if I quit, I can't get severance pay
and that is more important to me than my health. I think
this manic episode has been a long time in the making and
there is nothing more I can do to avoid it. Unless you want
my work to suffer, I think it's best you let me*

The email ended abruptly. The draft was sitting in her
inbox unfinished. It was probably when Emily had signed
out of her accounts, cutting the hacker off. She was about to
email Horace when she saw there was a new message from
her therapist, Dr. Wright.

Dear Emily,

*I find it hard to believe this is actually you, so I'll address
the sender of the email. I don't know who you are, or what
the intention of this message is, but I have recorded the
message, and Ms. Gray's legal representation has been
notified.*

Emily felt paralyzed. She was starting to think her weird
experience over the weekend wasn't a prank at all. She
scrolled back to the original message:

Dr. Right,

*I know you are in love with me, and you've been stalking
me in your spare time. Someone broke into my house this
weekend, and I know it was you. I have cameras all over*

my house and they show you entering my home and causing havoc with my things. You don't believe me? I'm happy to send over the footage. I am going to send this footage to the psychologists board and get your license revoked unless you do the following:

1. Tell my boss that I am mentally ill. He refuses to fire me even though I have stated repeatedly that I need a break.
2. Cancel all of our appointments.

You have until the end of day to do both of these things. Please CC me on the email you send to my employer, Horace DeVilliers at Flamingo Press. If not, I will release the footage of your obvious obsession with me, and you'll never work again.

Sincerely,
Emily Gray

Emily was horrified. She wasn't sure what to do or whom to call first. Should she call Horace and tell him this wasn't a mental breakdown at all, that she was still completely sane and had no idea who had sent those messages—or did she email her therapist to tell her the horrible comments in her email were from a hacker?

Emily felt stunned and could do nothing but stare at her computer in disbelief. Who was targeting her? Teddy couldn't be doing it—he knew anything he did to hurt Emily would just be brought up against him during court. Besides, he didn't know where she worked. Emily didn't appear on the Flamingo Press website, so there was no way he could get her email that way.

If it wasn't Teddy, then who?

After Emily scrubbed her computer with every cybersecurity measure she could think of, she called Horace. Luckily for her, he was still awake.

"I know it's late, and this is probably inappropriate, but—"

"Emily, I never thought those emails were from you," Horace said. "The spelling and grammatical errors were so out of character, it was almost comical. I am sorry if I made you nervous, but I wanted to make sure the company's security department was made aware of the hack; they'll probably contact you tomorrow to tighten up your security."

"Thank you," Emily mumbled.

"I know you are going through a somewhat high-profile divorce. I don't know if this is related, but I think you have a cyber stalker. If you haven't already, make sure to start documenting anything strange that might be happening, even the most innocuous stuff. Trust me, I used to deal with this when I worked in newspapers."

"Thanks, Horace, I'll do that."

"If you need time off to deal with it, just let me know. I'm going to let you go, I'm afraid I'm at a dinner with some publishing agents, and if I spend another minute on my phone, one of them is going to think I'm ready to publish his authors."

Emily hung up, packed her things and returned home. She sat in the darkness of her living room. She had checked the windows and doors, twice each. She checked the cameras, even looking to make sure the tapes hadn't been erased.

Her comforting routine suddenly felt completely futile. If this didn't protect her, if her stalker could break through and touch her on a different plane, then what was the point of all this? Why was she fighting it?

14

*You think this is bad, Emily? This is just the beginning.
Your life is going to get worse. I overplayed my hand, I'll
be the first to admit it, and that was definitely a mistake,
but you? You can fix it all. Just change your passwords
back, and everything will go back to normal.*

The email was sitting in her inbox that Wednesday,
waiting for her to wake up. Emily had spent the
previous day scrubbing her internet presence.
Gone were her social media profiles, any piece of information she had online, even her online banking profiles. There
was nothing this person could touch. Emily had worked
with a security expert to make sure she'd thought of
everything.

That also meant each and every little convenience she
had was gone too. Was that what her stalker meant by her
life getting worse? Now she was stuck with a little notepad so
she could record her passwords; another book to write down
what she spent and where. She was going to have to go into

the bank to pay her bills or check her accounts—services they now charged a fee for, since everyone did their banking online. She was tempted to answer the stalker and tell them she was *determined* to show them she wasn't afraid. Her life was finally her own, and no one was going to take that away from her.

The messages continued throughout the week, not only to Emily but to her boss and therapist as well. At her weekly session she apologized to Dr. Wright, who waved it off.

"You're not the first patient of mine who has dealt with abuse like this. The internet is a blessing and a curse—it's the information superhighway, with a fast lane for abusive partners and stalkers."

Horace was just as understanding. He set up an email filter for Emily that automatically moved all the stalker's emails into a folder where they could be documented, and had a copy sent to the security department.

The support she received made her want to cry; there was a time in her life when she thought if she left Teddy, she would be so deeply alone. While Dr. Wright and Horace weren't exactly friends, it felt good to know they were willing to fight her corner.

"Wait, I don't understand—why can't I pick you up from your house?" William asked.

Emily was trying to plan their next date, but didn't want to bring William into the fold of her stalker's crazy behavior. "I'll explain more at dinner, but I think I have a stalker, and I don't want him to get your license plate."

"Is he outside your house? Why don't you call the police or—"

"No, he's a cyber stalker. He—or she or whatever—already hacked into my email and sent weird emails to my boss and my therapist. They clearly know their way around a computer system, so I worry that if they have your license plate, they'll start harassing you as well. I'll meet you at the restaurant. I promise it'll be fine."

William kept talking about protecting her, but that wasn't what Emily needed. She needed William to protect himself so he could continue to be an island of calm for her. It wasn't getting through.

Even during dinner, William acted as the bold and angry boyfriend, the protector of the damsel. "I can stay with you for a while, but what you're saying doesn't sound like a stalker. I have a friend who got hacked; they attack people with no abandon; it's nothing personal. I honestly think you may be blowing this out of proportion."

She had expected William to be a little more support-ive. Emily didn't want to share what she had done that week or how she was feeling if William was going to shut her down. The paranoia she felt *was* real; it came from a very honest place. It was a normal reaction to feeling like someone had broken into your home, played a strange prank on you, and then gone on to start threatening your boss.

"Still, I don't think those are connected," he continued. "You said so yourself, Laurie was probably the one who messed up your house as a stupid prank. The hang-ups sound like butt dials or telemarketers who lost their nerve. Everything can be explained, Emily, and I want to help you, but I do think at least some of this is your imagination. You said so yourself, that feeling of someone being in your house was a nightmare, right?"

"Right—but someone hacking into my email is very tangible. Sending threatening emails, escalating their attacks, all that is very targeted behavior, don't you agree?"

"Sure, I just don't think it's a stalker. With the divorce going the way it is, maybe your subconscious is trying to personalize what isn't really personal."

Dinner ended very soon after that. Emily lost her appetite for romance. She got in her car and cried quietly all the way home.

When she got home, her phone pinged. It was a voice-mail from her stalker using one of those voice-changing apps so it sounded robotic and was almost as chilling as the words they spoke.

"Red dress, knee-length. Not too slutty, which is good for a date with your little suitor. The black heels don't really match. I would have chosen something to match the dress, or something a little lighter and more casual. I like you in natural makeup; it enhances your natural beauty. Though I would say—your highlights need to be touched up. I'm starting to see a little bit of the roots come through. Also, nice bag—wouldn't think you could afford designer with how modestly you live, but I guess there are some perks to being frugal. How was Tropicalia? I've always wanted to try Brazilian food—was the caipirinha everything you hoped it would be?"

Emily screamed and threw her phone into the living room. She had been on alert, made sure to have a table with a full view of the restaurant. She had parked down the street, walking a few blocks just in case someone was following her and she could catch them, but it was all useless. Someone was stalking her, following her every move, judging everything she did—but who? Could it possibly be Teddy?

She shook her head. The only person she'd seen that night, the only one who knew where she would be and what she was wearing was William. But he couldn't possibly be the stalker.

Could he?

15

The weekend felt about a month long. Emily continued to be harassed by her cyber stalker, and had no clue how to work out their identity. She tried doing a reverse IP address search, but the instructions she found online got overly complicated really quick. She googled the email address, only to find that it was randomly generated off a very disturbing website for prank hackers. There was no clear way forward apart from giving in to the stalker's demands. She tried to figure out who it could be. The only possible culprits were William and Teddy.

That was how she put it to Sheldon when she met with him on Monday.

"I don't quite understand," Sheldon responded. "You're saying Teddy or William got into your email and started sending threatening messages to people? How did he get a hold of your computer?" He meant well, but he was not exactly computer savvy.

"No, somehow they figured out my password. He tried to

change it so he could take over my email, but luckily, I managed to log out of my accounts before he could. I don't know who it could be, but I wouldn't put it past Teddy to do this. He's incredibly smart, and I think he'd be capable of hacking into my accounts."

"Do you think Teddy is the one following you too?" Sheldon asked.

"Maybe. I'm not sure. All I know is that I've had this weird feeling that someone has been following me. And he's been sending threatening emails as well as leaving voicemails with a robotic voice, including the one I got on Friday night. It details everything I wore and where I went that night."

"How can Teddy be following you if he doesn't know where you live?" he questioned, but then looked thoughtful. "Unless he followed you home or had someone else follow you." He shook his head, frowning.

"I suppose that's possible. He could have hired a private detective to find me." Emily realized she'd been naïve to think Teddy couldn't find her if he wanted to.

"I'm the first to admit, computers aren't my expertise, so I'm not sure how to monitor it. I'll reach out to some of my contacts on the police force, and some reliable private investigators I know. Either way, I'll have someone keep an eye on Teddy—both virtually and in reality."

"If it makes you feel any better, after this your cybersecurity will be impeccable." She smiled weakly, then left Sheldon's office.

Emily arrived home and immediately went through her updated routine. She swept her car for any tracking devices, checked the locks on her doors and windows, and checked the camera system—including the tape that was in there—and monitored her internet activity for the day.

Everything seemed normal, yet when she sat down in her living room, her television turned on by itself, blasting the song "Somebody's Watching Me."

16

A few days later Emily sat across from Sheldon with a report open on the desk in front of her. It showed the internet activity at her house, which looked normal, as well as Teddy's reported activities for the days in question.

"A personal investigator friend put the report together," he said. "There isn't a single sign of Teddy being behind this."

Emily was in shock. For days the cyberattacks had been steadily escalating, and she was sure she'd find out it was Teddy. Teddy playing these mind games and trying to get her to give up—give up on her job, her therapy, and maybe even the divorce.

"Is he sure?" she asked. "Did he really follow Teddy everywhere he went?"

Sheldon sighed. "He kept an eye on Teddy in person, and he has a guy he works with who is a cyber wiz. Trust me, these men are experts. If they say Teddy hasn't been anywhere near you, hasn't spoken with anyone who is in your vicinity, I'm inclined to believe them."

"Could Teddy have hired someone else to do it?"

"That is possible," he admitted. "The investigator didn't rule it out completely."

"Were they at least able to track down where the random emails are coming from? It's been getting worse—" Emily cut herself off before she burst into tears.

"Hey," Sheldon said, handing Emily a box of tissues, "this isn't the end of the investigation, it's just a check-in. If it turns out it is Teddy or someone he's hired, he's bound to mess up, and that's when we'll catch him. But in the meantime, we have to entertain other possibilities—if only for your own safety. Is there anyone else who knows your address, your employer, and your therapist?"

Emily bit her lip, hesitant to admit the truth. The only person in her life who knew that much about her was William. She didn't talk with her father about her therapist, and Laurie didn't pay enough attention to recall the name of Emily's boss.

Emily was faced with a question she desperately didn't want to ask. Could William be her stalker?

EMILY WENT HOME that night and hid from the world. She didn't even bother to do her security routine, she just crawled under the covers and waited to fall asleep.

It was so tempting to give up. She knew, deep down, that if she gave in to Teddy's ridiculous demands and stopped fighting for what she was owed from their marriage, what she deserved for having suffered his abuse, it would all be over. But she couldn't do that. At the very least, she wanted what he'd taken from her—her career and the condo she had owned and worked for. But was it worth the fight anymore?

Laurie called her a few hours later. "Sheldon called Dad, and Dad called me. You think Teddy's stalking you?" she asked, her voice gentler than usual.

"It has to be Teddy. If it isn't Teddy, then it might be William, and I just can't bear thinking it could be him."

"Why? He's just a man; there are plenty more of them around."

Emily sighed; she didn't know how to convince her sister that it was actually hard for her to find a decent man. She liked William, she'd just begun to trust him, and she wanted it to stay that way.

"It's not about that. I just wanted the first person I dated after Teddy to be different. I wanted to be able to confide in him and not feel like that was going to be used against me later."

Laurie was quiet for a while. "I hear you," she finally said. "It's hard for us to trust people. It's harder for people to earn our trust back after they've broken it. Honestly? I know you may not want to hear the answer, but I think you need to ask William. If it isn't him, great. If William gets cagey about it, then you can cut him off."

Emily sniffled in her bed. She didn't want to agree, but Laurie had a point. If this was William showing his red flags, it was better it happened now, before Emily was truly committed to him.

"We had a good time," she said. "He has taken me to a bunch of restaurants I would have been way too nervous to go to by myself. I finally had sex again, and it was good. He's funny, and we joke around a lot, and he took me to see that movie."

"See what I mean? You have good memories to hold on to until the next guy comes around. There's no reason for you to be holding on to a person who has proven himself not to be worthy of you. I'll be around if you need me, okay? But please promise me you'll confront William and actually *listen* to what he says. Don't just brush it off."

Laurie had a point; there were still positive memories for Emily to look back on without having to stay with a man who could be dangerous.

"I AGREE WITH YOUR SISTER," Dr. Wright said.

It had been a couple of weeks since their last appointment. Emily didn't feel comfortable going to her therapist's office until she felt more secure that Teddy wouldn't be waiting for her outside, and she didn't want to get hacked in the middle of a Zoom call. Dr. Wright understood and made sure to mark Emily's case as highly sensitive so that everyone in the office knew she was having problems with both her ex and a possible stalker.

"William is the one new person in your life," Dr. Wright continued. "This activity started around the same time. Logically it could be that he is the culprit. It could also be that you're attributing all this to him because, subconsciously, you're still a little hesitant to get more serious with William. Either way, it wouldn't hurt to ask. Asking him could reveal a major red flag—that William will treat you the same way as Teddy—or it could assuage your fears. No matter the outcome, I think asking the question is a good idea."

Emily hated it when her sister and her therapist agreed. It meant she had to ask William if he was the one stalking her, or at least if he could explain why all this started happening when they started dating.

This whole situation was exhausting. Emily wanted it to be over, and asking William for the truth was a step in that direction. Still, even with all the moral support, Emily wasn't sure if she was brave enough to ask William point-blank.

"ARE you the man who has been cyberstalking me for the past month?"

William blinked, clearly stunned. They'd been having a nice, quiet dinner when suddenly Emily blurted out the question that had been on her mind for days.

"Wh-what?" he asked, the color draining from his face.

"Are you the man who has been cyberstalking me? If you are, I have to leave. I can't continue having a relationship with you if you're going to behave like this. If it isn't you, please tell me if you know who it is because it's driving me crazy, and it's unfair to drag my therapist and my boss into all this." Emily took a deep breath and then a long drink of water.

William was staring at her like she had just turned into a ghost. "What are you—"

She took another deep breath. "Also, the prank was not funny. It was really disconcerting coming home to a house that was just a little *off* from usual. It drove me crazy. It felt like I was back with Teddy, and he was gaslighting me. Why would someone do that?"

William's face was frozen in a blank expression. "Are you accusing me of messing with your furniture?"

"I'm not accusing you. I'm—"

"We were both drunk that night, Emily, and that was the whole reason we got a hotel room. Are you saying you think I got out of bed, sobered up, went to your house, messed with your furniture, and then came back?"

"No, I don't think—to be honest, I don't think anything at all. I've been getting these weird phone calls, and now someone is trying to get into my email and trying to get me fired, and you're the only person in my life who...can. Who knows everything—"

"You honestly—why would I do that to you? What reason do I have?"

"I don't know—"

"You seriously think I would do those awful things to you?" William was starting to raise his voice, and his face was getting red. "I'm not going to be the scapegoat for your paranoia."

Emily felt nervous; she wanted to get out of there and back into the safety of her own home. This was the reaction she had been dreading. "I don't *know*. I'm not trying to—"

"No! You're accusing me of something I haven't done—I'm not following you. Believe it or not, I actually have a life beyond these weekly dates. I've done everything you wanted, and now you're going to sit there and accuse me of *stalking* you? Is this just some ploy to break up with me? Because if it is, I have to say, it's pretty pathetic. I would have thought you had more of a backbone than this."

"William, I just needed to know if you were involved. The fact is, the weird stuff that's been happening, the annoying phone calls, the cyberstalking, has all happened since we reconnected. I asked you because you were the common denominator in all of this. Last week, I got an email describing *exactly* what I had been wearing to dinner and where we had eaten, even what I ate. You were the only person who knew all that. I'm sorry if you feel I'm accusing you. I really don't mean to do that, but the fact is I have to ask."

"You didn't have to ask. You didn't have to do anything at all," William said, standing up from the table. "I'm leaving now. I've lost my appetite." He pulled some cash from his wallet and dropped it on his plate. It was enough to only cover his meal, she noticed.

Emily watched as William left the restaurant and went back to his car. It felt like she had been slapped in the face.

Her worst fears realized, Emily sat in the restaurant and picked at her food for a while, as the waiter kept coming over to ask if she was okay.

"I'm fine," she sniffled, "really, I am."

He comped her meal after that.

Emily went home, replaying the scene at dinner in her mind. When she had confronted William, he was immediately defensive, and the color had drained from his face. Was that a sign? William had avoided talking about the cyberattacks, focusing on his outrage. He'd also mentioned being drunk the night her house had been messed with, but could he have been faking? Suspicion ballooned in Emily's chest. He was the common denominator, just as her sister and therapist had said.

He refused to even entertain the logic of the situation, instead focusing on Emily's emotional state and how offensive the implication was. He said she was accusing him, but she never really accused him of anything. She asked, point-blank, and laid out the reasons for her suspicions, but left enough room for William to plausibly deny what had happened. Instead, William lasered in mostly on one part of her argument and got angrier and angrier about the suggestion that maybe he was involved.

Teddy used to do that sort of thing all the time, Emily remembered. Especially when it came to his affairs, Teddy always turned the blame onto Emily, acting as though he was offended that she would think of him in that way. Of course, Emily's instincts turned out to be right in that case.

Were they right again about William?

THE NEXT DAY Emily sent her therapist an email detailing her evening with William.

Dr. Wright immediately called her, which was surprising since it was the weekend. "I know this does not feel very good. You may even be feeling that you're at fault, but you have to remember that you are not in the wrong in this situation."

"I realize I did accuse him of messing with my furniture. Is that bad?"

"No, you still offered him a chance to have a reasonable reaction, didn't you? Instead he was focused on turning the blame around onto you, which isn't healthy relationship behavior."

Laurie agreed with Dr. Wright when Emily called her after speaking to Dr. Wright.

"Honestly, it sounds like you dodged a bullet. It's not your fault he's a shitty guy, Em. It's not your fault he freaked out when you asked him a few questions, and *abandoned you* at the restaurant. The only other good thing about that night was that the waiter thought you got dumped and comped your meal. Actually, I might steal that idea for myself, see how many free meals I can get out of it." Laurie laughed.

Together Emily and Laurie decided on a new plan. Sheldon already had someone tailing Teddy and made sure his police buddies kept an eye out for any suspicious characters hanging around Emily's house. Emily would contact Sheldon and get him to add William to their list along with a protection order. That way, if a man matching William's description was seen around her house from then on, the police could charge him for harassment.

At first Emily was hesitant, thinking this course of action was a little harsh, but Laurie pointed out that it was better to nip this behavior in the bud before it could escalate.

"It doesn't sound HARSH, exactly," Sheldon said.

Emily called him on Sunday to bring her lawyer up to date.

"I want it to be harsh. If it is him, I want William to know I'm not a pushover, and I won't stand by and just let him ruin my life for his own amusement. I've been through it before, and I won't do it again." Emily was on the verge of tears, but she refused to let them fall; she was stronger than that. Leaving Teddy had made her resilient. She would stand up for herself against William.

"I'll let the investigator know about William. We'll make sure he can't get to you. Has he tried to contact you at all this weekend?"

"No, he hasn't called or texted, and I haven't seen his car."

"Good, that means he's keeping his distance. He probably doesn't want you getting more suspicious of him. I'll pass this along to the investigator, and if he notices William creeping around, he'll let me know. We can get the protection order started too. Once you sign that, we can take it from there, okay?"

Emily agreed. It broke her heart to have to put William on her bizarre watchlist, but she needed to be safe. She thought he would be the one—a casual friend, a sort-of boyfriend, someone she could confide in and have a little fun with on the weekend. She didn't want to dive into another personal drama in the middle of her divorce from Teddy.

"In the meantime, Teddy has still been coming up clean. His mother has him on a tight leash; the man isn't even going out to bars these days. We're still not entirely sure about his online presence though. It seems the Gaunt family has a tight network, and it's hard for the investigator's cyber guy to get in through their firewall and see anything. I told him to avoid doing anything illegal so we don't compromise your divorce negotiations."

Emily didn't say anything. Teddy wasn't doing anything out of line, and it appeared William was probably stepping far over it.

Meanwhile, Emily was left staring at her ceiling, wondering when her instincts had gotten so bad.

17

Emily woke up the next Saturday after an uneventful week, determined to live her life without fear. She got out of bed and meditated on the mantra "I am gentle with myself. Setbacks do not define me; they nudge me to new awareness."

"I am gentle with myself. Setbacks do not define me; they nudge me to new awareness."

Emily repeated that to herself while listening to binaural beats. Then she did breathing exercises while letting the words settle over her. She wanted to have a day free from her past, but if that wasn't possible, she wanted to at least feel less imprisoned by it.

That feeling didn't last long.

After a long meditation and an even longer shower, Emily went downstairs to her kitchen to make an extravagant breakfast. She wanted to make blueberry waffles from scratch. It was one of the cherished memories she had with her father, from when she was a little kid. Her father was a great cook, and not once had Emily realized he'd had her help with breakfast to keep her away from her mother in the mornings.

Emily opened her pantry and recoiled at what she saw.

Bugs everywhere. Little crickets and beetles filled her pantry and contaminated everything in it. There were crickets buried in her flour, beetles shoved in a jar of fancy olives. Emily screamed as she pulled everything out of her pantry, only to find the dead insects had infested all of her food. There was nothing she could eat that wasn't plagued by death.

Emily scrambled away, grasping for her phone. "L-Lau-Laurie, I-I, it's ruined, it's all ruined. Oh my God, it's in every-thing—I don't know—"

Her sister didn't wait for an explanation. She hung up the phone.

Fifteen minutes later, Emily was sitting in the corner of the kitchen, staring at the contents of her pantry spilling all over the floor, when Laurie burst into the room.

Laurie screamed. "Oh my God. I'm calling Dad."

Emily didn't answer. She just stared as the few live bugs died. *There must be poison along with the bugs,* she thought, but it was as though she were outside herself, watching everything, hearing everything.

Laurie put the phone on speaker. "Dad, I'm at Em's. Somebody's been in her house—"

"Stay put," he said. "I'm calling the police, and then I'll be right over there."

"Come on, let's go in the living room," Laurie muttered as she helped Emily to her feet.

Emily complied, still feeling as though she weren't really there. It was almost like she was floating.

"Emily, do you know who did this?" Laurie asked.

Emily just shook her head. It had to be whoever was messing with her. William or Teddy or someone Teddy hired. But she couldn't make her voice work.

The police arrived a few minutes later, along with her dad. She was still in a state of shock. Observing but not reacting anymore. It was all so surreal to her.

"Ms. Gray," an officer began as he came toward her, gingerly stepping into the living room, "I'm Detective Mike Jackson. I know this is a difficult time, but can we talk? Your sister and father can be here if you prefer."

Emily nodded. All she had wanted was a calm morning at home, she wasn't quite ready to confront the chaos of what was going on in her life just yet, but it looked as though she needed to gather her will and be cognizant before she was really ready.

She took a couple of deep breaths and tried to bring herself back to the present. "Is my kitchen okay? Was anything else ruined besides my pantry?"

"I have a couple of officers in there now, but it looks like most of your food was destroyed." Detective Jackson removed a notepad and a pen from his pocket. "Do you have any idea how this happened?"

She looked at the detective. "I'm being stalked. I've been getting mystery phone calls, and then someone hacked into my email account and sent embarrassing emails to my boss to get me fired. They also tried to fire my therapist for me, and when I discovered it and changed my passwords and tightened my security, they started sending threatening messages."

He took notes. "What are they threatening to do?"

"I don't really know what's in them," Emily said. "After

the first couple, my boss and therapist got involved, and they have email filters set up so I don't see them anymore. They're saving them in security files. I can give you their contact info if you need it."

"Do you know who is doing all this to you?"

Emily nodded. "I think it's my soon-to-be ex-husband. As I'm sure you've read in the papers, I'm divorcing Teddy Gaunt."

Detective Jackson's eyebrows shot up. "Why do you think he's behind this?"

Emily shrugged. "He was abusive when we were married, not entirely physically, but emotionally. He would gaslight me, twist things. Do things to make me think I was losing my mind. This would be an escalation of that. My lawyer is looking into it."

"Okay, we'll look at what your lawyer's got."

"But it's possible it's another person I recently reconnected with, William Summers. When I first tried to leave Teddy, I got together with William, but Teddy—" Emily started, trying to figure out how to explain her connection to William.

"Teddy conned her into coming back to him," Laurie said, "and she broke it off with William. When he found out about the divorce, he reached out to my sister again and asked her out, but he's been weird."

"What do you mean?" the detective asked.

"He wasn't weird at first," Emily said with a frown.

Laurie turned to the detective. "Strange things started happening after he apologized for ghosting her for three weeks. When she confronted him about it, he yelled at her and jetted, leaving her at a restaurant."

"Is that true, Ms. Gray?" Detective Jackson asked, his tone much softer than her sister's.

"Yes, it is. While I was away from my home, I'm pretty sure someone broke into my house and moved my furniture around."

"Describe that for me. What was moved?" Detective Jackson asked.

"It was subtle. The kind of thing you wouldn't notice unless you spent all your time at home, which is exactly what I do. At first, I thought it was just my front table where I put my keys. I thought maybe I bumped it, but then the angle of the TV was off, and the couches were slightly off. Everything was shifted the tiniest bit."

He nodded and scribbled in his notepad. "Was anything taken?"

"Nothing that I noticed, but after that is when the email stuff started. So maybe they got to my computer at that point."

"Right. Okay, I'll check with your lawyer, therapist and boss to get those emails and the information on Mr. Gaunt. You just relax. I'm going to check on the officers in the kitchen; they should be about done. There may still be a mess for you to clean, but they'll remove the tainted foods."

"With the bugs dead, will they check for poison?" Emily asked.

"Yes, that's protocol. We'll want to be sure something else wasn't going on."

"Thank you." Emily watched him head to the kitchen.

"There's a huge mess; maybe we should call a maid service," Laurie suggested.

"It'll be fine. We can take care of it," Dad said, causing Laurie to huff.

The rest of the morning was a blur. All Emily wanted to do was lie down and start over. Maybe if she closed her eyes tightly enough, this would all turn out to be a dream and she could actually make herself the waffles she wanted in the first place. Of course, it wasn't a dream. Emily could never be so lucky.

Still, with her dad's and Laurie's help, they cleared out everything in her pantry and cleaned it with a mix of distilled white vinegar and hot water so the cabinets wouldn't be ruined. She scrubbed each and every cabinet while Laurie washed all the containers. Her dad took care of sweeping and discarding all of the food and bug bodies the police had left behind. Once it was all cleaned, they went home, leaving her to rest.

Three hours later, when she woke from her fitful nap, she realized the thought of cooking dinner made her stomach revolt. Not that she really could have anyway when most of her food had been pitched in the garbage. She decided she would order takeout or go out to eat until she could handle being in her kitchen again.

It's just what he wants, to force me out of the house and draw me into the open.

With her kitchen in that state, William, Teddy, or whoever was behind this knew she'd never eat there. Contaminating all her food was a ploy to get her out of the house or to at least open her door for takeout or grocery delivery and into supposed neutral territory—but why? Was he planning on terrorizing her at home and on the streets? There was no way to tell at this point. Emily was navigating a nightmare with no way to wake herself up.

She changed her clothes and then drove in circles, trying to lose anyone who might have been following her before finally pulling into the small parking lot of a diner. She waited several minutes to see if anyone else pulled into the lot, but didn't notice anything unusual.

Glancing around, she hurried to the diner door and walked in. There was a sign telling her to seat herself, so she took a booth away from the windows but facing the door so she could see anyone coming in.

"What can I get you, hon?" the waitress asked, tapping her foot.

Emily scanned the menu. "A burger and a coffee, please."

"I'll have to make a new pot. Is that alright with you?"

"That'll be fine. I don't mind waiting."

The waitress nodded and walked away.

Emily noticed a tall man sitting at the end of the counter. He hadn't been there a moment ago. He was reading a newspaper, but for a second, Emily could have sworn he was looking right at her. The man was tall with dark wavy hair—just like William. But despite some unsettling similarities, it wasn't him, of course.

The waitress returned with her order. "D'ya need anything else, hon?"

"Uh, no, I'm all good, thanks," Emily muttered.

She'd lost sight of the guy at the counter while talking to the waitress. She looked around for him, but he was gone. Maybe she'd imagined him from the start. She looked around again, but didn't see him.

Eventually, she felt she could relax and eat her burger. She didn't feel as though anyone was watching her. She could see all around her. Everything was going to be okay.

Sure, you can see all around you, but you didn't actually see him leave, did you? He could be hiding in one of the booths up ahead, your view blocked by the leather seat back.

Emily barely tasted her burger after that. It was devastating to feel unsafe everywhere she went, to always be looking over her shoulder, worried about whom she'd see. And maybe she'd been wrong, and it was William playing some game that was meant to make her feel crazy. If that was his goal, he was succeeding.

This is ridiculous, Em. He knows where you live, so there's no need for William to follow you around. You're letting your paranoia take over. Get up, leave some cash, and go home.

She slowly got up and, training her eye on the door, calmly paid her bill. There wasn't anyone who looked like the mystery man sitting in the booths, but still, the eerie feeling that someone was watching her was back, and it coated her skin like grease. She tried to shake it off, but that seemed to make the feeling worse.

She left the diner and went out to the parking lot. Behind her, a set of footsteps fell in line with hers. Heavier than her own, it could only belong to a man.

Emily quickened her pace and headed toward her car at the other end of the lot. She didn't want to run and give the man a reason to chase her, but she didn't want to stop and give him a chance to attack her.

The footsteps got louder.

Emily's heart jumped into her throat. She reached her car and braced herself. Emily whipped around and—

No one was there.

There was no William, no Teddy, nobody who could have been making those footsteps. Nothing that could explain the looming danger she felt eating alone in public.

"Who are you?" Emily called out. "Why are you following me? Why are you tormenting me?"

Her words seemed to echo through the half-empty parking lot.

Nobody answered, and yet...Emily continued to feel as though someone was watching. Some menacing person was taking pleasure in her feelings of anxiety.

"Leave me alone!" she shouted as she opened her car door.

Whoever was doing this to her was close by. She knew it just like she knew they weren't going to stop. She didn't know what their end game was—to drive her to insanity maybe?

The fact that Emily didn't get into an accident on her way home was a miracle. She was shaking the entire way, taking surprise turns, and speeding up at random points to make sure she wasn't being followed. She was paranoid of any car that trailed her.

By the time she arrived home, Emily was in an intense state of paranoia. Still shaking, she called her therapist. "I don't know what to do. I feel like I'm going absolutely crazy. I woke up this morning to find someone had broken in and put bugs in my food. Everything in my pantry was contaminated. I couldn't eat here, so I went out, and I felt like I was being followed, but nobody was there. I don't know if it's all just my imagination. Maybe I'm hallucinating? Maybe breathing in all that vinegar and water is causing hallucinations? Or maybe there's a gas leak in my house? Could that be the explanation for everything?"

"Emily, please calm down. Follow my lead and breathe with me, okay?" Dr. Wright breathed in deeply and then slowly exhaled.

Emily followed suit in her own ragged way, trying to

follow Dr. Wright's loud breathing through the phone. Eventually it worked, and her racing heart slowed.

"You've had a very overstimulating day, and I think you need to force your body to relax. Maybe go to a hotel. Hotels have security, you can feel safe there, and no one will know you're there unless you tell them."

"Are you sure? Shouldn't I be in a place where I feel safe so I can calm down?" She was starting to panic again.

"Emily, you don't feel safe in your own home. Your life is full of stressors and triggers; all I'm saying is that it might be good for you to go somewhere different, to force yourself to reset. Tell your father and sister what you're doing so they can keep an eye on things. Call a cab and go, stay for a night or two at a hotel. It could be like a mini-vacation. Get a massage, visit the pool, treat yourself to room service—anything to get out of your house while you navigate this panic attack."

"Okay, I will." Emily hung up the phone and packed a bag. She moved through the house as though she was being watched, keeping away from windows and tiptoeing to make less noise. She found a hotel downtown—an independent place that had no association with the Gaunt family. She called a cab from her computer using a VPN and gave the cab company a fake name.

She was descending into madness, and this was the last stop before she couldn't go back.

THE HOTEL, thankfully, had self-check-in. She waited in line until a kiosk opened up, and a man immediately slid into the spot next to her. She froze, unsure of what to do. She didn't want to type in her name or her confirmation number, just in case. She'd taken every precaution on the way here, but was it enough?

Emily pushed away her fears and quickly checked herself in, waiting for the key to program itself with her room number. She scurried away from the man, who immediately followed her out of the reception area. He was too close. How would she get away?

18

Emily was in full panic mode as the man continued to follow her. She headed toward the small café to the right of reception, intending to hide in there.

Suddenly, the guy turned abruptly and embraced a woman. "I checked us in. Have you found a place for dinner?"

"Yeah, there's a tequila bar nearby," his partner replied.

The couple trailed off as they headed toward the elevators, hand in hand.

Emily's heart stuttered in her chest and resumed beating at a normal pace again. Her therapist was right. She needed this mini-vacation, or she really was going to lose her mind.

EMILY TOOK advantage of every amenity the hotel had to offer. There was a small spa with a jacuzzi, an infrared sauna, free yoga classes, and a bar with a new signature cocktail every day. She slept in Sunday morning and again this morning and had stayed up late both Saturday and Sunday night, talking to different guests at the bar.

This morning, which was Monday, she worked from the hotel's remote office setup, happily taking some of their complimentary stationery and free snacks. It was exactly what she wanted—a mini-vacation where she didn't think about the men trying to ruin her life.

After three days of rest, relaxation, and actually getting some work done, she went home. She used her key on the front door and closed it behind her, feeling relieved that she'd made it home and could relax. As she turned toward the living room, she realized something looked off. The house had a strange feel to it.

Emily had entrusted her father to keep an eye on things while she'd been gone. He had said he'd come by every day and check everything just as Emily had shown him. Every day he had called to tell her he was proud of her, and to say that nothing out of the ordinary was happening at her house.

And yet, Emily once again found that everything was just slightly out of place.

Had her father done it while he was here? But why would he? He knew how particular she was about her things. He wouldn't have done this, would he?

The doors and windows were locked, so there was no way anyone could have got in without a key—but here she was surveying her home where every object was askew. As she went around her house, moving things back into place, she noticed there were a few new objects in her home. New picture frames with new pictures in them, tucked in behind the old so they weren't as obvious.

Emily's heart began to pound. No. Her father definitely

wouldn't have added those. She hurried through the house and came to a stop in the doorway to her kitchen, her mouth agape.

There was a bottle of wine on the counter, wrapped with a large bow. It could have been a gift—something her father would never touch—but no one had given it to her. Emily clenched her teeth as she unwrapped the wine, carefully peeling off the bow, the wrapping paper, and then it dropped to the floor.

Inside a fake flower pinned to the gift was a tiny pinhole camera, the kind people put in teddy bears to use as nanny cams.

Seeing that, Emily was determined to tear the house apart until she found each and every camera, cursing whoever was doing this as she did. Inside the new picture frames were tiny cameras and microphones. Her house was plagued with them—there were microphones hidden in the couch and pinned to her linens; cameras embedded in every single room of her house. Every time she found a new one, Emily screamed at the top of her lungs and threw it against the wall.

When she thought she was finished, she called Detective Jackson, and he came with several officers to sweep her house from top to bottom.

"Is this everything you found?" he asked, holding the bag of tech that Emily had collected.

She nodded. "These were the obvious ones I found. But I think there's more. He probably wanted me to find these so I'd be paranoid about what else could be hidden away."

"You did a good thing calling us, Emily. Is there some-where else you can stay?"

"I just came from a hotel."

"Why don't you go back there. Give me the details, and when we're finished, I'll have an officer come pick you up, and we'll debrief down at the station. You should probably inform your lawyer so he can come down in case we find who has done this and it turns out to be your ex."

"I don't understand why I'm not catching this person on my surveillance cameras," she said, frowning.

"We'll look into that. Make that reservation and head on out. I'll have an officer follow you, just in case."

And just like that, Emily was back at the hotel, only this time she didn't feel like taking advantage of the sauna or the jacuzzi or pool. Emily was angry, and she wanted to find whoever was doing this. She called Sheldon, her sister, and her father, who all came to the hotel and joined her as they waited for Detective Jackson to send for her.

"If this is Teddy, he's going to pay for it," Sheldon muttered, pacing the room. "But if it's William, it will be a pretty cut-and-dry case. He took advantage of a woman he already knew was vulnerable, and tortured her. My question is for what? What is his motive?"

"I'm so sorry, dear." Her father paced in the opposite direction. "I should have paid closer attention. The wine was left on the porch, and I brought it in. I thought it was a gift from your boss because of all the confusion...I checked the doors and cameras every night, but there was nothing on them. The rooms remained the same. Nobody came in or out. I don't understand how they did it. I did exactly as you told me to do and watched the tape on fast-forward, but I didn't see anything. I-I'm so sorry, Emily."

"It's okay, Dad. It's not your fault. I think it's more complicated than I imagined. He must have found a way to get around my security system. He must be doing something to it so it doesn't show him being there and changing things. Who knows, maybe some of this spyware has been there longer than I thought. If William is behind it, well, I had invited him in at least twice, and he came by to pick me up a couple of times too. Maybe he took advantage and planted the cameras then."

Emily couldn't decide if she wanted to scream in frustration or go find William and tear him apart.

Before she could figure it out, her phone rang. It was Detective Jackson telling her he was sending a car for her.

"WHAT DO you mean there's no fingerprints? Nothing to trace them? There's nothing?" Emily demanded. Earlier, an officer had dropped Emily off at the police station, where she now sat with Detective Jackson and Sheldon.

"When you ripped them out, the cameras stopped transmitting," the detective explained. "You were right, the ones you found were the surface-level pieces; there were a couple embedded in your speaker system that my crime scene team had to dig out with tweezers."

"He had enough time to embed cameras in my speakers, and my surveillance cameras caught nothing?" she asked.

"I think he knows all about your cameras," Detective Jackson responded. "Because they're old school, he's just rewinding the tape and taping over his visit. If you're watching on fast-forward, you're not going to notice the glitch of time being jumped."

She always watched the tapes on fast-forward, looking for anything or anyone who shouldn't be there. Detective Jackson was right. She wouldn't have noticed a glitch.

Emily sighed. "So how was he using the cameras? Where were they broadcasting to?"

"Our tech guy says there's a couple of ways the perpetrator could have set them up. One is that the cameras were on a Bluetooth-based stream, meaning they sent a file at the end of each day via Bluetooth to a receiver nearby, and that receiver was bouncing the footage somewhere else. The other possibility is that the cameras and microphones created a subtle network around your house, and it was all sent like a live stream to this perpetrator. Being Bluetooth, it's hard to say exactly where the feed was going, but it had to be fairly nearby for it to work."

"So this person has been close to me the whole time?" That sent a sliver of fear through her.

"It appears that way," Detective Jackson replied. "We'll follow up with the cameras and microphones and see if we can track the purchase. You should be able to go back home tomorrow, but I recommend having a family member stay with you for a few days, just in case. If this *is* your ex...well, exes are always a little more hesitant to try something when there's family around. If it's not your ex, then hopefully having family around will be a deterrent to them, and they won't escalate things." He patted Emily's hand and left the room.

It wasn't reassuring at all. She hadn't even been thinking about things escalating. How much worse was this going to get?

Sheldon drove her back to the hotel and shared the news. Laurie was outraged, her dad looked dejected, and Emily could only see red.

After dinner everyone went home, and Emily tucked

herself into bed, exhausted. She stared out at the city, worrying about this person's next move.

She thought about William. How he wouldn't admit blame and how he'd lashed out at her and twisted her words at the restaurant. She couldn't help but see the same pattern she'd experienced with Teddy. Granted, Teddy's had taken years to manifest.

But maybe she was wrong? Maybe William honestly was hurt and disappointed when she accused him? Maybe his only real fault was lashing out at her with his words and walking away from her.

What if she'd made a terrible mistake? What if it was Teddy this entire time?

Could it really be Teddy? Teddy knew he couldn't come anywhere near Emily. Not only did she have a restraining order against him, but if he tried to attack or harass her, he'd never get his way in their divorce settlement, and that was the thing he cared about most. The money didn't matter. It was winning that mattered to Teddy. Getting his way and destroying her because she had the gall to walk away from him. And what if he was using William to do it? she wondered. Was that possible? Or was William an innocent bystander? She couldn't be sure.

However, the possibility that Teddy was somehow behind it all played heavily in her mind.

19

The next morning Emily emailed Horace, apologizing for her disappearances lately, and asked for another day off. She was sure what she needed to do wouldn't take long, but she wanted the day to rest. She took breakfast in the hotel's restaurant before calling Sheldon.

"I think the private investigator needs to be on my house," Emily said. "Obviously the security system is not working because whoever this is got into my house multiple times without being seen. Tracking the calls didn't work. Following Teddy around is getting us nowhere, so I think it's best we shift gears. I want evidence of whoever is coming into my home, in case we go forward with pressing charges."

"That makes perfect sense. Emily, how are you handling this...financially? I ask because the investigator's rates are pretty—"

"Honestly, I have no idea, and I can't think about it now. It's probably worse if I get killed, right? In that case no one is getting paid." Emily didn't hide the strain in her voice. She didn't want to be thinking about *finances* right now. She knew she was digging herself into a deeper hole by asking the PI to be stationed near her house, but what else could she do? Every day she came home to a new horror. There was only so much time she could spend away before her stalker found her again.

Later that day, while she was sitting in the infrared sauna, the spa attendant approached her. "Excuse me, Ms. Gray?"

"Is something wrong?" Emily asked.

"It's just your phone has been ringing nonstop." She handed over the phone, which she'd left at the counter with them. "I figured if they're calling this much, it must be important."

A feeling of dread filled her. She wondered if it was the anonymous caller badgering her. Emily took the phone and saw it had been William calling over and over again—and again, the phone started ringing in her hand before she could thank the attendant. Whether it was instinct or shock she didn't know, but Emily answered the phone as the attendant left with a nod.

"Emily! You answered." William sounded out of breath and paranoid.

If he needed to talk to her this badly, why hadn't he left a voicemail, or at least sent a text? She had noticed in those few seconds she'd held the phone that she had neither.

"What is it, William?"

"I need to talk to you." He sounded panicked, as if their meeting was a matter of life or death. "I know I'm probably not your favorite person, but I really want to find a way to explain or at least hash it out. I feel like I freaked out and ran away and didn't even give you a chance to explain why you thought—"

Emily had had enough. She interrupted him. "You've answered everything by now. Your behavior this past weekend was enough—"

"What are you talking about? I've been at the hospital since Saturday morning. I worked a double and then slept in the on-call room before starting another shift. I haven't even been home all weekend."

The panic in William's voice caught Emily off guard. He sounded like her—paranoid and in hysterics. She didn't know what to believe. She'd already half-convinced herself that William was working with Teddy, and he was the one behind the mess at her house. The one making the anonymous calls...everything.

"William, are you telling the truth? You know I can call the hospital and find out."

"Call them! I swear I haven't been anywhere near you. Please, can we just talk? We can go somewhere public, and I promise I won't cause a scene."

Emily chewed her lip and thought about it. She wanted to believe William, and that was what made this decision so difficult. If William weren't clever and funny and so easy to be around, she would have hung up the phone and returned to the sauna by now. This could also be a moment to catch him in a lie. She could record him on her phone, just like she had with Teddy during the accident. That way if he said anything incriminating, she'd turn the recording over to the police, and they could arrest him.

"Fine. I'm going to call the hospital and ask if you were actually at work for the past several days. If you were, I'll be at Cherry Bomb Cafe on Main Street at 3 p.m. If I find out you lied, I won't show up, and I will not be answering so much as a homing pigeon from you ever again —understood?"

"Understood. I'll see you there," William said.

Emily hung up and went back into the sauna, eager to undo what that phone call did to her nerves.

EMILY CALLED the hospital and confirmed that William had indeed been at work. When she'd explained her situation, the head nurse had assured her that William had worked a double shift and had gotten read the riot act by several other nurses for how he'd treated her when he'd told them he'd left her at the restaurant. It had made Emily feel a little better about seeing William.

At 3:00 p.m., Emily was at the café, waiting, but there was no sign of William.

At 3:05, there was still no sign of William, and he hadn't sent a message to explain that he'd be late.

At 3:10, Emily waved away a waiter asking if she wanted another drink—she wouldn't be staying much longer.

At 3:20, just as she was getting up from her booth, a disheveled William walked through the door. The five-o'clock shadow made him even more handsome, and heads turned as he crossed the café.

"You're late," Emily said.

"I'm sorry. There was traffic on the way down here." William sat down quietly.

They stared at each other until a waitress came by to take their order.

Even after the waitress left, Emily didn't say a word. She

just continued to stare at William, waiting for an explanation.

"How's your week? I heard the trial got delayed again."

"Teddy's up to his usual antics. My week has been stressful, as I'm sure you know."

William winced. "I thought maybe, if you decided to meet, that meant, you know—"

"Whether or not you were at the hospital, it doesn't take away the fact that I still had a stressful week. Not everything is about you, William," she snapped.

They fell silent again.

"Do you still think I broke in and moved your furniture?" William eventually asked, playing with his sugar spoon.

Emily didn't bring up what had happened most recently. Not yet. "If not you, then who? My sister is petty but not *that* petty. Teddy wouldn't dare. He has a court order barring him from contacting me, and he doesn't even know where I live—as far as I'm aware. All these things started happening after you reappeared out of the blue and we started dating."

"But, Emily, you know me. I wouldn't do that to you. For starters, it's risking my job. I work at a Catholic hospital, and they're incredibly strict when it comes to their employees' moral behavior. I also have never, *ever* given you any indication that I'm a dangerous guy, have I?"

Emily was frustrated. The steely facade cracked, and angry tears began to pool in her eyes.

"Please don't cry," William continued. "I hate seeing you like this. I just need to know why you thought it was me. We have a history, and I thought it was one of mutual respect and comfort."

"I want to believe you. But I can't think of anyone who

would do this to me. You are the only one who has had the opportunity—"

"But what could my motive possibly be? I have been there for you in every way I can think of. I've tried to cheer you up after shitty days, and I've been your sounding board when you need it. Why would I try to destroy that?"

Emily dodged his hand as he reached out to her, still unsure if she could actually trust him. He was right, though. He didn't have any motive to harass her that she could see. "Somebody planted cameras in my house," she said, deciding to trust him. "That's why I asked where you were these last several days."

"Emily," William said, his hand creeping toward her on the table, "I am not Teddy, I promise you. I don't want to hurt you, and I'm not the one behind this harassment. I didn't plant any cameras. You can ask anyone you like. I'll give you my coworkers' numbers; they'll tell you I'm not that kind of guy."

"Then why is it that when I asked, you got *so* defensive? Didn't you realize that would make me think it was you?" Emily questioned. "I asked you point-blank, with no agenda, and you said I was accusing you. You said it as if I had already made up my mind, and then stormed out. The waiter thought I'd been dumped."

"I thought you were accusing me. I thought you had made up your mind, and I felt backed against a wall. I'm really sorry for reacting that way."

"You acted like a guilty man. Even now, I feel like you haven't actually given me a reason to believe you. You keep asking me to ask other people to prove where *you haven't* been. It feels like a convoluted argument."

William cleared his throat and looked everywhere except

directly at Emily. "I'm not trying to make this argument convoluted, I just feel a little desperate. You're so determined to write me off, and I am just trying to hold on to you, Emily. I'm telling you what I can to make you believe me. I'm not the person harassing you. I never have been. I'm sorry I ghosted you for a few weeks, but I promise that doesn't make me a stalker. I'm just a busy man, with his own stressful life."

Emily still didn't know how to react or what to think. Just this morning she had been half convinced that the person stalking her was William, and now she just didn't know. William was incredibly charming, but she could tell he was hiding something.

What was behind William's charisma—and was it going to stab her in the back when she least expected it?

20

For the next few days Emily woke up holding her breath.

She left the hotel and went home. Her first order of business was to create a new routine. She still checked the locks on her doors and windows, but she took some time to recalibrate and readjust her security cameras, moving the setup so it was under lock and key in her bedroom closet. She changed the settings on her IP activity monitor to be more sensitive to unusual activity, and then tested everything. Overall, it took hours, and she was exhausted by the end of it all.

Nothing happened the first morning or the second. Emily figured the police presence had scared the harasser away.

Good, they ought to know I'm not going to be the victim again.

When she had a moment, she sent a long email to Horace, apologizing for her erratic absences at work. Now that she had a few calm days, Emily was able to get back into the swing of things and was even more productive than usual.

Emily,

No need for you to apologize. Seeing as the abusive emails have continued to escalate over the past week, I figured you were dealing with personal matters that were a little more serious than my correspondence and scheduling. I'm glad you're doing well, and you're more than catching up on what you've missed. Incidentally, a police detective reached out, and I've had our security head send all of the abusive emails I've received to them. I wondered if you would like me to have them sent along to your legal representation as well. Not sure what will come of it, but I figured it would be a smart move, no?

At some point Emily must have done something to earn more karma than she ever deserved. That was the only explanation she could have for landing a boss like Horace. She got him to send all the emails to Sheldon. Emily was unsure what would happen with them, but she figured it was better to keep them on hand than to leave them in the cybersphere. She included that in her tasks of the day, and soon she was finished with her work.

For good measure, Emily went around the house and did her routine again.

Windows and doors, checked.

Internet activity, checked.

Security cameras, checked.

To some this would feel like a prison of their own making.

Emily stayed away from her windows, barely went outside, and didn't bother ordering in. Her groceries were delivered straight to her door, and she always had the delivery person knock twice and wait for her to go through them to make sure they were what she ordered and were untouched before she brought them inside. At night, either Laurie or her dad came over to check on her and make sure she was still alive.

"I'm afraid you're going to get scurvy or something if you don't get out of the house," Laurie remarked.

"That isn't how you get scurvy."

"Whatever, the point is, how long are you going to keep it up?"

"For as long as it takes," Emily responded. "I don't want to be caught off guard again, and I don't want to be living in fear anymore."

"I could never live like this," Laurie muttered. "I'd drive myself crazy."

"I'm doing this because there's someone out there determined to drive me crazy."

After her sister left, Emily went over her house once again.

Windows and doors, checked.

Internet activity, checked.

Security cameras, checked.

She lay in bed and stared at the ceiling until morning. Emily barely got any sleep these days; she was busy waiting for the slightest noise to wake her and force her to check her surroundings. One night, a tree branch kept tapping on the window of the spare bedroom, so Emily reached out the window and snapped part of it off. She sat at the window, guarding her house for the rest of the night.

"HAVE YOU BEEN SLEEPING AT ALL?" Dr. Wright sat across from Emily, who was unable to hide her distress.

"Not really. I usually get a couple of hours, but I don't wake up feeling rested at all. I'm just scared; this feels like a false sense of security. I feel like the second I let my guard down, I'm going to wake up to the next plague. Ever since I met with William, I feel as though I've been holding my breath and waiting."

"Waiting for what?"

"I'm not sure. Proof, I guess, that he is or isn't my stalker. That this is all over and I can go back to worrying about one terrifying man in my life, and only that man. Or I'm waiting for whatever the stalker is planning next. He can only be working up to something big, right? That's the other explanation for this silence."

"Have you been going outside, taking walks, running errands for yourself?" Dr. Wright asked, closing her notebook.

Emily flinched. "No, I haven't, other than coming here. It's too dangerous. I don't know who might be watching me. I've been reading a lot, which is nice. I got through this new fantasy series in three days since I didn't have as much work to do at my virtual assistant job. I have graduated to sitting by the window, but I don't like to do it for very long because I feel too exposed."

"Are you afraid that if you leave your house more often, something bad is going to happen?"

"Wouldn't you? Considering my life lately?"

Dr. Wright didn't answer that. "Let's do some breathing

exercises. There's an app you can use as well, but I know you're trying to stay away from technology right now."

THE APPOINTMENT RAN LONG. Emily wished she had insisted on doing a virtual appointment so she didn't have to leave her house. Now she felt worried someone would be waiting for her outside Dr. Wright's office. She'd taken a cab there and didn't want to stand on the street for too long waiting to hail another. She hid in the lobby and called her father to come pick her up.

Her therapist hadn't been much help. She was so focused on what Emily was doing to stay secure, which Emily felt was pretty reasonable considering the circumstances. Emily didn't *want* to go outside, because she didn't want to come back to a house that was doused in pig's blood or something. She didn't want to stand or sit near her windows because it always felt like someone was watching her, somewhere in the distance.

She was beginning to feel that the people around her didn't believe that she was still in danger. But Emily knew that she was. She'd seen it happen before with Teddy. For months on end their marriage seemed perfect, and Teddy acted as if he had seen the error of his ways and was getting help. Then, over dinner or even while watching television, everything would change on a dime.

"How was your appointment?" her dad asked as she got in his car.

"Good, she gave me something to help me sleep." Emily's eyes darted the street. "Can we go? I have to get this prescription and then go home."

Her dad drove her to the pharmacy. When they reached her house, he stayed while she went through her routine.

Windows and doors, checked.

Internet activity, checked.

Security cameras, checked.

Her dad made her a chamomile tea and a mug of warm milk with cinnamon. "I wasn't sure which you'd prefer. You used to love the milk and cinnamon drink as a kid, but I figured chamomile is a bit more grown up."

"Thanks, Dad," Emily said, tucking herself into bed. She glanced at him. "You're staying, right?"

"I'll be here. You're safe, Em." He walked out and closed the door.

Emily sipped the tea and took the pills, then waited for them to kick in.

It was incredible what a week could do. The anxiety meds were starting to do their job—Emily was finally sleeping and wasn't waking up to nightmares. She was still jumpy, but she was starting to find a bit of comfort in her own home again.

Emily noticed that Horace hadn't been sending her his usual workload. Recently it was less about having meetings or booking restaurants and flights and more about giving a second opinion on manuscripts to potentially publish. When she asked him about it, Horace was evasive. He said that it might be a little less pressure-filled than her usual work, and sandwiched in a compliment about her book taste. Emily worried that Horace was buttering her up just to fire her unexpectedly.

That Wednesday, Emily went out to her mailbox,

expecting a manuscript from Flamingo. Horace had emailed the night before, saying he was going to overnight the newest draft of a fantasy young adult novel. *A Venetian Oleander*, working title, was the second in a series about a fifteenth-century Italian countess who discovered she had the ability to transcend dimensions and bend time. Emily didn't want to admit it, but she had just finished reading the first book, *The Olive of Mandarino*, and was *dying* to know what happened next. She sprang out of bed and ran down the stairs, waiting by the front window for the mailman.

The second she saw his van, she ran out to greet him. "Hi, is there something for Emily Gray? A big something, perhaps a bit heavy?" she asked. Emily sounded like a teenager—nothing like a fantasy novel written for teen girls to bring that out in a woman.

"Uh, yeah, there's a bit for you, actually. Sign here."

Emily signed, and the mailman tipped his hat and handed her two massive envelopes. One heavy, one incredibly light. The heavy parcel had the Flamingo Press stamp and letterhead all over it.

The other envelope was addressed to her, with no return address. But on the corner of the envelope was a small embossed stamp with the initials "TG."

Her blood froze in her veins. Teddy had found her.

21

How was this possible? Emily thought as goosebumps rose on her skin. She had been so sure that Teddy had no access to her, so confident in the stupid no-contact order, she'd let her guard down, and here he was. Teddy Gaunt, reminding Emily that no matter what she did, he always had access to her. She should have known he'd find her.

She whipped around to scan the area around her. The mailman's van had already turned the corner, and all her neighbors were at work. Emily was alone.

She rushed inside and locked the door. Obviously, this letter violated the no-contact order, so she had to call Sheldon. But first Emily needed to open the letter to confirm it was really from Teddy. She didn't want to appear even more paranoid to her lawyer, who had already hired a private investigator to act as personal security for her.

It could be a trap, Emily thought. *Teddy could be trying to lure me into violating some other part of the prenup or of our court orders against each other.*

Emily knew Teddy's team had slapped some kind of reciprocal orders on her, but she hardly paid attention to them. Emily wouldn't contact Teddy even if she could; she wanted as little to do with the man as possible.

So Emily decided to play it safe. She set the envelope aside and called Sheldon's office.

His secretary answered.

"Um, hi, uh…it's Emil—"

The secretary transferred Emily over to Sheldon's line before she could even ask.

Minutes later Sheldon came on, and Emily sputtered out an explanation of her morning.

"Emily, I—wait, he delivered—is he there now?" Sheldon's voice started to rise.

"No, he isn't here; it's just a letter. There's no return address, but it was delivered through the post. He definitely has my address."

"And you're sure it's from Teddy?"

"I haven't opened it yet, but yes, pretty sure. There's a little stamp that says TG on the envelope. I don't even know if there's something in here, or if this is just a message. That he knows where I live, and he can touch me if he wants to."

"Bring it to my office. This is a violation of the no-contact order, and he clearly knows it. Take a photo of the stamp; maybe we can have it blown up or…Emily—are you okay? Do you need me to call someone to go over there?"

Emily stared out the window in a daze. Her excitement for the book was gone; her excitement for anything was gone. Outside felt like a giant empty minefield.

"I'm fine. I'm going to take a quick shower, and then I'll drive over." Emily hung up and immediately checked her windows and doors.

Emily finished her shower in record time, dressed and headed to Sheldon's office. His secretary showed her in immediately, and she handed over the envelope.

Sheldon took a picture of it before opening it. He removed a letter and began to read, then abruptly stopped. "Perhaps you should read it," he said, offering it to her.

Emily took it tentatively and read.

Dear Emily,

First, I want to apologize for this letter. I know it will come as a shock. But there is obviously no other way for me to contact you. I can't come by or call, so it was either this or smoke signals, and I think Mother will have my head if I try to do that.

I realize the process of our divorce has been mired in confusion and resentment. My lawyers, while very good at their job, are not at all sensitive. They're like bulls charging to the finish, not caring about trampling anyone who is in their way. I want to formally apologize for them. I knew what I was doing when I hired Carson Ciel, but I never imagined the impact he would have on you, nor did I think he'd draw the process out for this long. It's getting ridiculous, even I know that, and I'm a selfish prick who doesn't quit until he gets his way.

I was prompted to write this letter because of your behavior the last time we were in court. I saw you crying, and I noticed that you ran off with your sister right after it was all done. I'm truly worried about you, my love. I think this is the effect of Mr. Mason's attempts to slander my name—I think that deep down in your heart you hate the way he's gone about it. I know you better than anyone, and I know you'd never stoop so low, so I have to think it's your lawyer persuading you to do this. He knows he'll get good press—the whole David vs Goliath thing always goes far—and it's obvious he's using you to attract other clients. You would never see that because you've always had the ability to see the best in people. It's one of my favorite qualities of yours.

I think you know what he's saying is a lie, and it's affecting you physically. You were never a very good liar, after all. I want to implore you to rethink your counsel. He's working for you, remember? That means he has to have your approval before slandering me, calling me names, and throwing me to the wolves. I, unfortunately, don't have quite as much control over Ciel, especially since my mom is paying for him. I'm a little down on my luck at the moment, so I don't think I have the power to control Ciel the way you can guide Mason.

This divorce was never supposed to get this bad. I know you were angry, and I suppose my hubris made me think it would all blow over and I could have you back in my arms. I miss you, Emmy. I miss your smell and the way you used to cuddle up to me at night. My bed feels empty, and I feel alone—I think you are feeling the same thing. I'm truly sorry that I've caused you this much pain. It's hard to communicate in a letter the remorse I feel, and how I feel this whole debacle has gotten carried away.

Mom is particularly indignant. I suspect she's been directing Carson to bring out the big guns because you've hurt her ego by standing up for yourself. Frankly, I think you've been doing a great job—she needed to be brought down a peg or two, and I'm proud of you for being the woman who could do that.

The next part of this letter feels impossible to write because I feel like I already know your answer. I just want all this nastiness to end. I've been going to intense therapy to help me with the trauma I went through and how I basically passed it on to you. My attempt to set boundaries in my life caused confusion and exasperation for you, and that was unfair. You are the love of my life, and I want to try again—for real this time. I want to commit to couple's therapy, and I want to find a way for us to continue on this path together, whatever that looks like. If you want to continue living apart for a while, that works too. The only thing I ask is that you have your lawyer stop with the slanderous talk that I know you don't condone. It's the only boundary I ask you to respect —I can't move forward if I keep hearing stuff like I abused you and stole from you. We are a partnership, and it hurts me to think it's been broken in this way. Please, I hope you can consider this letter to be an extended apology. I was never the writer in this couple, so I doubt I've been able to convey my true emotions on this paper.

I hope this letter reaches you, and I hope you read it with the open heart I know you have. I really am sorry. I'll do what I can to make my legal team ease up. I hope we can find our way back to each other now that we've both

healed a little bit. Thank you for reading it this far. I love
you, I really do.

Yours, forever, under every circumstance,
Teddy

It was possibly the most poetic thing Emily had ever read. And most likely absolute bullshit. She handed the letter to Sheldon and stared at him, analyzing his expression, as he read the rest of it.

"He ought to be a politician," Sheldon finally said. "This is spin some people pay good money for."

"What do you think I should do?" Emily asked.

"Nothing. I think you've done enough by bringing me this letter. This violates his no-contact order, and I'll submit it to the judge, as Teddy is clearly trying to coerce you to end the divorce settlement."

"Why is he doing this? Why now? He's always so...he just sits there staring at me with that smug look every time we're in court together. Why not stop Ciel when he can?"

"He wasn't lying, his mother is footing the bill, so maybe he doesn't feel he has the power to stop Ciel. His lawyers submitted his financials as evidence he doesn't have money to settle with you. I've been working to prove that his fortune, even the money he's made since marrying you, is in a trust, waiting for him when this is all over. He's probably tired of living under his mother's thumb while the divorce drags on. Not to mention how embarrassing this has been for him."

"How embarrassing could it be? I'm the one who looks like a deer in headlights all the time."

"Yes, but you are a very alluring, beautiful deer in

headlights. The longer the trial goes on, the more Teddy looks like a philandering troll. His outbursts in court make him seem like a spoiled brat, and the gossip pages have enough lurid stories of his debauchery to keep them running for another hundred years. The settlement is starting to fall in your favor, and I'm guessing Teddy's pride is hurt. Not only does he not have access to his money right now, but he's also being made out to be a fool."

Emily thought it over. She had to wonder if the entire letter was him gaslighting her again, or if even a little bit of it was true. Was he really in therapy? And was this letter the only form of contact he'd made? That seemed a bit suspect to her. Especially since he wasn't supposed to know where she lived. It scared her that he knew where to find her. How did he find her? Had he hired a private investigator? Probably. That seemed like something Teddy would do.

"I would never have thought subtlety was in Teddy's wheelhouse. There was a time when he'd just show up at my door before I moved to this house and demand to see me, regardless of the no-contact order."

"We still don't know if he's the one behind all of the things that have been happening to you."

Emily nodded. "It could still be William or someone Teddy hired..." She frowned, not feeling any safer than she had before.

"We'll keep on it, and we'll figure this out, Emily, I promise."

"DID you get the parcel I sent? I hope it's not too much. I just wanted your thoughts on the book." Horace had called shortly after Emily arrived home.

"I did. Unfortunately it came at the same time as a letter from my soon-to-be ex-husband, so I haven't glanced at it today. I'm really sorry. I swear I'm not usually this flakey; it's just—"

"It's just that you happen to be going through an unusually tumultuous time in your life; that's totally understandable. We've all been through something like that. I remember breaking up with a long-term boyfriend who refused to move out of the apartment despite the fact that I had paid for the damn thing. He just kept showing up and acting as if he still lived there, and would *complain* when I didn't get groceries for him."

"That's insane—why would he think he could stay?"

"He was angry that I broke up with him, didn't think he deserved to be dumped. It took me putting the apartment on the market and hiring a lawyer to point out he'd have no rights to the place before he stopped harassing me. So trust me, I understand having a roller-coaster ride of a breakup."

"Without this job I truly think I'd be spiraling into madness. Honestly, Horace, please understand that I am committed to my job, and I can handle whatever you throw at me."

"You're doing a great job. I can book my own restaurant reservations for a couple of weeks, and there's a couple of interns here who are far too happy at their jobs. It's time they were tortured by an unreasonable boss, you know? I'll keep sending you my rejections to take care of, and if I need a second opinion, I'll let you know. All those things aren't urgent, so you can work at your own pace."

"Thank you. I'm so grateful for this. Especially the copy

of *A Venetian Oleander*—if that can't get my mind off my contemporary troubles, nothing will."

Emily hung up and started on her routine.

Windows and doors, internet activity, security cameras. Windows and doors, internet activity, security cameras. Windows and doors, internet activity, security cameras.

22

Venetian Oleander was even better than Emily expected. She spent the next three days reading the book cover to cover, and when she was finished, Emily went back to *The Olive of Mandarino* for clues to what would happen.

She was reading when she heard a commotion at her door. Emily jumped, so engrossed in the story that she forgot, for a few hours, to be paranoid. She crept to the door and listened.

"Emily," someone said, "Emily, please open the door."

She looked through the peephole and saw it was William slumped against her doorframe, his hand raised to knock on the door.

"William, what is going on?" Emily threw the door open just as William tumbled forward into her hallway. He looked even worse than the last time she saw him. The dark circles under his eyes were deeper, and his hair was tangled. He was drunk—he was *wasted*.

She looked to see if the police had picked up on him

being here, but they weren't around. Maybe they'd gone on patrol and would notice his car when they came through?

Emily didn't know what to do but follow him as William stumbled through her house, finally landing on her couch. He collapsed forward with his head in his hands and started sobbing uncontrollably. Emily took the opportunity to pour him some water and throw a coffee pod into the machine. She debated calling the police to alert them, but then figured he wasn't going to harm her, not when he was this drunk.

"William, what's going on? Are you okay—did you *drive* here?" Emily stared out the window at the car parked askew on the curb. She was amazed he'd made it here in one piece.

"I'm so sorry, Emily. I'm so, so sorry. I just don't know what to do anymore. I am so out of—I'm not controlling any —" William cut himself off and moaned.

Emily didn't know what to do except rub his back. That was what Laurie liked when she was too drunk to sit up properly. "It's okay, William. You don't have to do anything; just sit, okay. Here, drink some water."

"No, I don't deserve it."

"It's water; you don't need to deserve it," Emily said, forcing the glass into William's hand. She'd started coffee for him too, but it wasn't ready quite yet. She watched him gulp down the water, choking back sobs as he did.

"You don't understand," he said when he was done. "I didn't know what it would—he made me, okay? They both got together, and—now my life is—I'm sorry, okay? I'm so sorry; please, I need you to understand that. I need you to understand that I am so *sorry*."

"Sorry about what?" Emily asked as she returned with his coffee and handed it to him. *Who got together, and what did they do? What kind of trouble had William got himself into?*

"Everything, I'm sorry for leaving you and because you asked me to tell you, but I can't tell you what there is to say." He hiccupped. "I left you to protect you, but that wasn't enough. The bastard pushed me into it, do you see? It's all *his* fault, and now it's following me."

A bastard pushed him into not seeing her? Who was William talking about?

"Who is the bastard?" Emily asked, handing him the water again.

"Randy. Or one of Randy's *friends*. They're following me now everywhere; I can't go outside. I had to escape, so I came over when I could. Emily, I can't believe it. I can't believe what they're up to, it's *crazy*, and now I seem crazy. I can't eat, I can't sleep, I can barely focus when I'm at work."

"What are they making you do?"

"Everything, anything. I'm trapped, Em, I'm trapped." William broke down in tears again. "If I don't do it, my life will be ruined. My life is over anyway, I shouldn't even be here, but I had to tell you—I'm sorry." William fell over and lay on the couch, crying.

He sounded like Emily during the worst part of a panic attack. Paranoid delusions and fear of the world took over, and she rambled so incoherently that she couldn't even think straight. William was definitely drunk, but Emily thought his behavior might be a combination of other things, enhanced by his drinking. William could be taking drugs—prescription or not—that interacted weirdly with alcohol. Or whatever stress he was feeling had come to a head and sent him over the edge. Combine that stress with alcohol and he was a ticking time bomb for delusional thinking.

She didn't know what to say or what else to ask. She

doubted there was only one answer, because it was rarely that simple. Emily did what she could to make William feel comfortable as he cried and rambled on her couch. She served him coffee alternating with water to sober him up and keep him from getting sick in her living room. She hadn't been someone's drunk babysitter in a while; the feeling was calming. William was easy to take care of, unlike Laurie, who was always lashing out and trying to pick a fight or run away. William just needed someone to listen, and apparently for Emily to accept his apology.

After an hour of William's drunk and tearful ramblings, he suddenly stood up. "It's late. I have to go." He marched toward the door.

Emily got up to stop him. "What on earth do you think you're doing? You can't go anywhere; you're drunk. Sit down."

"I can't sit down. I've overstayed my welcome. I'm disgusting; just let me go."

"No, I'll call you a cab if you want, but you have to sit down."

"I can't."

This went on for some time: Emily trying to stop William and William trying to get past Emily without touching her. Then Emily saw her opportunity. She pushed William onto the couch, his keys came tumbling out of his pocket, and Emily kicked them under her couch. He could go out to his car, but there was no way he could drive it. In this state, William was more likely to drive his car into Emily's house than to find his way back home. When he fell backwards, his first instinct was to curl up into the fetal position and cry. It was so...pathetic. William was usually so self-assured. Seeing him like this broke Emily's heart because she knew it must be something extreme that had got him to this state.

"Okay, William, you can go. If you really want to leave, I can't stop you, so just go."

William slid off the couch and stumbled to the door.

Emily watched through the living room window as he searched for his keys in his pockets and then in Emily's lawn. He soon gave up and tried the doors of his car. The back seat door was open, and Emily watched William crawl inside and curl up into a ball.

At least he's safe and not driving, she thought, as she checked her house and called the non-emergency number to alert them that William was sleeping in his car in front of her house, and she was okay with it. It took some convincing before they agreed to let her handle him, and then she got ready for bed.

THE NEXT MORNING Emily woke up earlier than usual. She made a pot of coffee, along with an extra greasy breakfast to help with his hangover. Then she fished his keys out from under the couch and went outside to his car.

William was still asleep in the back seat. In this light, his body curled onto itself, he looked like a little kid. Emily could see the innocence splashed across his face. Something was bothering William, and it ran deeper than what their relationship could be. She gently tapped on the glass to wake him.

William woke with a start, clearly confused. He opened the door and let Emily onto the back seat.

"I brought you breakfast and coffee," she said, handing him the plate and mug. "How are you feeling?"

William sighed and managed a small smile. "Oh, I feel swell. I could run a marathon if I wanted to."

Emily giggled. "I found your keys. I'll admit, I kicked them under the couch last night. I didn't want you to drive home. I just wanted you to be safe. I would have let you back in but—"

"It's okay. It's probably for the best that I slept out here."

They sat in silence as William ate. Emily sipped her coffee and stuck her head out the window to get away from the stale air.

"I should go," William said. "I've intruded on your kindness long enough."

"It's okay, you can come in for a refill if you want."

"No, really, it's fine. You've been great, Emily, thanks for, um...watching out for me last night." William reached across her lap and opened her door.

Emily shuffled out of the car and onto her lawn. She was left standing there, empty dishes in hand, as William drove off.

It was so weird, last night he'd been so tearful and apologetic, and now in the cold light of day he was back to the stoic version of himself. Emily was dumbfounded and unsure what to do. Should she call him and make sure he got home okay?

It felt like a dream. William coming over drunk, rambling incoherently about an apology, and then disappearing just as suddenly as he had appeared. His behavior was oddly suspicious, completely different to the William she knew and had feelings for. This William was so paranoid, running around like a wanted man.

Emily wasn't sure what to make of it. Clearly, last night wasn't just from alcohol, but she knew William wasn't the type to abuse drugs. Emily couldn't figure out what had happened to William to make him break down like this. With Emily, it had been her abusive ex-partner and the threat of a stalker. With William, it was anyone's guess if this was the inevitable decline of an unhinged man, or stress playing with his psyche.

Emily couldn't decide if she had dodged a bullet, or if William needed her help now more than ever.

23

Two days later, Emily received another special delivery.

Dear Emily,

You didn't respond, so I thought I would send another letter. I know this isn't allowed, but I had to find a way to get a message to you, and I don't trust that my lawyer will convey what I want him to. I figure, since this worked the first time, I would try again.

Emily, I want to say again that I am sorry for everything that happened. I understand now that I put you through a lot in our marriage. I didn't have the language or capacity to communicate my needs before, and now I do. After a lot of work on myself and a commitment to self-care, I've found that I can forgive you, and I hope you can forgive me too. I know that I'm not exactly in your good books at the moment; hence, why I need to mail you a

letter like some serial killer rather than being able to call
you or come over, but I hope that can change. I only want
what's best for you, and my arrogance made me believe I
knew what that was. If there was something else you
needed, I wish you would have just told me about it. But
like I said, communication was not our strong point. If we
get back together, maybe that can finally change.

These letters have probably come out of the blue for you,
but I have been writing and rewriting them for months
now. I am not as talented as you are with the written
word, so it's taken me a while. I've been trying to find
ways to reach out, but I just can't figure out how to get
through to you. This was a last-ditch effort, and I have
never been so glad to find out that it worked. I could have
cried! I know I was supposed to feel bad or like I was in
the wrong, but I was elated! Finally, I could reach out and
tell you about all the progress that I have made, and that I
am now in a better position to be your partner. I don't
have to be your husband. We can date and start to get to
know each other again. It's been so long since I've had you
by my side.

There is one concern I have. A little birdie told me that you
and William Summers have rekindled your "relationship."
Just like last time, this is a very bad idea. You don't know
the real William Summers. He's a liar and a cheat who
will not stop until he gets what he wants, and then he'll
disappear just as quickly as he came back into your life.
He is more interested in poaching other men's wives than
having a real emotional connection. That's because he is
so self-centered and vain that any deep emotional connec-

*tion will completely break apart in his hands. When you
were in the hospital, he seduced you and drew you away
from me. You can't let him do it again, my love. He won't
treat you right, and he's bound to get you caught up in his
emotional maelstrom.*

*I will contact you again soon, but I think this is the last
time I can write a letter. I swear my mother is going to
start going through my mail. She hates every mention of
you, and sometimes I think she is driving me insane. Can
you be brainwashed by your own mother? Because I think
that's what happened to me. If you are willing to stop this
divorce, I can help us escape, go somewhere completely
alone where other people, like my mother, can't touch us,
and we can finally solve all of our problems.*

Farewell, my love.
Teddy

Emily read the letter twice. The first time, the whole
thing made her laugh. Teddy had clearly read some Jane
Austen while they were apart. That was the only explanation
for the flowery, overly romantic language in the letter. It was
absolutely ridiculous, down to the brainwashing and the
slanderous comments he was making about William. He was
back to gaslighting and projecting his actions and feelings
onto William. Did he really think she wouldn't see through it
all now that she was wise to him?

The second time Emily read the letter, she had to run to
the bathroom to throw up. While the letter was overly
embellished, Teddy had hit the nail on the head when it
came to William. Well, partially. William had shown up out

of thin air, pursued her, and then disappeared when she returned his affections. Then, when William finally reappeared again, he came back more emotionally volatile than before. The volatility came to a climax when he showed up at her house, drunk and muttering strange apologies.

Either Teddy knew that William was volatile and had been waiting for this situation to blow up, or Teddy was trying his best to manipulate Emily's feelings for William. Either way, Teddy had been keeping tabs on Emily. The letter made her feel as though he'd been watching her from the shadows this whole time, waiting for her life to fall apart.

These letters weren't about Teddy pleading for Emily to end the divorce; it was a way for him to prove that she'd never escaped his clutches.

She didn't understand how this had escaped her security measures. She especially didn't understand how this had escaped the private investigator Sheldon hired.

EMILY DROVE to Sheldon's office, determined to get some answers. She looked over her shoulder every time she took a turn, always convinced the car behind was following her. When she arrived, the receptionist claimed that Sheldon was out of the office. Emily waited in reception for him to return.

After some furtive actions from the receptionist, Emily began to wonder if she'd lied about Sheldon not being in. She stood up and walked over to her desk. "You lied to me. He's here, isn't he?" she demanded.

The receptionist looked at her nervously, then at Sheldon's door. "Look, he said he didn't want to be dis—"

Emily pushed past the receptionist's desk and opened Sheldon's door.

"Wait!" The receptionist jumped up to stop her, but she was too late.

"Emily," Sheldon exclaimed, "I didn't—do we have a meeting that I forgot about?"

"No, and I'm sorry for barging in when your receptionist said you weren't here, but I came as soon as I received this." Emily dropped the envelope onto Sheldon's desk with a glance at the man sitting in the chair opposite Sheldon. She was in too big a rush and focused only on what was going on in her world to recall that he had other clients. "Sorry," she muttered to the man.

"Seems important. I can wait. I'll just step into the waiting area." The man got up and walked out before Sheldon could stop him.

"What is this, Emily?" Sheldon asked, picking up the letter.

"Just read it, please. And I'm sorry for bursting in, but I couldn't wait."

The letter wasn't long, but it was buried in a stack of blank pages, evidently to get past Teddy's mother. Sheldon took his time reading the single page of text, the crease in his brow getting deeper with every line. "When did you get this?"

"This morning, it came by courier."

Sheldon nodded slowly. "Who's the little bird?"

"I don't know. I was hoping you could tell me. Sheldon, please tell me the truth; are you—"

"Emily, stop right there. Take a deep breath. I can guarantee I am in no way affiliated with the Gaunt family, *especially* not Teddy."

They sat in silence as Sheldon reread the letter and started making notes.

"I'm going to make a copy of this," he said gravely, "and I'm going to highlight every time Teddy mentions something personal and current to you. It's another violation of the protection order, and I won't let him slither away from it."

"Sheldon, I feel like the past several weeks I've been psychologically tortured, and I have to wonder if maybe it's been Teddy all along."

"The investigator said there's been no sign of Teddy doing any of this."

"Could Teddy be stalking me in some other way? Do you think the investigator is working for Teddy too? Maybe that's how he got my address in the first place."

"I thought I could trust him, but maybe everyone is corruptible when you start adding zeros to a check."

"I don't understand how Teddy could know all this if he isn't the one harassing me."

"Emily, you know this letter is the rambling of an extreme narcissist, right? Teddy is trying to manipulate reality so much it's stopping him from making much sense."

"I know that, but he's also right about the way William has been acting. Teddy is using real stuff that's happening in my life to try to manipulate me, and I don't know if I can handle that." She took a long, ragged breath and turned pleading eyes on Sheldon. "Please, can you start using a different PI? I just don't trust that this one is telling the truth anymore."

Sheldon tapped his pen against his desk. "Do you recall the name of the police detective who is on the case of the break-in?"

"Yes, Detective Mike Jackson. I have his card."

"I'll call Detective Jackson and see if he has any updates on the situation with your home, and in the meantime, I'll fill him in on what's been happening with Teddy. He might have another perspective on it, and maybe he can help me uncover who the 'mole' is. I'll also call the private investigator and give him a very *stern* talking to about what it means when I pay him to keep an eye on your home and check if your abusive ex-husband is stalking you. How does that sound?"

Emily shrugged; it was as good an idea as any. It was likely better than her own idea—to run far, far away and never come back. Maybe she could start a new life in Greece as an olive farmer or something.

"Emily, it's better to fight this than run away," Sheldon said, apparently reading her mind. "If you run away, Teddy can find you, and he knows he has power over you. If you fight for what you deserve, you show that you won't go down without a fight and that you have people in your corner who believe you, support you, and won't let Teddy walk all over you."

Sure, Emily thought, *but where have they been while Teddy watches my every move?*

24

Agoraphobia (noun): extreme or irrational fear of entering open or crowded places, of being in places from which escape is difficult, of leaving one's own home.

Emily read the definition over and over again after her sister accused her of becoming an agoraphobe.

"It's not normal, Emily." Laurie sighed. "You can ask your therapist if you don't believe me. You have to *live* your life; that's the only way you can prove to Teddy that he isn't getting to you."

It was easy for her to say—Laurie was carefree and almost reckless when it came to relationships after the abuse she'd taken from her first boyfriend, always claiming that she wasn't going to let someone steal her power ever again.

Still, Emily knew her sister had a point. She had to start living her life as normal before she became confined to the walls of her small house. Her father kept inviting her for coffee, but Emily kept avoiding him; his wasn't the support she wanted right now. She wanted to feel independent not indebted.

She decided to test her agoraphobia. After a little bit of a pep talk, Emily gathered the courage to leave her house and spend her whole workday outside her own little jail cell. She went to the one public place she felt safe—the co-working space at the hotel. It was basically an extension of her home —she'd slept at the hotel enough times to feel truly comfortable—and had the security she needed, being a higher-end hotel.

Partway through her day, when Emily had relaxed into the advance copy of what was supposed to be the next big prestigious literary novel, she got a call. At first, she ignored it—she was deeply engrossed in the book and didn't pay much attention to her phone as she let it vibrate in her pocket.

When they called back almost immediately, Emily sent it to voicemail without even looking to see who it was. She figured it was probably that hang-up caller again.

When the phone rang for the third time, she actually pulled it out to see it was Sheldon calling, and quickly answered.

"Hi, Sheldon, is something wrong?"

"We need to talk. Can you come to my office? We—I need to show you something." He sounded urgent and a little disturbed.

Sheldon had implied there was someone else attending the meeting. That was unusual. Normally it was just the two of them going over his strategy for the day. "Is it that important you need me there immediately?"

"It's extremely important. I need to show you something

as soon as possible, and I'd like you to hear it from me and not someone else. You need to come to my office right now."

EMILY ARRIVED at Sheldon's office an hour later to find Sheldon and an older man she'd never seen before. The man was tall and broad, wearing an old leather jacket over jeans. His eyes were hidden under a pair of heavy eyebrows, giving him the look of someone who was suspicious of everyone and everything.

"This is Nic Evalds," Sheldon told her. "He used to work for me as a paralegal before going off and getting his private investigator's license and throwing away a potentially very lucrative career in a law library."

Nic laughed—he sounded like a robot who had been given the command with zero context. He turned to Emily and held out his hand. "Nice to finally meet you."

"Um, you too," Emily said. Her heart started racing. "Why are you here? What is this about?"

Nic and Sheldon looked at each other gravely.

"Maybe it's best you sit down," Sheldon said.

Emily did as he asked, taking a seat in the chair next to Nic. She tried to steel her spine as she waited for the dreaded news.

"As you know, Nic has been keeping an eye on you and your house. We've been mainly focusing on Teddy, trying to find evidence that he's observing your activities. So far, there's nothing on that front. Nic has an associate who was trailing Teddy for a while, and according to him, Teddy is holed up in his mother's house."

"He isn't exactly a prisoner," Nic interjected. "He leaves sometimes to go out partying and comes back with a woman or two on his arm. Not exactly discreet behavior."

"Yes, we've been logging all that as evidence Teddy isn't the gentleman he claims to be. But today, Nic observed something that is important for you to know." Sheldon opened a file and laid out five blown-up photographs.

William turning the corner by Emily's house.

William walking up to the door.

William taking a set of keys out of his pocket.

William using the key to open her door.

William in her living room.

William upstairs in her bedroom.

William all over her house, looking for something, turning over couch cushions and looking behind curtains.

"What's he looking for?" Emily asked, stunned.

"I was trying to figure it out," Nic answered, "but I couldn't get much closer without making it obvious that I was watching him."

Emily picked up a photo of William holding a picture frame. *It's probably the cameras,* she thought. *He's looking for the cameras and the microphones; that's why he's behind the curtains.*

"Emily." Sheldon nudged her hand. "Do you know what he might be looking for?"

Emily wasn't paying attention; she just shrugged. She'd been right to question William. He'd somehow stolen her keys and copied them, broken into her house and planted the cameras all over the place. William was the one who had been torturing her. Maybe he was even the one who'd told Teddy where she lived.

"We need to call Detective Jackson," she said.

Nic shuffled in his seat. "I don't know if we need to bring the police—"

"Detective Jackson needs this information. You're a licensed PI; there shouldn't be a problem. You can still keep watch over my house if all you care about is a paycheck," Emily said, more sharply than she intended. "This is evidence for his investigation, which will do more good than just collecting evidence for my divorce. William has nothing to do with my divorce, remember? The police can actually *do* something."

"Of course, Em, I had planned to let Detective Jackson know as well, but we wanted to show you first," Sheldon said. He looked at Nic. "You weren't suggesting anything else, right?"

The PI muttered something under his breath about a waste of taxpayer dollars before nodding.

"I didn't want to tell you over the phone in case you went into shock," Sheldon continued. "We'll call Detective Jackson from here and brief him on what Nic has observed and give him the photographic evidence."

Emily didn't know what to say. She kept staring at the photograph of William standing in her living room, holding a picture frame. She couldn't quite make out the photo in the frame—was it the one of Emily and Laurie as young girls, ready to go off to camp? Maybe it was the family portrait Emily kept, the one her dad had insisted on taking when the girls were both in their twenties, so they could have a photo of their family that wasn't triggering for any of them.

She wondered what was going through William's mind as he broke into her home. Did he feel guilty at all? Was that why he came over to her house drunk and apologetic? All around her the new, good men in her life were acting to keep her safe from the romantic partners who kept disappointing her, while Emily sat in the eye of the storm, unsure of where to go.

Sheldon called Detective Jackson and arranged for him to join them. He arrived within ten minutes.

"Do come in, Detective." Sheldon directed him to the chair his receptionist had brought in for him while Emily had been staring at the photos.

Detective Jackson sat down. "You said you have photographic evidence of who has broken into Ms. Gray's home?"

"We do." Sheldon handed over the photos, all except the one in Emily's hand. "Em, can you give that one to the detective as well?"

She nodded and handed over the photo.

Detective Jackson looked at each photo and then listened to Nic, who seemed just a tad resentful to be telling him what he'd seen, but he did so without complaining.

Jackson said he'd make sure to pick up William for questioning, but without proof or a confession, they couldn't charge him with the original break-in. And seeing as he had keys in the photo, it would be a he said/she said as far as this was concerned.

Emily didn't know how William had gotten her keys in the first place.

"Emily, do you want to be escorted home?" Detective Jackson asked, his hand on her shoulder. "I can have an officer stationed close by to keep an eye on you and your place."

Home was the very last place Emily wanted to be.

"No, I don't want to go back there. I want to go to the hotel. I have to finish my work," Emily mumbled as she thought about the book and review notes she needed to get done.

Detective Jackson nodded. "Would you like to stop at your house and pick up anything?"

Emily paused. She did need some things if she was going to stay at the hotel. "Yes, please."

Jackson escorted her to her house to grab a bag of clothes and her essentials, and then took her back to the hotel. He met with the head of security to explain her situation. Emily stood beside him, listening.

Jackson turned to her. "Please let me know when you leave the hotel grounds. You can call Mr. Mason if you can't reach me directly, and he'll pass it along. I know it probably makes you feel like a prisoner but—"

Shaking her head, Emily said, "It's fine. I get it; this is just my life for now."

"My officers are bringing William down to the precinct as we speak. I'll call to update you later. I am very hopeful for a confession once he's confronted with those photos. Mr. Summers is somewhat cooperating, at least," Detective Jackson said. "He insists he's innocent. Even when faced with the photographs, he claims we can check with the hospital, but the photographs are time stamped and don't lie. Despite the chance this will end up in a he said/she said situation, the DA has decided to push forward and press charges for breaking and entering. Maybe if he spends some time in the county lock-up, he will finally start telling the truth."

"That's good," Emily muttered. "I can't stay in this hotel forever. It's getting too expensive."

"Are you planning to return home tomorrow?" he asked, sounding concerned.

"No. I'm going to my dad's."

"Officer Corbridge and I will escort you there in the morning."

"Thank you, Detective." Emily said.

She looked around the hotel room, feeling somewhat secure. She just wished that feeling would last, because she was afraid this was going to be the last good night's sleep she was going to have for a while.

25

The next morning Detective Jackson and Officer Corbridge arrived at nine and drove Emily to her dad's house. Officer Corbridge drove her car while Emily rode with Detective Jackson. The ride was a quiet one, but Emily didn't mind. She was lost in her own thoughts and barely registered him escorting her to her dad's door and handing her the keys to her car.

"Hi, Dad. Thanks for letting me stay," Emily said softly as she entered the house.

"Of course." He showed her to the guest room and then said, "I made tea if you want it. It's in the kitchen. I'll be here in the living room if you need anything."

EMILY SAT in the living room, drinking tea with her dad. "I can't believe it came to this. I thought I was finally getting my life back after Teddy, and then I end up in a similar situation with William. I just don't know what to do."

"If you need help, you can always stay here for a while, or we can find you another place to live. And remember, William's still in jail—he can't leave without it being all over the news, and that'll give you a bit of a head start, don't you think?" He smiled.

Emily laughed in spite of herself. "I just don't understand how I got this way. How did I end up having the worst luck with men?"

"It isn't bad luck," her father said, "it's my fault, really. I should have left your mother years before I did, but I wasn't sure I could handle you and Laurie without her. Your mother made me believe I was incompetent as a father, made sure there was enough distance between us that you girls wouldn't trust me as much as her. She impeded my career and—well, I don't need to talk about that with you. Only that I wish I could have given you a healthier example to follow so you would know what to look out for."

"It wasn't you, Dad. You did the best you could, and I see that. I really do think it is bad luck. Teddy was so kind when I met him. It wasn't until after we married that a switch was flipped. No one could have seen that coming."

Her dad was quiet.

Emily looked at him and realized her words weren't true. Someone had seen it coming. Someone who had been through the same thing.

"You saw it coming," Emily said softly. "You tried to tell me. I should have listened, but I was just so angry about everything that happened with Mom. I was angry that you didn't do anything, and I was angry at myself because I didn't stand up to her sooner."

"That's the thing about manipulators—they make you think you don't have any options."

AT ABOUT FOUR, while Emily and her dad were quietly watching a show on the Discovery Channel, Laurie burst through the door, carrying more takeout than the three of them could ever eat.

"I'm sorry I'm late, I wanted to pick up your favorite Thai in case you were hungry, but they were closed, so I went to that Chinese place nearby, the one I like, because I knew it would be open, I hope that's okay," Laurie said, all in one breath, before sitting down and setting everything on the coffee table. "You okay?"

Her dad clicked off the TV, then went to the kitchen to get plates and utensils for them.

"Thanks for this," Emily said, gesturing to the food. "I didn't think I would be hungry, but now I realize I'm starving."

"Figured you hadn't really eaten with everything going on. Dad told me about William."

Emily nodded. "I didn't want to believe it was him," she admitted.

Her father came back into the room and fixed each of them a plate. She felt like she was suddenly able to see him in a different light. He had helped her so much, from buying a house in his name for her to live in, to referring her to Sheldon, and all he wanted in return was the occasional dinner with his daughters. He hadn't been able to stand up to their mother when they were kids, but he had managed to recover from their marriage over time.

Emily knew that was the kind of strength she wanted in her life—a gentle unshakeable sturdiness.

LATER THAT NIGHT after their dad had gone to bed, Emily and Laurie stayed up watching trashy reality television.

Laurie glanced from the TV down to her phone. "Do you want to watch another show?"

"I'm not tired yet. I'll probably watch another, but you don't have to stay." She was grateful to her sister for being there for her, but she knew Laurie had her own life and didn't need to be caught up in all her drama.

"You've had a long day; you should sleep." Laurie didn't move from the couch, merely stared at her.

Emily smiled. "You know I don't need a babysitter, right? I'll be okay if you want to leave. I know Dad basically demanded that you come over today and spend time with me, but it's fine. I finally realized something today. Through everything, Dad has had my back. I don't think I understood until today how much he's really done for me."

"I have your back too, you know." Laurie arched a brow at her.

"I know, but sometimes it feels like you think I'm taking advantage of you."

Laurie squirmed in her seat and shifted to look at her. "I'm always here to help when you have a breakdown or a panic attack. I don't think it's very fair for you to say Dad is the only one helping when you know he was never around—"

"He wasn't absent from our lives, Laurie, he was always around, but Mom took up so much of his time—"

"Exactly—"

"Laurie! You're not hearing me. Mom was a narcissist. She took up so much of his time because she wanted to be the center of attention. It's why we always had to cater to her. She was the same as Teddy. If I wasn't paying attention to him, he would get *angry* with me—can you imagine how that must have been for Dad? He wanted to do things with us, but Mom wouldn't allow it. Do you not recall how she'd yell at him, hit him, anytime he got something for us? The older we got, the more he had to pull away because Mom got violent."

Emily sighed. "I know you're angry with Dad, I know you're angry about our childhood, hell, you can be angry with me for having such a fucked-up marriage, but you can't look me in the eyes and tell me Dad, who was in an abusive marriage with our mother, was an absentee parent. He did the best he could, while our mother tried to isolate us all from each other and manipulate us so we had no choice but to rely on her version of the truth."

Laurie looked stunned, and her mouth hung open slightly as she stared at Emily.

"I'm going to bed," Emily said. She left her sister in the living room and went upstairs. Emily was tired; she was tired of being scared and apologetic. She was tired of being angry with her dad for surviving a marriage similar to her own. Laurie could live with her anger for a day or two—maybe it would help her see that their father wasn't the enemy.

As she climbed into bed, she heard the front door slam shut. Her sister had left.

———

Emily didn't hear from Laurie after that. She stayed with her father, and they talked for the first time about their mutual experiences in abusive marriages.

"I loved your mother deeply—I'm sure you felt this way with Teddy—I just couldn't be with her anymore. I couldn't keep sacrificing myself for her. It was unfair to me and to the two of you. The hardest day of my life was leaving your mother for good, because I felt like I was giving up on her. I had a breakdown because it felt like I had failed."

"I understand that. I always feel like I failed and have nothing to show for it. I sacrificed everything for my marriage, and I still failed—but to hear Teddy's lawyers talk about it, you'd think I had succeeded in some ultimate plan to ruin him. So I sit in court completely confused. Am I a failure, or am I a success? Should I have just kept my head down and let Teddy cheat on me, gaslight me, isolate me from everyone? Would that have been better?"

"Absolutely not, sweetheart, it would not have been better. You're still young; and take it from me, there is no age limit on starting over. Therapy helps."

Their conversations were healing, and Emily actually looked forward to her days spent sitting in her father's living room and reading the books Horace needed help with.

The nights were a different story. Every night Emily went to bed knowing she was about to have the same nightmare as the night before. It started off the same way: she was at home, making herself dinner, when she heard footsteps from somewhere above. Emily gripped her knife tightly and tiptoed out of the kitchen on the hunt for the intruder. The footsteps got louder and louder as she approached the stairwell. The intruder was running now, but it was never clear if they were running toward or away from her.

When she reached the staircase, the footsteps started to change. They would be upstairs, and then a second later she would hear them in the living room. By the time she got in there, the footsteps were back by the stairs. No matter how quickly or slowly she moved, the person was always *just* out of reach.

She crept back to the foot of the stairs and stopped. "Fine!" she yelled. "You win! I'm giving up. I'm putting the knife down!" Her heart raced as she set the knife on the bottom step.

The footsteps were steady, slow, and heavy as they came down the stairs, unaccompanied by a body.

Emily could feel herself shaking with fear, bracing herself for what the ghost would do when they were finally face-to-face.

Finally, the footsteps reached the bottom of the stairs and stopped.

Emily lurched forward, reaching out to where the ghost should be. Sometimes, she swore she felt something as her fingers reached out into thin air.

For the most part, she would fall on her knife and immediately start bleeding, lying on the stairs as her blood seeped into the carpet.

Sometimes, she reached out and grabbed onto a flannel shirt, but when she looked up, the stranger in her home didn't have a face.

Then, other times, she would look up into William's dimpled smile before he dropped her onto the knife and watched her bleed to death in front of him.

26

F inally, they reached the end.

The living nightmare that was Emily's three-year-long divorce was finally at its conclusion, and there was hope at the end of the tunnel.

Judge Adisa contacted the two legal teams to say he'd heard enough evidence from both sides regarding the prenuptial agreement and the considerations against it, as well as the accusations of abuse from both Emily—which were sound—and Teddy—which were facetious. Judge Adisa declared their next court date to be the last, and he would be immediately dismissing all additional appeals.

The day of the final court date, Emily and Sheldon met for a more casual lunch meeting. She was exhausted from lack of sleep. Last night she'd had the same nightmare that had plagued her for weeks, except this time it was Teddy staring down at her as she slowly bled out and died. She'd looked even worse than she had the night of the car crash.

"This is good," Sheldon said. "I think the only reason Adisa would put his foot down like this was if he decided against maintaining the prenuptial agreement, and is coming down on your side. I really think the recording of the car crash swayed him. Teddy's need for control is undeniable, *and* he's violated your protection order twice—which proves he has nothing but contempt for the court and believes himself to be above the law."

It sounded more like Sheldon needed the pep talk than Emily. He was reassuring himself that all this work wasn't for nothing, that maybe there was one judge who could see that there was a deep power imbalance in this relationship, and there needed to be a correction now.

Emily hoped he was right. "Thank you, Sheldon. I honestly don't know where I'd be without you. No matter how it goes today—and I think it's gonna go well, but I still need to say it—thank you for all your support and for just believing me, even when you didn't need to. There were plenty of other lawyers who didn't care, who just took Teddy's lawyer at his word. I really appreciate how much time you took on my case."

Sheldon smiled and patted her hand. "You're a good person, Emily. I hope this means you can finally move on."

Their lunch didn't last long, as they had to get to the courtroom. After they took their seats, Emily glanced around the room and saw Teddy and his legal team, along with journalists from the city's major newspapers.

"Thank you all for coming," Judge Adisa began. "And thank you for your acknowledgment and consideration of my letter. It is my belief the decision I make today is fair and equal to both parties and takes into consideration the terms of their marriage, including the length and commitment made by both Thaddeus Anthony Gaunt and Emily Amelia Gaunt, née Gray—which is

how she'll be referred to during the rest of this
decision."

You could cut the tension in the courtroom with a dull
knife. Emily felt as if everyone was holding their breath. She
looked back at the viewing gallery, searching for her family.
Her father was there and gave her a thumbs-up. Laurie was
nowhere to be found, and that made her sad.

"I've reviewed the prenuptial agreement and have
decided to uphold it, with some amendments," the judge
continued. "The prenuptial agreement states that both
parties will maintain the properties held in their name *at the
beginning* of their marriage, as well as the debts and inci-
dental costs associated with them. This remains the same,
meaning Mr. Gaunt is ordered to vacate the condo originally
purchased by Ms. Gray; and Ms. Gray is required to repay
Mr. Gaunt the total amount he paid during the period in
which they were married."

Emily wanted to throw up. Out of the corner of her eye,
she could see Teddy grinning at her—he knew this was
going to go his way.

"In the event that Mr. Gaunt has already sold the property, Mr. Gaunt shall reimburse Ms. Gray for all financial
contributions she made to the property. I will also uphold
the stipulation that Ms. Gray is no longer legally entitled to
use the Gaunt surname on any personal, professional, or
legal documents, and that Ms. Gray will receive only $1,000
per month in spousal support from Mr. Gaunt until either
she marries again or five years have passed, and that this
divorce shall sever all ties between the two."

Emily felt herself deflate.

Teddy's lawyer tapped the table with his stupid fraternity
ring, and Teddy did the same. They were already celebrating

their success—one more woman being ground into the floor thanks to their partnership and roguishness.

Sheldon took a deep breath beside her. She didn't know how to comfort him since she could hardly comfort herself.

"Now, for the amendments—I've decided on the following departures from the original prenuptial agreement based on facts presented during the mediation and subsequent court hearings for this divorce case."

Emily braced herself.

"I find that Thaddeus Anthony Gaunt engaged in abusive, controlling, and dismissive behavior in his marriage, including but not limited to the psychological abuse of his wife, stalking her after their marriage had ended, and unfaithful behavior during their marriage. The following decision takes into account the fact that Ms. Gray applied for a protection order against Thaddeus Gaunt, which was repeatedly violated—most recently by Mr. Gaunt sending personally addressed letters to Ms. Gray at her new home address. It also takes into account the fact that Ms. Gray put her career on hold during their marriage and, according to the testimony of various household staff, recommitted herself to taking care of her husband and the house they lived in."

The tides were starting to turn a little bit. As Judge Adisa outlined Teddy's many infidelities and the accusations of abuse, Emily could hear his legal team muttering amongst themselves. Could they even keep this going? Everything that Judge Adisa was saying was going on the record, and all the journalists they'd invited were about to print it in their newspapers. If Teddy appealed the settlement now, it would be a horrible look for the Gaunt family. Ultimately, his team was employed by *Belinda* Gaunt, who prized her reputation above everything else. She likely wouldn't risk it so her son could get his way.

"In conclusion, it is my decision that Emily Amelia Gray be awarded half of Thaddeus Anthony Gaunt's financial assets, and that all legal costs associated with this divorce settlement be reimbursed by Mr. Gaunt—"

"This is complete and utter bullshit!" Teddy shouted as he jumped to his feet. "Who the fuck do you think you are? You idiotic—"

Carson Ciel pushed him down into the chair.

Emily looked over and saw that Teddy's face was bright red, and he was being held back by his legal team.

"Mr. Gaunt, this behavior will not be tolerated in my courtroom."

"Your courtroom? This is *my* courtroom. Do you know how much money my family gives to this city every year? We're the *entire* economy. I'll have you out on your ass by this afternoon!" Teddy went on to accuse Emily of gaslighting and physical abuse and called her every insult under the sun.

During his rant, Emily sat in her chair, unmoving.

Judge Adisa banged his gavel and said he was going to hold him for contempt of court if he didn't stop. Within seconds, he asked the bailiff to remove Teddy from the courtroom.

"You'll *pay* for this!" Teddy shouted as he was dragged away. "I will not rest until she is *buried* in the fucking ground! You hear me? I want that bitch buried in so much debt that she won't be able to fucking *breathe*!"

After the outburst, Judge Adisa had trouble getting the courtroom back in order. The journalists were already scribbling away and calling their TV news counterparts. Belinda

Gaunt was crying in a corner, distraught that her "precious baby" was having a nervous breakdown. Emily heard her claim that Teddy was suffering from depression, anxiety, bipolar disorder, and obsessive-compulsive disorder—anything to distract from his erratic behavior and the clear fact of the day—that Teddy was an abusive husband who deserved exactly what came to him.

The judge banged on his gavel for several minutes before getting the courtroom's attention. "We'll take a short break. When we come back, this will be a closed courtroom. All observers can wait outside as I present the rest of my decision."

BY THE END of the day, Emily was a rich woman.

Judge Adisa had settled the divorce in her favor, awarding her half of Teddy's financial assets, extending the protection order, and forcing him to give back the money he'd made on the condo that had been sold out from under her.

Carson Ciel begrudgingly shook hands with Sheldon, and the matter of her divorce was finally resolved.

Emily was finally free of Teddy and the Gaunt family.

"It doesn't end here, exactly," Sheldon explained. "Teddy is required to make his financial commitment in three installments over the next three years, so that's going to require some finesse with his legal team. He may try to sue you in civil court, but it sounds as though Judge Adisa made that long speech about his infidelities so that it goes on the record and his appeals won't hold up."

"How long will the protection order be extended?" her dad asked.

Sheldon rummaged through the papers to confirm the answer. "At least three years—I assume to coincide with your involvement with each other. If he's still trying to find you at the end of all that, we can ask for another extension, but hopefully by then he'll have moved on."

He'll never move on, Emily thought. Teddy could hold a grudge like no other, and he would always be angry about the fact that she *beat* him in court.

"For now," Sheldon continued, "we can celebrate. I'll contact Teddy's lawyers in the morning to move forward according to the settlement, and you don't have to worry about Teddy since he's in jail for contempt of court. Finally, a little good news, right?"

Emily smiled weakly and cheered to her success. She couldn't help but feel that this was all about to be pulled out from under her.

Maybe tomorrow it will feel real. Today seems like it could be a dream.

Two DAYS later and still not a single word from Teddy. He had been released from jail thanks to his mother's influence, and seemed to go into hiding after that. Emily's updates came from the news channels and Sheldon's communications with Teddy's legal team.

It seemed they weren't going to bother with an appeal, as it wasn't likely they'd win. Belinda Gaunt apparently decided it was easier to throw money at Emily until she went away.

That worked just fine for Emily; with any luck she would never have to see Teddy again.

The world was finally Emily's oyster. Maybe after a few years she could travel. She wasn't bound to one place by the divorce proceedings; she could live her life how she wanted. She trusted Sheldon to deal with the financial aspects of the settlement, and was ready to wash her hands clean. For the first time in years, Emily wasn't responsible for anyone except herself.

There was only one thing standing in her way—William.

Detective Jackson came to collect a formal statement from her about the break-ins at her home. She asked him what was happening with William, but he couldn't tell her anything of substance.

"William has continued to deny that he was behind the destruction of your kitchen or of planting the cameras and microphones. He admitted that it was him in the photos, and that he did take your keys, but suggested there was more to the story. He's been charged and arraigned, but he made bail." Jackson shook his head. "That's all I can tell you right now."

But Emily had to wonder, *What else could there possibly be?*

27

The next day, Emily was halfway through a stack of rejection letters when she got a call from a private number. Without thinking twice, she answered and was blown away by who was at the other end of the line.

"Emily, I need to see you. It's important."

EMILY SHOWED up to the coffee shop ready to run. Her car was parked right outside the doors, she called her dad to tell him where she was, and she texted Laurie even though her sister hadn't answered any of her texts since she'd blown up at her a few weeks ago. She knew this was a stupid idea, but the phone call and her own morbid curiosity drove her to meet him. She came alone, just as he'd asked, and hoped she was prepared.

William was sitting at a table, nursing a coffee. She sat down across from him.

"This feels weird," William breathed. "I want to hug you or something."

"I don't think that's wise, considering everything." She folded her arms over her chest and stared at him.

William looked even worse than he had the night he showed up drunk at Emily's house. His beard was starting to come in, his hair was unruly, and he looked as though he hadn't slept in weeks. Emily waited for what he had to say— he'd made it seem so urgent on the phone, but now William appeared nervous. His eyes were darting around the shop as he opened and closed his mouth without saying anything.

"I guess I'll go ahead and speak since you seem unwilling to," Emily said. "You've changed so much from the person I once knew that I'm not even sure I remember him right. Were you always this disgusting and devious? Maybe I just didn't notice it because my brain was so rattled from dealing with Teddy. If you weren't, then what the hell changed? Did you get some sick pleasure from watching my emotional breakdown? I feel crazy, and I feel like I can't trust a single soul because the second I went out on a limb and trusted you, you *tortured me.*"

Emily was seething. She wanted this to be over; she wanted William and Teddy to go away and never bother her again. She wanted so badly to not care about William. She wanted to be anywhere but at this coffee shop, sitting across from William, hoping for an explanation.

Yet, she stayed.

Because she also wanted answers. She wanted to know *why.*

"Emily, I understand, I really do. I know what it's like to be punished by someone in your past and never know the real reason why. Randy's done it to me. I would never want to hurt you like that—"

"But you did! And every time you deny it, you hurt me a little bit more."

"I swear on my own life, I didn't *do* any of it. I-I—" William bit his lip and looked away.

Emily could see tears forming in his eyes—what could possibly be going on? What game was he playing now? "You feel guilty, but that doesn't make you innocent."

"No, you're right. I'm not completely innocent. I could have said no and suffered the consequences, but I didn't. I'm just not that strong," William mumbled.

"Fine. If you're not the one involved, then you have to tell me who is. Is it this Randy person? If you tell me, then maybe I can help you. I have a great lawyer, someone I trust; maybe he can help you too."

William shook his head. "No, no, I can't do any of that. I'm in too deep now; you just have to believe me."

"Believe what? You haven't explained anything. I can't just believe you at your word. You've broken my trust many times over. If you can't tell me if Randy is controlling you, at least tell me how you're involved in what's been happening to me. You have to give me something, or else I'm just going to call the police and have them deal with you—"

"No!" William exclaimed.

Everyone in the café turned around and looked at them.

"No, I really don't want that," William said, lowering his voice. "They were relentless. I almost—listen, all I wanted to do was tell you that I'm not doing this because I want to, okay? I'm not doing this to be malicious. Randy is making me do this, and I don't have a way to stop them, not now." Suddenly he stood up, knocking over his chair.

Emily could do nothing but blink up at him as he struggled to get the chair up. William was shaking, glancing around the café.

"I shouldn't have done this. This was a dumb idea. I have to get away before he finds out that I—Emily, I'm sorry. I'm truly so sorry for everything that's been happening, and I'm sorry for being involved, and I'm sorry that I can't tell you why. Maybe someday I'll—" William never finished his thought. He scrambled away, leaving upturned chairs in his wake.

She didn't know what, but something had changed in the man. Was it this Randy he kept mentioning? Something or someone had turned him from the charming, collected, handsome nurse that she knew into a paranoid, jittery mess. Was it him? Was Randy even real? She didn't know the answer to that. Could it be drugs? He did show up at her house unannounced, drunk out of his mind. It could be something else, another psychotic break that followed a period of mania where he decided to call up an old girlfriend and charm her into loving him again.

"I'm not doing this because I want to."

"THAT'S WHAT HE SAID?" Laurie asked.

Emily called her sister when she got home, desperate for her advice. They hadn't spoken in weeks, but this wasn't the kind of thing Emily wanted to take to her father. Out of habit, Emily dialed Laurie's number and was surprised when her sister actually answered.

"Yes. He kept saying he was innocent, that it wasn't him

behind all these weird...pranks, or whatever you want to call them."

"And he was saying someone was forcing him to do all this?" Laurie clarified. "Someone named Randy?"

"Yes, and that someone would be angry if they found out we met up. He didn't clarify if Randy was that someone, or someone else. He seemed confused and half out of his mind."

"Emily, the man sounds insane. I'm sorry, I know he was kind of the perfect guy, but he's taken a dive off the deep end since. I can't tell if he's paranoid because there's someone *actually* following him or if this is all in his mind—did you say he hadn't showered?"

"Yes, and I know it was him because someone got up and moved away from our table when they caught wind of it."

"Yeah, that sounds more like some kind of paranoid schizophrenia or something. Maybe he had a manic episode, and that's what you saw at first—the sexy, charming, manic persona—and now he's going through the decline. If that's right, you can't exactly blame him; it's just his mind telling him that all this behavior is normal. Maybe Randy is one of his alternate personalities?"

"But William's a nurse. You can't treat patients if you have to be a patient yourself, can you?"

"Of course you can—he works at a hospital; there's no shortage of doctors who can treat a mental health condition like that. But why are you pushing this? Do you really want to jump into a relationship with someone who can't keep track of reality?"

"I don't want that anymore with him. I feel like now I just want to know that William is okay. All this behavior is out of character for him, and I'm not just saying that because I kind of fell for the guy. I remember when I was in the hospital how the other nurses would talk about him like he was some kind of superhero. He was so patient and kind. The fact that he's changed this much in just a few months is so...I'm just concerned, okay?"

Laurie sighed. "I was thinking about what you said before. All that stuff about Mom."

"Yeah?" Emily whispered. It was off topic, but Emily craved their reconciliation. "What were you thinking about?"

"I was just thinking about Mom and Dad's relationship. I feel like I could never see the truth of it because I was so young; you and Dad managed to shield me from the worst of it. Because of that, I feel like I grew up in an entirely different house than the one you grew up in. Sometimes when you talk about Mom and the way she manipulated us, I feel like you're talking about a stranger, and I get so angry. She was our mom! She should be remembered for her virtues not her faults. But then I recalled the few really bad memories, and I got to thinking. For every bad memory *I* have, you probably have double that. And for every bad memory you have, plus the ones I have, Dad probably has at least four times as much, since he was with Mom before we were born. It made me feel embarrassed to realize that you and Dad have it so much worse than me."

It's not exactly an apology, but it's a start.

"Anyway, I feel like I got away really lucky, so it makes sense that you and Dad are gravitating toward each other right now. You can relate to all the bad memories he has because you have bad memories of your own with Teddy."

"Laurie, that's all I was trying to say. I was just trying to convey that not everything we remember about Mom was the whole story, and that it's more likely she was wrong more often than you realize, and the way she treated us is most likely the reason you fell for that jackass who treated you like shit. It was what you knew; it was how Mom treated us. But you were strong and got out before it took too big a hold on you. I admire your strength."

"You do?"

"Of course I do."

"Thank you." Laurie paused. "Anyway, I just thought you should know I forgive you for yelling at me. I know I deserved it, so I'm sorry for being bull-headed. I know I wasn't at the courthouse, but that's because I was still mad, but I heard it went well."

"Yeah, it went really well. The judge ruled in my favor in the settlement, so I should get a bit of a windfall from Teddy in the next few weeks. It's kind of cool. I might take myself on a trip or something."

"A trip? Wow, sounds fancy. Where are you going to go?"

Emily hadn't thought that far. She mentioned the first city to pop into her brain. "New York. I'd like to meet my boss in person, maybe go to a writers' convention or something. I don't know, it just seems that I can really start my life over again. There's nothing tying me down here, so why can't I leave for a little while?"

"I see," Laurie said.

Emily could tell her sister was either chewing on her lip or on a nail. "Laurie, stop chewing. You're ruining your lips or nails—I can't tell which one."

Laurie laughed. "I'll have you know I was chewing on a plastic straw. I try not to bite myself when I'm at work so as not to seem too unprofessional. Not all of us can have cushy day jobs where we basically read teenaged books all day."

And just like that, they were back to normal.

"I can't even apologize. I know I have the best job and a more understanding boss than I could ever deserve, and I feel really lucky these days. The fact that this divorce is finally *over* makes me feel like I'm actually capable of dealing with William and whatever lie he's telling himself."

Laurie was quiet for a moment, back to chewing on her plastic straw. "What if he's telling the truth?"

Emily shook her head. "There's no way. He's acting so suspiciously; he was *so* defensive. I just don't think—"

"If he's telling the truth, then it should be obvious to you why he's been defensive. He doesn't know what's *actually* going on. The person who is planning all this hasn't told him the details. William has a guilty conscience—you can tell because you're both weak like that—so whatever is happening to you is making him sick to his stomach. He can't tell the police because this other person has him dead to rights."

"Laurie, I don't live in a soap opera. That kind of thing doesn't happen in real life—there's no one walking around holding him at gunpoint, forcing him to break into my house. No, there's a simpler explanation for all this, and I'd rather not even think about it. All I want is to get William some help."

"Fine, maybe I'm just playing devil's advocate, but I stand by what I said. Maybe William really is telling you the truth."

28

B etween work and the near-constant meetings to finalize the outcomes of her divorce, Emily was distracted enough that William wasn't her top priority.

Teddy's outburst was big news, and Emily was coming out the hero. All the journalists who attended the hearing published basically the same story—that Judge Adisa ruled in favor of Emily because of Teddy's abusive nature and philandering, and as soon as Teddy heard it, he freaked out and had to be physically removed from court. His mother's claims that it was all some kind of sudden mental illness were clearly unfounded—Teddy hadn't been to a therapist since the one time Emily managed to drag him to a couple's counsellor. It turned out he'd lied about that in his letter.

Laurie kept sending Emily articles and blogs about how she was being touted as a silent hero—the woman who stood up to her abuser in court and didn't let him win. A podcast producer contacted her about making a documentary-style series about her marriage, and a local fashion magazine wanted to do a photoshoot with her. She declined them all. Emily was ready to disappear into her own life and enjoy the feeling of being invisible.

Teddy, meanwhile, had disappeared. He was swiftly released from jail, thanks to Belinda Gaunt's money and influence, and no one had heard from him. His mother claimed he was in a mental health and rehabilitation facility to address his anger issues—but no nearby facilities could confirm that he had checked in.

Emily finally felt it was okay to go outside and start living her life. Her agoraphobia seemed to vanish, the weight and fear of the outside world lifted off her shoulders now that the divorce was over, and she went on walks around the neighborhood. The break-ins had stopped, and she felt safe enough to take down her security cameras. She removed some of the locks on the doors, though she did get the locks changed, and she stopped doing her routine.

On Saturday morning, Emily woke up to someone ringing her doorbell at the crack of dawn. She groggily stumbled downstairs and opened the door to a strung-out, middle-aged man in a rumpled suit.

"Emilia?"

"Huh?"

The man didn't wait for an answer; he slipped inside the door and slammed it shut behind him. Emily instinctively backed away, but he slowly followed.

"I saw your ad, and I just figured I'd come over. You look really familiar, by the way; have I seen you before?"

"What ad? What are you—who the hell are you?"

"Uh...John? Is John okay?"

Emily screamed and pushed the man against her wall. He was so on edge that his body crumpled when she touched him. Emily threw the door open and shoved him out, she had no idea who he was or what address he'd mistakenly punched into his GPS, but she had zero interest in finding out.

The guy banged on her door for another minute or so before giving up and leaving.

By that time Emily was so wired she didn't even bother going back to bed. Instead, she started making coffee. It was a lot earlier than she would have liked, especially for a Saturday.

The coffee wasn't even halfway brewed before another man showed up at her door.

"Hey, um, Emma, I know it's early, but I saw your ad, and I figured I'd just come over. That's what you said, just come over, we don't have to confirm."

"What ad? What the hell are you talking about?"

The man's face went white, and he looked around. "Is this a—wait, are there cameras here? Is this, like, one of those TV shows? Listen, I'm a decent guy—can you please not say anything? I'm sorry, here, take the cash and just—" He cut himself off and ran down the driveway to his car. He left four hundred dollars in his wake.

That was the second strange man on her doorstep, ready to pay for her time. They'd each mentioned an ad, but neither got her name right.

Maybe I got rid of the routine a little too soon.

Emily opened her computer and looked up her IP address information. There wasn't anything unusual happening there. She googled her own name, but she only saw the recent articles about her divorce, no "ads" for anything, even sex.

That doesn't mean much.

She knew she couldn't keep this paranoia up, not today. No, Emily was determined to live her life as normal; she wasn't going to let two strangers pull her back into the agoraphobic panic she'd been living in for months.

Emily decided she was going to get dressed and go to brunch. That way she could avoid the weirdos for a few hours, and maybe they'd realize no one was coming to the door and they'd leave.

HER PLAN DIDN'T WORK the way she thought it would. When Emily came back from brunch, she noticed there were cars parked up and down her street, many more than usual. She glanced over her shoulder as she walked up the drive and went into her house.

Minutes later, two men appeared at her door.

"Hey, we've been waiting."

"Waiting for what?" Emily asked.

"Waiting for you, obviously, your ad said you'd be around, but there was no one here. I think we should get a discount for our time; no one makes us wait this long."

"Excuse me?"

"I *wasted* my time waiting around for you, so I'm not gonna pay you for the full time. What are you gonna do about it, call the cops? You're the one doing illegal shit in here."

Emily slammed the door in his face, but the two men kept yelling and banging on her door, demanding that she let them in.

"Get the hell out of here!" she shouted.

The two men gave her the finger and ran off. There was no question they were both high and desperately confused.

Or were they?

It was clear now that these men thought she was a prostitute.

They weren't the only ones. Emily spent the next hour fielding men who showed up at her door. They all seemed to think they were welcome in Emily's home, as if it was completely normal to walk into a suburban home and demand sex.

Emily was revolted. She threatened to call the police on all of them, and some of the men tested her resolve. She finally called after one of the men pushed his way inside, took off all his clothes, and went up to her bedroom, completely ignoring her when she told him she wasn't a prostitute.

"I was surprised to see your call," Officer Corbridge said when he arrived with his partner. "I thought we'd resolved everything. Is it William?"

"No, it's been...other men all morning. He's upstairs in my room. Um...you can't miss him."

Minutes later Emily heard the naked man screaming at the police, first telling them that Emily had kept him prisoner, and then changing his tune and saying he was married to her. It took Officer Corbridge and his partner a full ten minutes to drag him down the stairs and out to the waiting car. In the meantime another man showed up at Emily's door. That one spit in her face when she told him she wasn't a prostitute, and he was mistaken about the ad.

"Two birds with one stone, I suppose," Officer Corbridge said as he cuffed the spitter, "but I don't think we can keep this up all day."

"What am I supposed to do? They've been coming all morning. Some are just embarrassed, but for every embarrassed man, there's a harasser behind him."

Officer Corbridge shrugged. "Do you know who's sending them?"

"They all said they saw an ad. I don't know where."

"I'll notify Jackson; this might be important for your harassment case against William Summers. In the meantime, I'd go to a hotel; they can't try to solicit you if there's no one here, right? Hopefully, that'll deter some of them, and they'll spread the word. See if you can find the ad and have it taken down—have any of the men mentioned you by name?"

"No. Well, one of them called me Emilia, and another called me Emma."

"That's a start—search your address and those names. Don't use a search engine; try social media. We've found that's how most prostitutes advertise themselves lately. Once you find the ad, forward it to Jackson so he can log this as evidence, then do what you can to report it and have it taken down."

Another night at a hotel, another night avoiding my own home. Emily sighed and waved Officer Corbridge off. It was good advice, but she had to admit she was sick of running away. She wanted to just dump ice-cold water on the men as they arrived at her door.

Unfortunately, Emily didn't have enough ice for that.

The men kept showing up. She ignored the doorbell as she prepared a bag and called the hotel. The staff knew her by name now and were always friendly when she called.

"We've upgraded you to a suite and added a spa package

free of charge. Thanks for always thinking of us," the concierge chirped.

Emily couldn't help but laugh—if only they knew this wasn't a night for Emily to pamper herself.

AFTER CHECKING in to the hotel, Emily immediately went to their co-working studio and got to work finding and deleting the ad. It didn't take very long. She typed her address into the search field of some social media sites, and it popped up almost immediately—Officer Corbridge was right, the prostitution market *had* moved online, and there was the ad smack in the middle of them. Whoever posted it had photoshopped her face onto the body of a bikini-clad, busty woman.

Seeing it filled Emily with rage. It was the most disgusting violation of her privacy, even worse than sneaking into her home and moving furniture around. This image could circulate to her boss, her therapist, hell, even her father could find this—and what would they think? Moreover, what would happen if and when this image found its way to the media? Today, Emily was being harassed by johns, but tomorrow it would be camera crews and nosy journalists parked outside her door.

She immediately flagged all of the images, emailed everyone she could, and managed to get the ad taken down within the hour. It was posted on a local online classified website—that was the easiest to get taken down, and it helped fuel the rest of her petitions. Within an hour the image was gone, but Emily couldn't relax.

She didn't know who could have done this. Was it Teddy?

Or this Randy that William mentioned? Did he even exist? If it was William...that thought had her pausing. Had he been gaslighting her this entire time? Manipulating her, trying to gain her sympathy so he could further abuse her?

I'm not going to call. I won't give him that satisfaction. I won't give him another opportunity for a teary apology.

AN HOUR later Emily's tune had changed. The ad was back, and it was so much worse. The harasser had changed the main image to something even more explicit and grotesque. This time the body looked more like her own, making the ad appear authentic. Not only that, but when she searched the classified website, she found that the ad was posted all over the local sex work classifieds. When she flagged one ad, five more popped up in its place. Her hashtag was trending; the ad was everywhere; Emily was losing her mind.

There was nothing else she could do but keep flagging the ad over and over again—but there was no way to keep up. The harasser must have set up a bot to automatically repost the ad whenever it was flagged for inappropriate content. The harasser was never going to be done with her; there was no way for her to stop this unless she went straight to the source. With tears in her eyes and rage in her blood, she called William.

"What the hell do you think you're doing?" Emily paced her hotel suite while she screamed at William over the phone. "You beg me for forgiveness, you ask me to *trust* you, to *believe* in you, to blindly accept that you couldn't possibly be my stalker, and then you turn around and do something like *this*?"

"E-Emily," William stammered, "what are you saying? I'm not doing anything. I haven't been near you since the café, I swear. Whatever it is, I am not the one doing it."

"William, I want you to leave me alone. I don't ever want to see or hear from you again; just take down the ad. This isn't a good way to get my attention, I just got out of an abusive relationship, and there is nothing you can do to make me go back to one. I don't care if this is a threat. I will fight you with every last breath. I—"

"Please tell me what's going on. I've been home all day—"

"Of course you have, you've moved on from harassing me at home, and now you're doing it exclusively online."

"What are you talking about?" he asked.

"The prostitution ad that I can't get rid of because every time I report it, another five pop up in its place. There are men coming to my door, spitting on me, throwing money in my face, and acting like I am—"

"I swear it isn't me. It's Randy; they're trying to frame me. They want you to think it's me, but don't you understand, I love you, and I would never do something like this to you."

That phrase made Emily's blood boil. She'd heard it one too many times: from her mother, from Teddy, and now from William.

"I just want them to stop," Emily said. "I'm sick of this."

She heard William sobbing on the other end of the line. *Of course, I didn't forgive him off the bat, so he thinks he can cry, and I'll crumble.*

"Emily, please let me help. Let me do one thing for you so you can believe—"

"No, I don't trust you. Don't come over; don't try to help; just stay away from me, okay? I'm at a hotel; the police know what's going on. There's no point. I only called because I want this to stop."

Emily hung up the phone and collapsed on the bed. Her phone rang, William's number popping up on her screen. She couldn't answer; she couldn't let herself get pulled in again. Instead, Emily set the phone to silent, turned over, and went to sleep.

29

Emily took advantage of the spa package at the hotel the next evening. She had a massage and a facial and relaxed in the pool and sauna until the place shut down for the night. She wasn't interested in going to the bar, she was afraid someone would recognize her, so she ordered room service and watched old romantic comedies until she fell asleep.

"WE HOPE to see you again soon." The concierge smiled at her as Emily left the next morning.

Thankfully, no one at the hotel had found out about the ad, or she was sure she'd have been kicked out. She'd stayed two nights, and by then she was ready to return to her house and get on with her life.

Emily went home, hopeful that maybe the harassment would stop. When she arrived at her door, she found

William sitting on her porch, a shotgun laid across his lap. She pulled her phone out, ready to call the cops on him.

"Wait!" he cried out. "I'm not here to hurt you. I'm just here to make sure no one thinks they can...do anything to you. Or with you."

The hairs on the back of Emily's neck pricked up. On the one hand, she was incredibly annoyed. She'd told William yesterday she didn't need his help, and he'd completely ignored her and listened to his own pride instead. On the other hand, she was grateful someone was there to protect her, even if it was William. William, who was obsessed with regaining her trust, and was being threatened by some shadowy figure he called Randy.

"I can move off the porch while you go inside. I promise I won't bother you." William put the shotgun down and raised his hands in the air, slowly moving away from the door.

She walked past him without saying a word—it was better this way. Once she was indoors, William took up his position again. She could probably have the cops come and get him for breaking the mandated order that he leave her alone, but she honestly didn't want to be on her own if those men continued to come to her house.

Emily thought about calling Laurie or her dad, but they still didn't know about the prostitution ad, and she didn't want to tell them. She was tired of being a burden to her family.

Besides, William seemed to have this under control. She watched as another shifty-eyed man came up her drive. He went up to William, obviously mistaking the man with a shotgun for Emily's pimp or something. William didn't even say much; he laid a hand on the shotgun and whispered something to the man, who immediately ran back to his car.

Maybe having William sitting outside wasn't so bad after all. And she could keep an eye on him and be sure that he wasn't photoshopping her face onto yet another ad for sex work.

FOR THE NEXT FEW NIGHTS, William sat on Emily's porch with his shotgun and waved off the johns as they approached the door. He didn't say a single word to her except to tell her when he was going home and when he arrived. It seemed the men only showed up at night, so she didn't need protection during the day.

They settled into a routine where Emily left a thermos of coffee out on the porch along with a few snacks, and William set the dishes neatly in front of the door in the morning. William usually came back in the middle of the afternoon to start another shift guarding Emily's door. She wanted to ask how he had the time to do this, what he was doing for work in the meantime, but Emily didn't want to interrupt their silent routine.

William was determined to win back her trust, but Emily couldn't figure out why. Their relationship, this time around, had been a roller-coaster ride with one extreme drop. What could be motivating William to keep coming back? she had to wonder.

BY THE TIME Wednesday came around, Emily's curiosity was getting the better of her. She worked for Horace during the day and in her spare moments tried to figure out a way to communicate with William without having to invite him inside her house. She still didn't feel comfortable talking to him face-to-face, but she had some questions that needed answers.

That afternoon, as she prepared William's coffee and dinner for the night, she added a small card.

Let's talk. 8 p.m.

AT EIGHT ON THE NOSE, William knocked on the front door.

Emily opened her living room window. "I think I'd rather do this," she called out.

"That's fair. I've done a lot to break your trust."

"I have a lot of questions for you. I can't believe you without an explanation."

William sighed and rubbed his temples. Emily noticed how much darker the circles around his eyes were.

"I'm not sure I can explain it all, but I'll do my best."

"You promise to tell the truth?"

"I promise," he said, drawing an X over his heart, "cross my heart."

"Was it really you breaking into my house?"

"Yes. Sort of."

She narrowed her eyes at him. It wasn't completely the answer she was expecting. "What do you mean?"

"I swear it was only once. I came in because you said your house had been bugged, and I was worried. I wanted to make sure it was all gone. There wasn't much I could do, but since you had already deactivated most of the feeds, it wouldn't be weird if the others got deactivated as well. I managed to find a couple you and the cops had missed, and I busted them, then threw them away."

Emily's breath caught in her throat. The feeling she'd had of being watched, it was real.

"How did you get my keys?"

William hesitated. "When I stayed over, I took your keys and made a copy. You told me you were staying home all weekend, so I came back the next day and put them back."

So that was why she hadn't noticed they were missing. And that was why he'd showed up unexpectedly with dinner the next day.

"I was coerced into taking the keys and making a copy..." William trailed off. "I stole the keys for Randy...he's blackmailing me. I wanted to tell you the truth, but I thought they would release what they had on me and...well, it's pretty damaging. Maybe not to you, but for me...my work, it's..."

Emily didn't know what to say.

"I want to be able to tell you everything, but I can tell you still don't completely believe me. I don't blame you. I've been acting like a sketchy weirdo. I don't want to hurt you, Emily; that was never my intention. It's just that...this all got so out of hand. I was so happy to see you again. I never thought it would escalate like this." He gestured around him.

Just then another car drove up and parked in front of her house. The man got out of his car. He saw William staring at him with a shotgun and ran off in the opposite direction.

"How can I know you're telling the truth? You've lied and gaslit me so much, how can I possibly trust what you're saying now?"

"You asked me to tell you the truth, and I did so to the best of my ability. You can't know much more without being in danger, so this is all I can say. I admit to breaking into your home. I didn't confess to the police because I worried it would put you in even more danger. I stole your keys, and I got your passwords off your computer, and I'm desperately sorry about that. That's all I can say; the rest is up to you whether you believe me or not."

Emily nodded and closed the window. William had a point; she was the one who initiated their talk, who asked the questions she needed him to answer. What else could William say? Emily could only take his confession at face value. The blackmail did explain his erratic and paranoid behavior; it finally put into perspective what he had been trying to tell her the night he showed up drunk.

She wondered who Randy was and what they had against her. Were they friends with Teddy? Were they blackmailing William on Teddy's behalf? She didn't know, but she wanted to find out the answer to that question.

She still wasn't sure what to do about William. If she up and left, there was a chance that she would never see him again, but the memory of their initial time together teased the edges of her imagination. He had been a good man once; he could be a good man again. The roller-coaster ride of their latest courtship couldn't be the end—or could it?

The barrage of men at night had slowed down, so William went home around eleven. When he left his dishes out for her, she opened the door and thanked him for his work that day. William weakly smiled, and Emily watched as he walked out to his car and drove away.

HOURS LATER, Emily was woken up by a strange banging noise. It sounded like someone kicking at her door and then banging on the drainpipes outside. She heard yelling and a dog barking in the distance, and then the knocking started again. It was one in the morning, and there was a man at her door.

Emily's first instinct was to call William, but he didn't answer. He usually took his gun home with him, and Emily didn't have her cameras anymore and hadn't gotten around to getting new ones, to get a good look at the intruder. She crept downstairs as the banging got louder.

The man was yelling, ringing her doorbell, and kicking at the door.

Emily ignored him and dialed 911, but when she heard a loud crash coming from her living room, she hung up and put her phone in her pocket. Emily started to hyperventilate as the man staggered into the hallway.

"You're way uglier than in the ad."

He was clearly drunk or high, probably both. Emily pressed herself against the wall and held out her hand. "I've called the police; they're coming."

"Called the police for what? I'll show them the ad, and they'll leave us alone." He took a step forward, and Emily backed up the stairs. "Are we gonna do this here? I'm not paying for staircase sex. Actually, I'm not planning on paying at all. When you *advertise a service,* you should be expected to perform it."

He kept talking, kept advancing, and Emily was so terrified she couldn't think of anything except to keep moving away. The man wasn't backing down; he didn't care about her. He was determined to get what he wanted, and he was angry that she had kept him out.

"If this is what you're like with me," she said, "I can't

imagine what happens when a store says they're out of stock in your size."

"That's it. I don't take lip from hookers," he said and chased her up the stairs.

Emily ran, but there wasn't anywhere to go. She whipped around into the bathroom, but the man grabbed the door before she could slam it. He pushed her against the sink and pinned her arms to her sides. She'd been in this position before with Teddy; he would get mad and hold her arms against her sides until she lost all feeling.

She found herself floating out of her body. *This is what Teddy used to do,* was the only thought that popped into her head. *It's just like what Teddy used to do.*

Suddenly, the door crashed open, and the man crumpled to the ground. It was all a blur—another figure, tall with dark hair, burst into the bathroom and dragged the intruder out into the hall. Emily fell to the floor. She could hear the sounds of someone being kicked and punched just outside in the hall.

"Get out! Get out, or I'll shoot!" The voice was familiar, but Emily couldn't place it.

She listened from the bathroom as her rescuer fought the intruder down the stairs and out the front door. The sound of their fight continued to echo up the stairs, but it was muffled now by Emily's sobs. She felt weak and tired; all she wanted to do was sleep, right there on the bathroom floor.

"Emily?" It was her rescuer's voice. "Don't worry, he's gone."

Emily blinked away her tears, and William came into focus in front of her. His knuckles were bleeding, and his eyes were watery. She recalled trying to call him before she'd called the cops, but she hadn't gotten through to him or them. "How did you know?"

"You called twice. The second one sounded like a butt dial, but then I heard the man threaten you, and I drove over. I...I wasn't too far away," he said.

Emily didn't care. She couldn't believe that William had saved her.

"He's gone, Emily. He's gone; you're safe." William held her in his arms on the bathroom floor, rocking her back and forth until she fell asleep.

30

Emily woke up in her bed the next morning feeling like she was hungover. She kept waking up during the night from the same dream—the intruder barging through her door and strangling her. Every time she woke up, she started to cry, and William would come into her room and soothe her until she fell asleep again. Finally, it was morning; she could get up, put on a brave face, and do something about what had happened.

Before she even made her breakfast, Emily called the online classifieds where she'd found the ads and demanded they remove the posts internally and block it from being reposted. She explained that there was a bot automatically reposting the ad whenever she flagged it, and after a lengthy discussion where she had to prove what she was talking about, the post was finally taken down. For the other social media sites, Emily had Sheldon draft a quick "cease and desist" order for her to send to them, but she merely told him it was for a character assassination attempt, not what was really going on; it was too embarrassing. By the time the afternoon rolled around, the ad was finally gone.

"You'll need to make sure it's properly scrubbed from the internet," William said when Emily came outside to tell him the good news. "I can help you with that. I've got experience in doing that sort of thing."

Emily hovered in her doorway, gathering the courage for what came next. "William, I need the whole story. I want to understand it all. I want to listen to you tell it. I need to know what this person has on you and why they are using you to ruin my life."

"Give me a little while to work up my nerve. Tonight at dinner, I'll tell you everything," he said before turning his attention to another john coming up the drive who clearly hadn't gotten the memo that the ad was no longer up.

EMILY STOOD IN HER KITCHEN, putting lasagna on two plates. She added garlic bread and opened a bottle of wine. She had a feeling she was going to need it, and William probably was too. She carried the plates into the dining room and then asked William to come in and join her.

"This looks good," he murmured.

They took a few minutes to eat, and then Emily sighed as she looked at him. She was waiting for him to start, but then realized she'd have to prompt him. "I need you to tell me everything, William. Now."

"Where should I begin?" William asked.

"The beginning, I guess. How did this start?"

William drew in a long breath and stared at the ceiling. "The blackmailer knew about our prior relationship and wanted me to pursue you again. I was elated to get to speak to you again, maybe see you, so I didn't really see a problem with it, and I didn't know what they had planned."

He set his fork down and stopped eating. "Once you agreed to see me, they had me do a few things—going out with you, distracting you a few nights, getting your keys and making a copy, and finding a way to access your computer. They wanted me to put a tracking device on your car, but I refused. I thought it would be too obvious that it was me."

"You were right that it would have been too obvious. I've been checking my car regularly. What I don't understand is why you were being blackmailed to do all of this to me. What could they possibly have on you?"

He winced. "That's a bit complicated."

"William, uncomplicate it because if you don't tell me, we can't go forward. I need to hear it all."

William looked as though he was about to break down. Finally, he whispered, "I'm bisexual."

Emily didn't understand. Who cared if William was bisexual? Why would it matter?

He must have seen the look of confusion on her face because he continued, "I've always been attracted to both men and women, and I've dated both. I didn't hide who I was —until about six years ago, when I moved here. I was running away from Randy, an ex who turned out to be obsessive and controlling. I didn't want anyone knowing who I was because I was afraid if they reached out to my old job, Randy would find out where I was, and he would come find me. I had worked in a clinic back there, but it was for the city. When I started searching for jobs here, I applied at St. Mary's. It was a really good job, but it's a Catholic hospital, and they have a morality clause, so—"

"So you hid that you were bisexual. I can't imagine how hard that must have been; no wonder I didn't know about this side of you."

"Yes, I did. I really love working there, and I didn't want to leave because of something like this. It wasn't exactly hard —I am attracted to women, so it's not as if I have been hiding anything exactly." William paused and took Emily's hand. "I want to make sure you understand that—I *like* you. I'm attracted to you. I'm not—"

"I know what being bisexual means, and we'll discuss that later. But what you've told me so far doesn't really explain why you did what you did." Emily leaned back in her chair, waiting for him to get to the real reason.

"You're right. The root of this blackmail goes back farther than that. Years ago, before I moved here, I was in a relationship with Randy. At first, he seemed like the perfect man. He was attractive, attentive, charming, and most of all—he wasn't judgmental. He just accepted me for who I was, and at the time I was craving that easy love. As our relationship progressed, his jealousy and anger issues got worse. He started 'testing' my love, making me jump through complicated hoops to prove that I loved him."

"That's how it starts," Emily interrupted. "Teddy did the same. 'If you really loved me, you wouldn't put your friends before me' was a big one for him."

"Yes. Randy would sometimes come to the clinic to 'make sure' I was actually there and not lying to him. I almost lost that job because he was so disruptive. At one point, he coaxed me into making a sex tape with him. I should have known nothing good would come of it, but I did it because he made me feel so guilty and horrible when I said no."

Emily understood. "He wanted to be able to control you with that tape."

"Exactly, but at the time I had no idea. I wish I had the clarity I do now; all this could have been avoided if only I—"

"If only you hadn't dated an emotionally abusive partner? Yeah, I know the feeling."

The pair chuckled a little at how alike their pasts were. For a moment, Emily forgot that this conversation came about because William had broken her trust.

"So, I get that somehow this tape is the reason you did what you did, but what does Randy have to do with me?" Emily asked.

William stared up at the ceiling. "To be honest, I'm still not sure myself. I know that after I broke up with Randy, he put the sex tape online on one of those revenge porn sites. I managed to have it taken down—I found a lawyer who specialized in that sort of thing who helped me scrub it from most mainstream sites. It left me absolutely broke, and it still pops up occasionally, but I've learned enough to get it taken down pretty quickly.

"A few months ago, I got a text from Randy saying that if I didn't do *exactly* as he said, he would re-upload the video using a bot to make sure it popped up every time I took it down, and that he would personally email the sex tape to the hospital director of St. Mary's. I was devastated that he would do something like that. That he knew where I was and where I worked. Then when he mentioned getting in touch with you...well, I thought maybe it would be okay. It wasn't until the rest of his demands came in after we reconnected that I panicked and did everything he said. Since then, it's just been a steep decline, and now I—" William cut himself off and started to shake, his eyes growing teary. He held his head in his hands, and his shoulders shook.

Emily ran over and held him. "It's okay, I understand. I get that fear of your ex and what they could do to you, believe me. I think about how lucky I was that Horace figured out I was being hacked and didn't take any of my emails at their word."

William gently untangled himself from Emily's arms and took a few deep breaths. "At first all Randy told me to do was call you and try to start up our relationship again. Once that happened, he began messaging me with more demands, sometimes more aggressively. Last night, I texted him back and told him I no longer cared what he did or who he told about our relationship. I am done. I love my job, Emily, but what he's done...what he's made me do, I don't deserve to keep it. I don't deserve you."

Emily stared at William. He was a shell of his former self. The handsome, put-together gentleman she knew was gone. In his place was an unrecognizable twin, someone who was more jumpy, paranoid, and run-down. She half-wanted to kick him out of her house, but she believed him. She knew what it was like to be under someone else's control.

Still she felt betrayed by him. He was in the club of survivors of abuse—shouldn't he know better than to break into her house and break her trust?

"I have to tell you one more thing," William continued. "The more I thought about it, the more I thought it was weird that Randy was blackmailing me to torment you. At first, I assumed it was because he found out we were together before and he was angry, but when things started to escalate and you confronted me, I wondered if maybe it was someone else pretending to be Randy. We hadn't talked on the phone; we only communicated via text message—I just didn't want to hear his voice ever again, so I didn't ever call him. Finally, I called the number and confronted my black-mailer. I'm not sure how to tell you this, but Teddy answered the phone."

Of course. Emily thought, *Of course it's Teddy; it's so obvious. It was right in front of my face the entire time. I don't know how I didn't see it.*

It was Teddy who wanted Emily to know that he would always have control over her. It was Teddy who wanted Emily to know when he was angry. And now, Emily had won half of Teddy's estate in court, so Teddy wanted Emily to know what he thought of her—that she was nothing but a whore after his money.

"I don't know how Teddy found out about the tape," William said, "but I think blackmailing me was punishment for me being with you after the accident."

Emily felt stupid for not catching it sooner. But how could she have known when he'd used William? Emily could connect it all now. Teddy was a very smart man. She knew that when he found out about William, he'd dug into William's life. He had to have found out about William's past and knew he could use it against him, against both of them. Obviously Teddy had contacted William's ex—a man who would have his own irrational reasons to hate Emily because he was a man just like Teddy.

All of a sudden Emily's doorbell rang.

"No, not again," she said, feeling frustrated. "We had the ads taken down."

"He probably put them back up," William said, grabbing his shotgun as he went to the front door.

While William dealt with the stranger at the door, Emily

called the online classifieds. "Hi, I'm the one who called earlier; my ex is posting my photo and claiming that I'm a sex worker."

"Is this a joke?" was all they said before hanging up.

"Don't bother with them," William said. "I'll contact my old lawyer and tell her to get in touch with yours. There's no point in going to the source; you need someone who can fight on Teddy's level."

Emily felt her blood start to boil again. Teddy was nowhere to be found, but still he managed to disrupt her life. All she wanted was one day of peace, and she was determined to get it.

"Tomorrow morning we are going to my lawyer's office, and we are settling this matter," she said. "If I have to, I will sue that asshole for the rest of his money. I want my life back, and I will *not* bow down to Thaddeus Gaunt ever again."

31

"Let me get this straight. Teddy has been placing ads on websites with your picture, name and address and offering sex?" Sheldon was livid.

"Yes, that's why I wanted that cease and desist letter from you. I've sent them, but the websites aren't taking them down even though I've called about it several times," Emily shared.

"You didn't tell me it was for this, though. I believe you said it was for something to do with character assassination?"

"I know, I'm sorry. I just thought I could handle it on my own."

"It's fine. I can try to contact them on your behalf; maybe that will work," Sheldon started.

"I can pass along the number of my old lawyer," William offered. "She has a lot of experience in this area and can help fight to get everything taken down, and collect evidence for whatever you're going to do with Teddy."

Sheldon looked at William. "I'll accept that help.

Computers aren't my forte. Now can you go back to how this all started? I mean, how you ended up involved?"

William explained how Teddy had impersonated his ex-boyfriend and threatened to expose his former life if he didn't do as he said.

Emily reached out and took William's hand. She had been wrong to think this was over now that the divorce was settled. Now that Teddy had nothing left to lose, the games were really going to begin.

"I told Randy—Teddy—that I don't care what he does to me now," William concluded. "I want to help in any way I can to stop him. I'll testify against Teddy if I have to, and I'll say on the stand everything I said here. I just want Emily to feel safe."

Sheldon eyeballed the two of them before turning toward Emily. "Do you really trust him?"

"I understand what William has been through, so I understand why he went along with it. I understand the feeling of being under Teddy's control. It's all-consuming and makes you act like a stranger to yourself. I believe that William wants to help, so yeah, I trust him."

Sheldon sighed. "We're going to press charges against Teddy for blackmail on William's behalf. I'll talk to your lawyer, but in the meantime, I'll send another more specific cease and desist letter to any online service that posts the ad, and threaten them with legal action if it isn't removed immediately—and yes, that includes any clones that pop up in its place. Right now, I'm going to call Detective Jackson. William, you're going to tell him everything you told me, and you are going to answer each and every one of his questions, you understand? For all intents and purposes, *I* am your legal representation."

"Yes, sir."

"Emily, if you'd like to go home, you can."

"No, I want to be here when Jackson questions William. I can help corroborate some of the story."

Sheldon nodded as he dialed the phone.

By the end of the day, Detective Jackson had taken a statement from both William and Emily and put out an arrest warrant for Teddy. Two officers were headed to his mother's home to arrest Teddy for trespassing, a violation of a restraining order, and blackmail.

Maybe it was almost over. Maybe they had avoided the worst of it and caught Teddy before he could cause any more damage.

Maybe, for the first time in years, Emily could finally feel safe.

32

There might have been a warrant out for Teddy's arrest, but they couldn't find him, and Sheldon might have sent letters threatening any website that posted the ad, but neither stopped the men from coming. Emily usually ignored them, and thankfully they mostly came out at night, so she never had to interrupt her workday, but still there were instances where the johns were aggressive.

William left her the shotgun. She didn't want to use it, but just in case, he showed her how to hold and rack it anyway.

"Even if you don't have anything in there, the sound of a shotgun being racked is enough to deter any pathetic loser."

So Emily waited. She lived her life as best she could, no longer afraid of the outside world but not keen to join it either. Sheldon and Detective Jackson both agreed that it would be best if she continued on as if nothing was happening, to show Teddy that this wasn't bothering her. He couldn't touch her anymore, even when he was getting anonymous strangers to do his dirty work.

The next night Emily went to her father's house for dinner with him and her sister. They celebrated her soon-to-be finalized divorce and talked about taking a trip as a family. Something they all wished they could have done when they were younger, but were excited about now.

"What are you going to do with the house you've been living in?" Laurie asked. "When you get it back, I mean."

"I'm not sure. I really like the house. I like how quiet and out of the way it is. But it would be nice to have building security again." Emily glanced at her father and could see the disappointment written across his face.

The house in the suburbs was closer to him, and Emily thought he felt a little closer to her emotionally when she lived there. He wanted the best for his daughter, and it was hard for him to admit that might be a condo, closer to downtown, with a concierge and security.

"I might rent an apartment downtown and maybe rent out the house for some extra income. Looks like I'm going to need Sheldon for a few more months, along with some other lawyers, so it will be good if I can pay for them. This is all assuming Teddy doesn't play some kind of trick to deny the settlement."

"Why are you going to need Sheldon? The divorce is over, isn't it?" her father asked.

Emily didn't want to tell him the truth, so she shook her head and smiled. "Yes, but there's still the collection of alimony and the three installments of Teddy's financial estate that I'm entitled to. Way easier to do that with a lawyer than try to deal with Teddy and his mother myself."

"Much safer too," Laurie added.

Emily had told her sister about her sex-worker ordeal before coming inside. She was so irate, Emily had to send Laurie on a walk around the block and tell her father she was stuck in traffic. It took Laurie twenty minutes to calm down before she could come in.

Laurie changed the subject and started talking about her newest boyfriend—he was the sous-chef at a trendy restaurant, who had a business on the side making elaborate cookie platters for weddings. "He makes artisanal cookies with famous paintings on them. People pay a fortune to have him paint a Picasso on a cookie to serve their guests—isn't that insane?"

Under the table Laurie squeezed her sister's hand. It felt good to have Laurie on her side again.

———

EMILY GOT HOME LATE, and despite all the measures she'd put in place, there were still mysterious cars parked on her street. That was the other problem with staying in this house —she was starting to become infamous in her quiet little subdivision. She might not be welcome to stay in the neighborhood, no matter what her father felt about it. She came inside, took off her shoes, and grabbed the shotgun from the umbrella stand.

As if on cue, someone rang the doorbell.

Emily answered holding the shotgun. "I know why you're here, but the ad is wrong. My insane, abusive ex photoshopped my face onto some other woman's body and put my address out on the internet so you could come harass me because he can't do it without violating a restraining order. Get out."

The man immediately ran away.

This was going to be easy.

Emily dragged one of her favorite chairs into her entryway. She brought down a duvet and a couple of books she had been meaning to read and sat by the door with the shotgun all night. *Somewhere out there, someone else is doing almost exactly the same thing.*

Every time the doorbell rang, she stood next to the door and said the same thing that she told the first man in a loud voice so they'd hear her through it.

The other men weren't quite as nervous or terrified as the first, but they went away.

Then at about two in the morning Emily woke up to the sound of someone slamming his hand against the door.

Emily opened the door and aimed her double barrel at him. "I will call the police and have you arrested for trespassing. I'm not a hooker, and I'm not going to let you into my house." She slammed the door in his face.

There was a pause. The angry man was obviously thinking about his next step. "I'm sure a nice lady like you likes to have sex too. I can pay for your time."

Emily rolled her eyes. "Just leave. Go home to your wife."

"I'm divorced, I'll have you know. Here." He pushed two hundred-dollar bills through the mail slot. "That's for the divorce. If your ex-husband really is that much of an asshole, you're going to need it."

EMILY SLEPT by the door for the rest of the night, but no one else disturbed her. She woke up with a crick in her neck and the imprint of her embroidered cushions on her face.

After stretching a little bit, she stumbled into the kitchen to pour herself some coffee and then called William.

"Hello?" His voice was groggy and confused. William had left his apartment the night before and was staying with Sheldon for his own protection.

"It's me. I just wanted to thank you for showing me how to hold the shotgun; it really came in handy last night. You'll be happy to know I didn't point it at my own face once."

"Is that so? I'm glad; you'll be a pro in no time."

"Thanks." Emily paused—she wasn't sure why her first instinct was to call William. It was still a little soon, she still felt hesitant to trust him, but it was nice talking to someone who had gone through a similar experience to hers. "One guy actually ran away as soon as he saw it."

"You're kidding!"

"Nope. I racked the shotgun and watched him run down the street. Another guy left me money to help with my divorce."

"No way—did he just leave it on the porch?" William laughed.

"No! He said, 'If your ex-husband really is that much of an asshole, you're going to need it'—isn't that insane?"

"I'm very proud of you, Em. It takes a lot of courage to do what you did. Standing up to men isn't for the faint of heart —even if you have a gun."

"Thanks, I really appreciate that."

In spite of everything that had happened, Emily still felt drawn to William—especially now that she understood why he had been acting so strangely. It was comforting to talk to him without feeling the need to flirt or fearing that he was hiding some part of himself. It reminded her of when she first met him. He was the kindest nurse who tended to her when she was in the hospital, in part because he treated her like a human being and not a delicate piece of porcelain. At that time, she needed someone she could laugh with, and William was a godsend.

It also hit her that William was the first boyfriend to say that he was proud of her. Teddy never expressed any pride in Emily. He always picked at her faults, and it slowly eroded her self-confidence. It shocked Emily how something as small as William saying he was proud she'd defended herself built her confidence back up. It felt good to stand up for herself, to fight the assholes who came to her door; and it felt even better to have that acknowledged.

"I have to go," William whispered. "Sheldon's awake, and he's super grumpy in the mornings before he's had coffee. Maybe I'll call you later to see how you're doing?"

"Sure," Emily replied, "that would be really nice."

33

Teddy hadn't been seen in days. His mother, Belinda, wasn't giving up anything about his whereabouts, according to her he was still in a "mental health and rehabilitation facility"—but no one believed that anymore. Emily wanted to find a way to draw him out. She wanted to be proactive and do something that would help, but something that wouldn't be too dangerous, if there was such a thing.

When she'd spoken to Sheldon, he'd suggested something that would get Teddy's attention, but would also be a help to others. That was what led Emily to sitting in her living room, Sheldon off to one side, under an extremely hot light, waiting as a makeup artist dusted her face with powder.

"Ms. Gray? I'm Helena Taylor. I'll be interviewing you today."

Emily had seen Helena Taylor on TV; her hard-hitting yet emotional interviews were the stuff of legend. Emily and her sister used to watch them on the evening news and then recreate them in their rooms. She couldn't quite believe Helena Taylor was standing in front of her and was about to interview her.

"Um, hi, Hel—Ms. Taylor. I've seen your work. I'm so excited—honored, really, that you would agree to this."

"It's a fascinating story. I feel like as much as the Gaunt family rules over this city, most people know nothing about them. Teddy's behavior in court was absolutely abhorrent, and I think my viewers are curious if it was a onetime outburst or if there is more to it."

"I think you'll find there's a lot more to the story; that's why I asked you aboard, Hellie." Sheldon smiled. He'd called in a favor to his old pal *Helena Taylor*. He'd told her it was important to get Emily's story out there and raise awareness of the many different types of domestic violence and spousal abuse.

It was also the perfect plan to draw Teddy out of hiding.

Sheldon and Emily both knew he wouldn't be able to stand the press generated from an interview like this one. His rage would get the better of him, and he was bound to make a mistake.

"And as soon as he does, Detective Jackson will be there with handcuffs."

"So, tell me more. You claim Teddy posted an ad with your likeness, promoting you as a sex worker?" Helena Taylor asked, leaning in to Emily. It made her feel like Helena was a long-lost friend.

They had been sitting there for the better part of an hour, under lights that made her feel like a roast chicken.

Helena was gentle and motherly, but she was still asking tough questions about Emily's marriage. Reliving it was dizzying.

"I want to be careful who I accuse," Emily said. "I don't want to sound like some angry, paranoid ex-wife."

"Based on what you've told me today, along with Teddy's recent public outbursts, I don't think any of our viewers would say that. How are you holding up?"

"I feel proud of myself, actually," Emily admitted. "I'm not hiding in my own home. I'm not scared of everyone around me. I'm fighting back. I've been working with my lawyers to get the ads taken down. I've contacted the websites directly, and we've sent out letters, but the online ads have been attached to some kind of bot. Every time it's flagged for being inappropriate, five clones pop up to take its place. It's been horrible."

Helena shook her head. "I can't imagine going through something like that. I can't even imagine how something like that could happen."

"Revenge porn is quite common nowadays," Emily mumbled. "It doesn't have to be an ex leaking real nude photos. I've never taken those kinds of photos, but he managed to make it look as though I did. It is someone else's body with my face photoshopped onto it. I think creating awareness that this is happening is only part of the solution. We all need to be more informed about our cybersecurity and how to keep ourselves safe. Teddy isn't the only abusive partner out there. Not every woman has the opportunity to come on this show and share her side of the story."

"I am so glad that you are here shining a light on this kind of abuse. Thank you for being an advocate for abused women. I'm excited to see where this new chapter can take you. And thank you so much for sitting down with me today, Emily."

"Thanks so much for having me and for letting me ramble a little bit."

THE SEGMENT AIRED THAT NIGHT, just after the evening news. Emily invited her father and sister to come over and watch. They were surprised to find Helena and her crew had left the interview pretty much as-is, with only a few minor cuts for brevity.

"I imagine you're not the only one to have had a nasty run-in with Teddy," her dad said. "I'm glad she didn't twist your words. I was worried about that."

"Are you sure I sounded alright? Did I appear confident and strong enough?"

"You sounded great," Laurie replied. "You came off as strong and resilient but still vulnerable, and because you weren't outright *accusing* Teddy, you don't seem like a vindictive ex who is just filming this for her own ego. The interview couldn't have gone better, if you ask me."

Good. I have to be confident, or Teddy won't believe it, and he won't be angry enough, Emily thought. She had done the interview to help other abused women in the hopes it would draw him out; now all she had to do was wait.

She was working hard not to allow fear to consume her again. Another exclusive was going to run in the Sunday edition of the newspaper, complete with photographs taken at the hospital after the accident where he'd intentionally tried to hurt her. At first, she thought that might be too much

—Emily was wary of jeopardizing the terms of her settlement, but Sheldon assured her it would be okay.

"We're not doing it to badmouth Teddy; the angle of the article and the television interview is that you're trying to raise awareness about domestic violence. Don't worry, I won't do anything that will threaten you in the long run."

But that was just it—this whole endeavor was threatening to her. She hoped Teddy would be caught right outside his home, or swept up by a police cruiser somewhere in the city, but she couldn't be sure. When Laurie and her father left for the night, Emily felt extremely alone.

William texted her just as she was about to call her sister back to the house.

> Hey, I saw the interview. Wanna chat about it?

> Sure, that would be nice.

"You were very well-spoken," he said, in lieu of a hello.

"Do you really think so?" Emily fretted.

"Yes, I do. You appeared very sure of yourself, and you said the right things without sounding rehearsed—it was eloquence to a tee."

Emily laughed. She and William talked regularly, but they still didn't bring up the elephant in the room—their dating status. It was better to leave it alone for now, especially with all this press.

"I'm just freaked out now that it's out there. It was intentional because I want to help other women, but now I'm *worried* about what Teddy is going to do. I'm scared he's going to show up at my door unannounced, and I'll be caught off guard. I wasn't so freaked out about this earlier today, but all that confidence is gone now; all I can think about is Teddy's anger bubbling over."

"You know how to protect yourself. You can stay with your sister or your dad if you're really concerned. And if you can handle a bunch of angry, horny men, I think you can handle Teddy."

It's just not the same, she thought, staring at the cardboard that still covered her living room window. Her window had been broken for some time now. Teddy was worse than all those men because Teddy made her weak inside. There was still a tiny shard of the Teddy that Emily fell in love with, and she thought about that shard every time she saw him.

"I have an idea," William cut in. "Why don't we go to the shooting range tomorrow. If you're truly worried about Teddy, there's no reason why you shouldn't learn a little projectile self-defense. I'll teach you how to aim with the shotgun."

"I don't want to go to jail for killing my ex-husband."

"You won't. For starters, I still doubt Teddy will be able to reach you before he is arrested. Secondly, if Teddy is attacking you at the time you shoot, then it is self-defense, and you won't even be arrested. After that Helena Taylor interview, everyone will know exactly why you did it. Thirdly—this isn't really so you can learn to shoot Teddy, it's just to give you a small boost of confidence. You can fight back, Em; you are a strong enough person; all you need is to trust yourself a little."

And that was how Emily found herself standing outside the shooting range on a beautiful Saturday afternoon.

She couldn't believe she was doing this. She understood the basics, but couldn't wrap her head around the rest—what was the blowback? Would she even be able to hold the gun up after she shot something? How could she know she had good aim? All these questions were tumbling around in her stomach and making her queasy. By the time William arrived, Emily was positively green with nausea.

"You'll be fine; everyone's a little nervous the first time." William winked.

Emily took a deep breath and followed him inside.

WILLIAM WRAPPED his arms around Emily and helped her aim. "Okay now, you know there's going to be a blowback, so you don't want to lock your arms, so you can absorb the shock, right?"

"And I don't want to close one of my eyes because I need them to see."

"Right. You're doing okay. Now the trigger isn't as light as you think, so make sure you're not putting so much pressure that it tilts the barrel down, or else you're going to hit the floor. You have to kind of show the gun who's boss."

"Relaxed arms; open eyes; can't lose."

William chuckled as he let go of Emily and stepped away. She felt a slight chill roll down her spine, as though her body was craving William's warmth.

"Go for it."

Emily pulled the trigger, and she stumbled back a little, the shot not quite hitting the target. The second shot she braced her feet, re-aimed, and pulled the trigger, this time hitting the man-shaped paper target. She reloaded and tried it again.

Once she got the hang of holding the gun properly, it was

pretty easy to hit where she was aiming, but it did take a bit of practice to accomplish. William was right; this gave her the boost of confidence she needed to confront Teddy if he showed up at her house. She wasn't going to shoot him; no, that would have made her feel too guilty, but knowing that she *could* shoot him made Emily feel just a little more powerful.

"Not too bad this round," William said as he pulled the target toward them. "Not exactly perfect, but you got a few shots in there close to the chest cavity."

"I got his arm and what might have been his spleen and maybe stomach? I think I missed more than I hit."

"You're the one who said she didn't want to actually hurt the guy. If you miss him completely, I can guarantee he will not be hurt." William laughed.

Emily rolled her eyes at William's cheesy joke. They were tucked in so close together she could smell his cologne, and it seemed familiar.

"Did you borrow cologne from Sheldon?" she asked.

"Yeah." William blushed. "I kind of like it. Musky yet still a little fresh—I think Sheldon has good taste."

Emily groaned. "Not you too. My dad is always talking about how Sheldon is very dapper."

"He *is* dapper. You wouldn't know it because he wears basically the same suit every day, but on his off time that man is *fashionable.* If he were into it, I think I'd be tempted to flirt a little."

"You don't think he is?"

"Absolutely not. Our hands grazed this morning while reaching for the coffee, and he started blubbering something about how he went to Stonewall once, thinking it was a karaoke bar, then he accidentally spilled coffee on the counter and said, 'Oopsie daisy,' before literally running away."

"Maybe it's because he has a crush on you; he just couldn't handle the electricity between the two of you when your hands touched," Emily drawled, twirling her finger on William's chest. She was kidding, making fun of the situation William and Sheldon had found themselves in, but she found herself leaning in to William's chest. His head bent down toward hers.

"True, he couldn't handle the natural chemistry between us," William murmured.

Emily drew closer to him; suddenly she remembered why she liked William so much. She remembered the feeling of his soft lips, and his large hands venturing down her back until—

"Um, we should really go," William said, pulling away. "We should go before I kiss you and ruin what has been a wonderful friendship," he stammered and stumbled away from her.

Emily stared at the target hanging in front of her and sighed.

She had very, very bad aim. And probably very bad instincts too.

OUTSIDE, William was more nervous than ever. He gave Emily a peck on the forehead and ran to his car, barely stopping to say goodbye. She felt like she had just been slapped in the face. Sure, he had a point, it was best they didn't take things any farther than friendship, but William's quick rejection was a bit embarrassing.

She arrived home to a text from William.

> Thanks for a fun day. Sorry I ran off. I just got nervous and didn't know what to do.

> Don't worry about it. Thanks for respecting my needs. You did the right thing, and I really appreciate it. Though I think you need to learn how to leave without leaving behind skid marks...

The text was happy, fun, flirty, friendly, and it killed Emily to write it. It shouldn't make her frustrated, but it did. She sat on the couch and screamed into a pillow. Her heart and her mind were pulling themselves in different directions, and Emily didn't know which she wanted to follow.

She didn't have much time to think about it. Just as she was about to call William and ask him to come over, she got a call from her father.

"Dad? Is everything okay?"

"I need you to come to St. Mary's. Your sister was attacked."

34

Emily arrived at the hospital in record time. Her father was waiting for her in the emergency room waiting room.

"How is she? What happened?" she asked as soon as she saw him.

"She was beaten with a baseball bat," he said as he led her to her sister's small room in the ER. "She's okay. The doctor said she doesn't have any internal bleeding, but she's got a few broken ribs and a number of bruises."

"Oh my God." Emily was frantic as they walked through the ER.

"She said she screamed at the top of her lungs and kicked at the attacker's legs, and he ran off after that, just leaving her on the ground. Can you believe she was just left there; is there no common decency anymore?"

"Dad, I don't think the guy who beat Laurie with a baseball bat was thinking about common decency—"

"I mean from bystanders. Not a soul came out to help

her. Laurie had to drag herself back to her car and drive to the hospital."

"Do you know where it happened?"

"It was on your street. She had parked down the street about a block away."

A block away from my house? No, it wasn't possible—

Laurie was waking up as Emily passed through the curtained opening. She looked worse for wear, her cheekbone was bruised and already turning a deep purple, and there were bruises on her arms.

Laurie winced, her hands going to her ribs as she tried to move. "Hi," she rasped. "I'm glad you came."

"Of course I'm here; where else would I be? Laurie, what the hell happened?"

"This guy came up behind me, kicked the back of my knees, and knocked me down to the ground. Then he kicked me, got me in the face, and started hitting me with the baseball bat, but I curled myself into a ball and protected my head just like the self-defense classes tell you to do. I'd rather have cracked ribs than a cracked skull. Anyway, I kicked at him and got him in the shin while he was ranting at me."

"Did you see who it was, dear? Do you have any idea who did this?" her dad interrupted.

Laurie blinked and looked up at Emily. "It was Teddy. Except he thought I was you. He kept screaming about how television was for whores, and how could you be so ungrateful to him. He said you'd never get away from him, that he'd always find a way back. I started screaming back at him and kicked him more; then he ran."

Teddy.

Teddy had attacked her sister from behind, thinking it

was Emily. Teddy had come at her with a baseball bat and had run away as soon as she fought back—he always hated it when women fought back.

"Oh my God, Laurie, I am so sorry. This is all my fault."

"It's not your fault. If anything, it's Mom and Dad's fault for having two daughters who look alike, heh." Laurie tried to laugh, but it was clear it was too painful for her. "I was going over to your place when he caught me unawares. Teddy really doesn't care about the restraining order. He wasn't sending those guys because he couldn't come; he just wants to ruin your life. Emily, you can't let him ruin your life, okay?"

Emily held back tears as she grasped her sister's bruised hand. "I won't, I promise."

THEY BROUGHT Laurie home to her dad's house an hour later. Emily and her father spent the evening trying to keep her comfortable. Emily didn't do much sleeping; she watched as her sister slept fitfully because she was in pain. It should have been her. It would have been her if she hadn't been at the shooting range with William.

This had to end, but Emily didn't know how to end it.

"I GUESS Teddy saw the interview, huh?" her dad said, staring at his salad the next afternoon.

Emily and her dad had gone to lunch at a small diner not too far from his house. They'd left Laurie at home to sleep, telling her they'd bring her back a meal. Emily was still tired from not sleeping much at her sister's bedside and yawned. She was going to need a lot of coffee today to get through it.

"I'm sure of it. That was the point, wasn't it?" She smiled at the waitress, who poured her coffee. Once she was gone, she continued, "We did it to draw him out of hiding by making him angry. The only hitch in the plan was that he was supposed to be caught by the police the second he left home, so why was he able to make it almost to my door?"

Whatever Teddy was going through, whatever furious thoughts he had, Emily guaranteed they paled in comparison to her own. What was the point of getting the police involved if they wouldn't even be able to protect her? Laurie looked so much like her; if the police had been doing their job, they would have been able to prevent the attack. They knew about the interview, they knew another article was coming out in today's paper—so where were they? Why hadn't they caught him? She had half a mind to call Detective Jackson and ask, to show him what had happened to her sister because his *officers* hadn't caught up to Teddy.

Teddy had managed to attack her sister and escape, and not a single person caught him. No one helped Laurie; no one even tried to stop him. What was the point of Emily going on TV and talking about how people needed to start paying attention to their neighbors, when the sight of a man beating a woman with a baseball bat didn't even make people step in to help?

"Do you think this was a mistake, Dad?" Emily asked. "Should I just pack up and leave town instead?"

"No," he said, slowly stirring his coffee with a spoon. "I think what you did was right, and that nothing is going to stop Teddy from coming after you, so you might as well make him fight like hell."

By the time they returned home, Laurie was seated on the living room sofa, holding a copy of the Sunday newspaper.

"You didn't hold anything back," she said. "I'm glad he did this to me yesterday, before he had the chance to read this."

Emily set down the take-out container and joined Laurie on the sofa as Laurie quoted some of the highlights to her. She didn't really care, she'd lived through the experience and reiterated it to the journalist—to be honest, Emily was starting to bore herself.

"I couldn't hold anything back, Laur; the less I told them, the more opportunity he has to deny everything. I can't sit there and let him get away with it anymore."

"Good, you're right. He doesn't deserve your consideration. Don't feel guilty about this; it isn't your fault. Just get him, Em. Get Teddy and make him understand that you're not going to be his doormat anymore."

Hours later, Emily's phone was blowing up with journalists and podcasters—even a television producer—who wanted a statement from her, or for her permission to turn her life into a TV show or movie. She said no to all of them and told the journalists to refer to the article; she was done talking about it.

She wanted to wait in her house for Teddy to come find her; she wanted to look Teddy in the face and spit in his eye. She wanted to shoot Teddy for having beaten up her sister. Emily had done those interviews to help other women, but also knew it would make Teddy's blood boil, but she'd never factored in her own rage when committing to these interviews.

Just as she was imagining impaling Teddy's head on a spike, Emily got a call from a private number. Thinking it was another journalist, she absentmindedly answered the phone.

"Who the *hell* do you think you are?"

It was Teddy, irate as ever, ready to violate her restraining order again.

"Teddy, what do you think a restraining order is?"

"I don't care about what the court says, you are my wife, and I can contact you whenever I want, especially when you are going around spilling our private issues to the press and the police force. Do you know how embarrassing it was to have the police arrive at my mother's house? She has no idea I'm back; she still thinks I'm at that godawful 'rehab' facility."

"Our issues aren't private." Emily tried to record their phone call, but the app wasn't working—typical, the second you need a piece of tech is the second it's bound to break.

"What do you mean they aren't private? They happened between you and me, not between us and Helena Taylor or us and the *Sunday Times*. Our problems are not for public consumption, because you know that the press will do anything to slander my family name. Did you even think about that before you talked to them? No, I bet you didn't because you only *ever* think of yourself."

"You don't deserve to have privacy. You don't deserve to have me protect your lies anymore. Our marital issues ceased being private when you became an abusive husband, followed by an abusive *ex-husband*, and when you coerced pathetic men to come to my house in search of sex. Our problems haven't been private in a long time, and even if they were, you forfeited that privilege when you attacked my sister in the street!"

"That wasn't you? What? Do you have your sister running interference for you now? You're going to be that hypocrite who calls me out for a silly little prank?"

"You absolutely deserve to be called out in the most public way possible, even if it's just to warn other women about you."

"I don't have a problem with other women; it's you who's the problem. You were never able to just let go and let me be your husband. You were never able to just be my wife. You always had to have your own life."

Emily had to get off the phone before she said something she would regret—who knew what kind of technology Teddy was using to record what she said on this call. She feared he could splice and dice her words into a lie.

"Teddy, I can't talk to you, and I won't do it anymore. You need to turn yourself in. The way you're going, you're bound to get hurt. You never know who out there has a—"

"Is that a threat? Are you threatening me?"

"I'm not threatening you, Teddy. I'm giving you sound advice. I know you're angry right now, but I think it would be best if you turned yourself in, and maybe if you actually went to that rehab your mother found for you, it could help with your anger issues—"

"You're going to pay for this, you bitch. I swear, you are going to *pay* for disobeying me," Teddy said, and hung up the phone.

Emily couldn't remember a time when Teddy was this angry. She had wanted to draw him out in a way that wouldn't be dangerous, she'd thought she'd be safe, but it was possible she was just poking a sleeping bear. Bringing their fight to a public forum had caused some kind of snap. He was now more dangerous than ever, and Emily had no idea what she was going to do.

She spent the rest of the afternoon reinstalling the old locks on the doors. Emily called a window company and paid a premium to have them fix her window that day. William had boarded it up for her, so it wasn't just open, but it would be nice to have it repaired. Luckily for her, one of the window installers recognized her from the news and waived the urgency fee.

"If you're doing this to protect yourself, we won't charge extra," he said. "My sister was almost killed by an abusive ex —broken windows like this can be extra dangerous. You might want to invest in a security system as well."

Emily tried to thank him with a tip, but he refused. It wasn't about the money, it was about keeping each other safe.

"It's like you said, it's our collective responsibility to keep an eye on each other."

Finally, late that evening, Emily sat down to call Detective Jackson. She ought to have done it right away, but she was so shaky she couldn't even dial the phone. No, it was better to explain now when she had a cooler head. Detective Jackson would understand.

"Jackson here."

"It's Emily Gray. I have some news."

"Ms. Gray, are you all right? I heard about your sister; your father called it in. He mentioned the two of you look a lot alike, and that your sister suspected the attacker was Teddy—"

"I know it was Teddy. He called."

"I see. When did he call you?"

"A few hours ago," Emily said, "but I only just calmed down enough to tell you."

"That's fine; you didn't manage to get his number, did you?"

"No, he called from a private number."

"What did he say?" Detective Jackson asked.

"He admitted to beating up my sister, but he thought it was me. He said that I was going to have to 'pay' for disobeying him."

"In what way were you disobeying him?"

"By taking our problems to the press. Teddy always said our marital problems were only between us, that I wasn't supposed to talk about them outside our own home because other people wouldn't understand our marriage. He also told me that his mother sent him to a rehab facility, but he must have snuck out somehow. I'm not even sure if she knows he's hiding at home now."

"That part I did know; we had a few officers go by the Gaunt home yesterday after we got word of what happened to your sister. Because she reported that the incident happened so close to your house, I figured it couldn't have been completely random, and there must have been a connection to Teddy. His mom claimed she had no idea why we were looking for her son, and that he was off at some rehab place."

"I guess she is in the dark. Her son's behavior is off the rails, and he is finally out from under her control. I don't know where he could be. I wish—"

"Don't worry about that; you've done more than enough for this investigation. For now, I recommend making sure your doors and windows are locked, just in case. He might not try anything tonight since he was able to get a hold of you over the phone, but it's always better to be safe than sorry."

Detective Jackson hung up, and Emily was left holding the phone, obsessing over the last words she heard him say.

"It's always better to be safe than sorry."

Wise words, she wished someone had told her that before she ever went out with Teddy Gaunt.

35

The phone call Emily had with Teddy renewed her anger and, with it, her confidence about the situation. She deserved better; she didn't deserve to be sleeping in her foyer with a shotgun. She knew she had done the right thing by exposing Teddy; if she hadn't, then he might start the whole process again with another woman—another undeserving girl who had no experience with a narcissist. She was determined not to let that happen.

Thankfully, at least a few men in the city read the news. The barrage of men coming to her house slowed to a trickle by that night. She posted a sign on the door that said her little spiel. It made the process easier and meant that Emily could finally sleep in her own bed.

At some point in the night, someone tore down her sign—Emily knew something like that was bound to happen. She went back to sitting in front of the door, holding the shotgun. This time she allowed herself to have a glass of wine as she waited for the men to come.

After turning a man away, she watched him jog back to his car.

That was when Emily noticed him—tall, standing across the street, leaning against an old BMW, wearing a large hoodie that blocked his face. She'd seen him earlier in the night and didn't think much of it. All of the men, even the most aggressive, were shockingly polite to their fellow johns. They seemed to have an unspoken queue that formed throughout the night. When she first saw him, Emily assumed he was just waiting his turn, but when the hooded man never showed up at her door, she assumed he'd left.

But there he was, leaning against his car, staring at her house. She waved at him, waited for him to come over, but he just waved back and waited.

Was he another john? Or did Detective Jackson or Nic Evalds send someone to watch the house? Jackson had said they couldn't spare a man to sit outside Emily's house, and she hadn't heard from the private investigator since the settlement was decided. Had they changed their minds? Emily wanted to call Sheldon, but she knew he wasn't going to answer the phone right now; it was long past the older man's bedtime.

AT 2 A.M. Emily woke up to loud banging on her door. She looked outside and found two men on her porch.

Emily pulled the chain and opened the door, sticking the barrel of her shotgun through the small gap. "Don't you watch the news? You're in the wrong place. Go bang down someone else's door; there are no sex workers here. Now get the hell off my porch before I start shooting you."

The men didn't move.

Emily was exhausted; she just wanted to sleep through the night and stop worrying about these men. They were like zombies, slowly and relentlessly going after her until she drove herself into the ground. She was just about ready to give up when she glanced across the street and saw that the man in the hoodie was still leaning against his car, watching.

Finally, the two men on her porch turned and walked away. Sighing, she set the shotgun down in the corner. When she looked back out, the man in the hoodie walked up behind one of the johns and somehow brought him to his knees.

Emily was shocked, but grateful. She must have been right—the guy had been sent by Nic Evalds to keep an eye on her.

She saw something out of the corner of her eye. It was dark, but there was enough light from the moon and the lights inside her house to see that where the man was crumpled on the ground, a dark spot spread outwards from his head. Emily shook her head, convinced she must be dreaming. The man wasn't making a sound, and the dark spot was getting bigger—but it was impossible; she didn't hear a shot—

Before Emily could turn around, the other man cried out. She whipped around just in time to see him collapse to the ground as the man in the hoodie stood over him, a gun in his hand.

Emily's entire body felt paralyzed. She wanted to run, but she couldn't. She could only watch as the two johns lay dying on her lawn, and the man in the hoodie walked up to her porch. She wanted to reach for the shotgun, but couldn't remember where it was. It had been in her hands just moments ago; what did she do with it?

Her life played out in slow motion. She watched as the hooded man pulled a can from his back pocket and sprayed her with it—pepper spray—it knocked her backward, and she stumbled into her house. The man shoved her inside, grabbing her shotgun from the corner by the door.

That was where she'd set it, she now remembered.

Emily tried to raise her hands, but the pepper spray blinded and confused her. Through her blurred vision, she saw him throw the shotgun out the door to the front lawn before slamming it behind him. Emily screamed and cried, worsening the effect of the pepper spray. It got on her hands and burned more when she tried to rub her eyes.

She could hear the man locking the door behind him, clicking each of her deadbolts one by one. She still couldn't tell who it was; his face was obstructed by his hood and her blurred vision.

Finally, he took a rough handkerchief and wiped her eyes. Emily watched as he lowered his hood. She would recognize the gray-blond hair and piercing gray eyes anywhere, even through her blurred vision.

Teddy grabbed her hair and pulled her into the living room. "I'm done waiting. You need to understand the consequences of what you've done."

36

T eddy threw a wet towel at Emily. "Wipe that across your face; it's got milk on it; it'll help with the pepper spray."

"T-Teddy?" she sputtered. "What the—where— wh—"

"I don't know why you're surprised; did you really think I wasn't going to *react* after all you did this weekend? Ridiculous. Obviously, my *wife* is going through some kind of psychotic break, and I, as her husband, have to help her."

His eyes were wide and clear. Teddy wasn't inebriated; he was drunk from his own anger. Teddy was practically shaking as he stood over Emily.

She needed to buy some time, she had to do something, but she wasn't sure what. Emily couldn't think—could she call Nic?

"Stop trying to get out of this. I can see the silly little plan forming in your eyes. No, this time you have to listen to me. You have to understand what it is to be a kind and dutiful wife. I'm sick of playing these games with you, the court case and the divorce was *fun* and all, but it ends tonight."

The man was serious. Teddy was truly under the impression that he could "win" back Emily by intimidating her, and he wasn't going to quit until she surrendered.

That can't happen, Emily thought. *I have to find a way out of this.*

Luckily, her phone was still in her pocket. She slid her hands behind her, as if to crawl backwards on the couch, and took out her phone. Without looking, she dialed one of the last numbers in her call history, thinking it might be her sister or father. With any luck, it was Detective Jackson, and she could get all this straight to the ears of a police officer. Emily prayed the person answered their phone—it was the middle of the night; the likelihood of someone being awake was low. Emily hoped a random call from her would perk up their ears.

"Teddy, please put the gun down, and let's talk about this rationally. You're upset—"

"I am far from upset, Emily. I am determined to make you understand exactly *why* our marriage wasn't working. I thought that this little divorce game of yours would make you understand that without me, you are nothing. You are worth nothing, and your life is meaningless, because once a woman marries a man, her role is then to be his wife. Do you remember committing yourself to me, until death parts us? Last time I checked, neither of us was dead. We are both alive and well, and with the exception of you, we both still have our mental capacities in order. So you are the one with the problem; let's see why that is."

Teddy sat down on the coffee table and brought his knees to Emily's. He held her down by pressing his hands against her thighs.

Emily whimpered as his nails dug into her legs.

"It was stupid of you to go through with this divorce," he said. "I tried to tell you that it wasn't a good idea, and then you went ahead and got a protection order against me and moved so that I didn't know where you were, which is an incredibly inconsiderate way to treat your husband. It took months, but I finally found you. I know it seems like I was angry, but I wasn't. I knew this divorce was all a game to show me you could be independent. Well, congratulations, Emily, you've done it. You've enjoyed your time away from me, but now it is time to go home."

"No, I'm not going anywhere with you—Teddy, you're insane."

"I am *not* insane. You are my *wife*, Emily. That doesn't end just because some judge decided—"

"It does. I'm not tied to you anymore and—"

Teddy slapped her across the face, hard.

Emily bit her tongue hard enough to taste a little bit of blood. Her body was shaking; all she could hang on to was the hope that someone, somewhere was listening to all of this.

"You fucking idiot, I was giving you a way out, don't you see that? This was all a test. All you had to do was say yes and you would have passed, but you've proven to me that you're not worth *saving*. I guess I'll have to live with an adulterous whore for a wife—yes, I know all about William. I knew about him when you 'separated' from me, and I know you were dating him now. I put him in front of you as a test, and you failed miserably; the first chance you got, you cheated on me."

"What about all your infidelities?" she asked.

"That's different. I have needs that you sometimes can't fulfill. I was protecting you, okay? I was protecting the sanctity of our marriage, and you didn't so much as *thank* me. No, instead you cuckolded me while acting as if you were single. I am your husband, and I will always be your husband."

"Is that really what you want? What are you going to do, chain me up in bed and only trot me out for public appearances?"

"No, Emily, if you don't come back home with me, you won't survive this night. I'm willing to stay here for as long as it takes until you admit that you were wrong. I want you to refute everything you've said to the press. Then *you* can go to 'rehab,' while my family releases a statement that you were suffering from a substance abuse problem. That was the only 'abuse' that happened in this marriage, you and your glorious glasses of wine. You'll call off the divorce, put everything—including this fucking dumpster of a house—in my name, and you will come back and live with Mother and me. Finally, Mother can teach you what it means to be a *dutiful, loving wife and mother.*"

Teddy shot the floor with his handgun after his last point.

Emily wanted to scream, but she couldn't let out any noise. Was this how it would all end? Teddy could shoot her and then say whatever he wanted to the press—Emily wouldn't be around to contradict him. Who was left to defend her? No one would listen to her mild-mannered father, and Laurie was too much of a hothead. Was Teddy right? Was this the only option she had?

I am his wife, and I will always be his wife, she thought. *That's just how these things go; there's no point in fighting it anymore.*

"I'm sorry, Emily," Teddy said, a single tear streaming down his face. "I can see how hard this is for you, but imagine how difficult it is for me? I knew you would only answer to one thing—cruelty. That is the language you speak, and the only language you're able to understand. I didn't want to do things like this, but you left me no other choice." He hung his head and cried into Emily's lap.

It was over. All the work Emily did, all the money she'd spent, it ended like this. She knew if she walked away, Teddy would follow her no matter where she went. She couldn't disappear because Teddy would find her. There was no way out.

Teddy took Emily's face in his hands, squeezing her head between them. "If you come with me, I'll forgive you. If you come with me, we'll get you cleaned up, and you can tell everyone that you had a mental breakdown, and that's why you've been trying to torture me."

Emily opened her mouth to answer, but was interrupted by the sound of a shotgun blowing a hole through her front door.

Teddy stood up and pointed his gun, pressing Emily's head to his side. "Who is it? This is my house, and you're trespassing!"

Another gunshot blasted through the lock, and Emily's hero kicked through the door. It was like a scene out of an action movie that she'd never asked for. Emily was so tired and confused that all she could think about was how she was going to call a locksmith in the middle of the night. She barely registered when William burst into her living room, carrying his shotgun.

Seeing him unlocked something in Emily, as if she finally realized this wasn't a nightmare and she hadn't been transported back in time. A part of her brain clicked, and she started screaming for help at the top of her lungs.

"Get away from her!" William shouted.

Teddy let go of her, rushing toward William, who reloaded and racked the gun, then shot at Teddy. It happened too fast for William, and the shotgun was too slow. Teddy dodged the bullet, and it soared past him into Emily's favorite lamp.

Teddy knocked William off his feet, causing William's gun to go flying. The two men struggled on the floor, William attempting to wrestle the gun away from Teddy while Teddy did his best to strangle William with his arm.

"You go after a perfectly innocent woman who's already married, is that what you do? Huh? I won't let you corrupt her!"

William managed to hold him off, tucking a knee under Teddy and prying him off.

As the two men continued to struggle, Emily dug through her phone for the right person to call. She didn't want to call 911; she wanted someone who would listen. She wanted to go directly to the source.

"Teddy, stop!" she screamed, and tried to get between the two men. "Stop! You're going to hurt yourself!" There was no point in appealing to Teddy's consideration for others; he only cared about himself, after all.

"He can't hurt me; he needs to go. Don't you see, he's what came between us. He brainwashed you, Emily; he made you think I was hurting you. I was never hurting you, but you needed to learn a lesson. This sad excuse for a man thinks he can take you away from me, but I know better—" Teddy cut himself off when he heard the cock of the gun.

Emily stood behind him, her whole body shaking, completely unsure if she was even pointing the gun in the right direction. Her eyes were blurry with tears, mixing with the last bit of pepper spray. She couldn't pull the trigger, not like this. She had known Teddy long before he turned into a monstrous version of himself. She remembered Teddy as a kind, charming man—the man she dated, not the man she married.

She heard his voice in her head saying the same thing over and over again: *"I am your husband, and I will always be your husband."* He was right. For the rest of her life Emily would feel the ghost of her marriage to Teddy Gaunt. They were tied to each other for the next three years and for as long as he paid alimony to her. She thought she was getting what she deserved in the divorce settlement, she thought that was the point of fighting for so long—to find an equitable end to their marriage—but really, she had just tied herself to the Gaunt family for even longer. There was no escaping the memory of this marriage.

"I knew you wouldn't do it," Teddy said, smiling at her. His eyes had darkened even though they were clear as glass, the fury bubbling inside and spilling out of him. "You can't murder your husband in cold blood. You can be a good wife, Emily. You can be a doting wife and loving mother, you just need someone to teach you how. Don't shoot me, shoot the person who ruined your marriage."

"No, Teddy, I won't do that. I won't hurt William, but I will hurt you if you don't get up. Move to the couch and sit down—now!" Emily screeched.

Teddy grinned, but he did as she asked, his hands behind his head. "What are you doing, Emily?"

"I'm keeping you off William until the others arrive. You've been wrong this whole time, Teddy. I know deep down that I wasn't the one misbehaving. I did everything for you as your wife, and I don't deserve this cruel punishment of yours. I loved you so much; that's why I have been so blinded. It was obvious that you were behind the cruel jokes being played on me. It's all in line with what you think of me, isn't it? I can't keep my thoughts straight, or I can't keep the house clean enough for you. I see it all now, and it breaks my heart. I'm not angry. I'm heartbroken because I know I'll never get the Teddy I fell in love with back; instead he's been replaced by this...monster. A man who is so consumed by himself that he can't see the world in front of him."

Emily was sobbing now. She had suppressed these feelings for so long, but they were true. There was a time when she would have done anything for Teddy, but as their marriage and then divorce progressed, he got angrier, meaner, and more irrational. There was no going back from here, she would never trust someone blindly ever again, and it was all because of the man sitting in front of her. A man she'd once stood across from and pledged to love for all eternity.

This person isn't the man you married, Emily. This is someone else entirely.

"It's time for you to be punished, Teddy. Hopefully your punishment won't be half as cruel as mine."

"Police! Nobody move!"

A swarm of officers streamed through Emily's battered front door, led by Detective Mike Jackson. They immediately disarmed her and grabbed Teddy. As the officers dragged him out the door, Teddy fought all he could, screaming obscenities to the men in uniform.

"Emily!" Teddy called. "You get over here right now! Come help me; tell them to get their dirty hands off me! Are you really just going to leave me like this?"

Emily fell to the floor, exhausted. Teddy's screaming rang

through her ears long after he was thrown into a police car and driven away.

She heard a familiar voice off to the side, talking with William, taking his statement about what happened that night. Someone was examining the gun, trying to figure out how many shots had been fired; a preliminary investigation had already begun to figure out who shot the men outside. William was in handcuffs and was being led away from Emily's house.

Emily sat in the middle of her living room, once again the eye of the storm, unsure how to move to safety.

THE POLICE STAYED the rest of the night, taking photographs and interviewing her neighbors. True to their nature, no one heard or saw anything. Most of them wore earplugs nowadays, to block out the noise of men coming up to Emily's door all night long.

With Detective Jackson's permission, Emily took a tranquilizer and went to bed. He resolved to take her statement in the morning. Since the house was now an active crime scene, and her door was pretty much off its hinges, Emily finally got her wish for an officer to be posted outside her door while she slept.

"DO you want to start from the beginning?" Detective Jackson asked. "The beginning of the night, that is."

Emily rubbed her eyes and tried to wake herself up. She

felt groggy and tired, and all she wanted was to forget the events of the night before.

Detective Jackson told her they'd taken William's official statement at the station and released him on his own recognizance; now all that was left was for Emily to fill in the blanks.

"I didn't notice him until later; it took a few hours before I realized the man across the street in a dark hoodie never came to my door. He stood there waiting all night long, watching as men came up to the door and I sent them away—"

Emily cut herself off. That was why Teddy had had enough courage to come up to the door. He'd watched her reject all those men to make sure she was ready to come back to him. In his twisted, selfish mind, this was another one of his tests. If Emily really loved him, she would reject the men who came to her door. If Emily could be rehabilitated, she wouldn't accept the sex that was offered to her. Her whole body shook as she sobbed into her hands. She knew Teddy would have killed her immediately if she'd invited one of the men inside.

It took Detective Jackson the better part of an hour to get a statement out of Emily. Her father arrived partway through the morning and held her as she described the details of the night to the detective. She told him how she'd dialed a number from her call history at random, and how William had burst through the door and got Teddy away from her. She described how Teddy had approached her, how he'd silently murdered the two men on the lawn. She left out the gritty details of Teddy's lecture to spare herself the trigger.

When they were finished, Detective Jackson told her he

would contact her in a few days to determine what they could charge Teddy with.

Emily barely nodded—what did it matter? Teddy was bound to come back for her.

———

LATER THAT DAY, Emily was settling into her room at her father's house when William called her.

"I just wanted to see if you were okay. They took me away and—"

"I'll be all right," she murmured. "Thank you for everything, William."

"Of course. I'll always be here, if you need me."

Emily sat down. "I know you'll be around, and I appreciate it so much—much more than I can explain, but I need some time to think. I need some time to heal."

"I understand. Maybe we can go to the shooting range again and—"

"No, you don't understand," Emily interrupted. "Last night I...I realized that despite everything that happened, I still feel...something for Teddy. It isn't love, but it isn't disdain either. I'm not saying I have to hate him to be friends with you or something, but I think I need some time to repair myself before we go on even if it is just as friends. I think I'm more damaged than I realized. I don't know. I'm not making any sense; it's just that I need..." She trailed off, wiping tears off her cheeks.

"Time. I understand. Goodbye, Emily."

"Goodbye, William."

Emily hung up the phone and cried. She just wanted all

this to be over, she wanted to be done, but as long as Teddy was alive, Emily was inextricably tied to her husband.

37

A week later, Emily had a fresh new door on her house and was starting to get back into a *normal* routine. She asked Horace for the dullest, most perfunctory work he had so she could lose herself in data and numbers and not have to think. Whenever Emily tried to think, her mind wandered to the night Teddy broke in, and she immediately broke down in tears.

Horace was understanding. "You mean I have someone who *wants* to write my boring expense reports? I never thought I could be so lucky," he said with a laugh.

She was happy to be that person. Horace understood that Emily didn't want to talk about it. So instead, Emily received back-dated receipts and punched the data into a long spreadsheet. She learned the ins and outs of Horace's financial life and then immediately forgot about them when she turned away from her computer. She thought about nothing except numbers for hours each day and lived in ignorant bliss until she closed her computer.

All of the charges against William were dropped

Emily refused to press charges for trespassing and destruction of property against him, so there was nothing the police could do. They all knew that William had been coerced by Teddy, and her front door being busted was because he'd been trying to save her. Putting William behind bars wasn't going to help her in the long run.

William sent her flowers to thank her for the consideration. In the meantime, William had moved out of his apartment, which he'd recently discovered was in a building owned by the Gaunt family. Apparently, once he returned there, he did a thorough sweep and found a couple of cameras and microphones that matched the ones found in Emily's home—after that, he didn't feel safe in the building anymore, even with Teddy behind bars. He moved into a condo near the hospital.

Emily missed talking to William, but she knew this separation was for the best. She needed time to work on herself before even attempting to decide if there was anything salvageable between them.

That Monday morning, she sat down to work and got an unexpected call from another private number. Emily stared at the screen, completely frozen. Detective Jackson had promised she would be notified if Teddy was released from jail, but she hadn't received so much as an email from them. Could it be that Teddy found a cellphone while he was imprisoned?

"H-hello?" Emily answered, immediately turning on a recording device on her phone.

"Hi there, may we please be connected with Mrs. Emily Gaunt?"

Emily shivered at the sound of her married name. "This

is, um...this is she, but I don't actually go by my married name anymore. I—"

"Please hold for a call from the Police Corrections Office."

Emily was immediately transferred, waiting on the line, listening to the pleasant sounds of hold music. This was the day she had been waiting for, the day Detective Jackson said could happen sooner rather than later. Teddy's family had a lot of influence; they could pay for very expensive lawyers; he'd told her this made it more likely that he'd be released on bond sooner than what was usual.

"Mrs. Emily Gaunt?"

"Actually, we're divorced, and I returned to my maiden name, so it's Emily Gray now."

"I see...I have Emily Gaunt on the intake form here..."

"What is this about? Was my ex-husband released?" Saying the words made Emily's mouth run dry.

"Ma'am, I'm sorry to be delivering this news over the phone, but I'm afraid there has been an incident. Last night, Thaddeus Gaunt was rushed to the infirmary, suffering from stab wounds to the abdomen and neck. He succumbed to his injuries this morning. I'm very sorry for your loss. Though I suppose if he's your ex-husband, maybe you don't want condolences?"

"What? I...Teddy's dead?" Emily was in shock.

"Yes, ma'am. I wanted to let you know that an officer will be in touch to explain what will happen next and what your instructions are for the body. Again, you have my condolences." Just like that, the officer hung up.

Emily pinched herself to make sure she wasn't dreaming. It was such an unexpected call that she wasn't sure if it was real. Before she worried herself into a panic attack, she called Detective Jackson.

"Is it true?" she asked before he could even get a hello in.

"Emily, I was planning to come and speak to you. Yes, your ex-husband died early this morning."

"What happened?"

"I'm still a little unsure of the details. The incident happened last night, and he passed early this morning, so the official report hasn't been drawn up yet—the department of corrections isn't exactly known for its diligent report-taking."

"They told me he was stabbed in the neck and the abdomen. Who did it? Why did they do it?"

"Teddy got into an argument with his cellmate, Hank Tribble. Hank said Teddy persistently bullied him, insulted his intelligence, and otherwise goaded him until he just broke. Turns out he made a shiv out of a toothbrush, filed down with a piece of metal from the bunkbeds, and stabbed Teddy repeatedly in the abdomen and neck. He hit the artery, and even though they attempted to save him by rushing him to the infirmary, they were unable to stop the bleeding. He's dead, Emily. You no longer have to worry about him getting out of jail and coming after you."

HOURS LATER, Emily sat in her therapist's office, completely exhausted. It had been a few weeks since they last saw each other. With everything that was happening, a therapy session had been the last thing on Emily's mind. Finding out that Teddy was dead caused a kind of breakdown Emily wasn't expecting, and thankfully Dr. Wright had some time for her that day. She sat down in her office and started crying, but she wasn't sure it was because Teddy was dead or if it was from relief that he could no longer hurt her.

"Do you want to talk about it?" Dr. Wright asked. "If you need a space where you can cry, please take as much time as you need. Sometimes a therapy session is just a private hour where you can cry."

"I want to talk. But it's just that I'm...I feel horrible."

"Why?"

Emily didn't want to admit it out loud, but she was glad Teddy was dead. She was afraid that thought made her an evil, horrible person, no better than Teddy.

"Emily," Dr. Wright said, "nothing you can say will make me look at you any differently. Grief is processed in a million different ways, and grief after a traumatic event is a strange and unique creature. You don't have to say a thing; all I ask is that you tell the truth when you're ready to say it."

They sat in silence for a little while longer as Emily decided what to do.

"I feel relieved," she finally said, her voice barely above a whisper. "I feel heartbroken and relieved at the same time. Does that make me a bad person? I feel like it makes me a monster and a victim at the same time. I'm glad he's dead. I'm glad he's dead because that's the only way I could ever be free from him. But I also keep thinking..."

"What is it, Emily?"

"I keep remembering this moment on our honeymoon. We went to the South of France and then to Italy on a little sailboat. It was sunset, and we anchored the boat out in a calm part of the sea so we could watch the sunset and see the stars as we fell asleep. I remember we made love on the deck and lay in each other's arms as the sun set on the sea. It was the best moment of my life, and I thought nothing could get any better than that. Little did I know I was right—the Teddy I went on that trip with, that's the person I kept searching for in my marriage. He was silly and sweet, and he was always finding small ways of showing me he loved me. That one memory—of watching the sun set in my new husband's arms—sustained me for years, and now I don't know how to feel about it. Was it all a waste of time? Is that memory a lie?"

"I think it's okay for you to be relieved," Dr. Wright answered. "You've lived in fear for many years, and it all culminated in a traumatic night where you saw your partner at his absolute worst. You've experienced every single side of Teddy, and it doesn't invalidate the beautiful experiences you two may have had. The fact is, Teddy was never going to let you go. He said so himself, didn't he? He was not going to let go of the idea he had, so it's okay to grieve the old Teddy, the one you fell in love with, and to be relieved you never have to meet the new Teddy ever again. You don't have to be a perfect person in order to be a good one."

Emily nodded. Dr. Wright had a point; Emily wasn't sad about the Teddy she divorced; she wasn't sad to lose the abusive man Teddy turned into while they were married.

The one thing she couldn't admit was that she was happy to be free of him and his bullying. Teddy had finally met his end when his bullying tactics backfired on him—he tried to bully the wrong person and suffered the punishment that went with it.

38

SIX MONTHS LATER

Emily walked into the hotel restaurant and greeted the hostess warmly.

"Ms. Gray, nice to see you again. Your usual table?"

"Sure, Hannah, the usual table will be just fine."

Hannah led Emily to a small booth by the window, perfect for people-watching.

"Your usual order? Rosé with a soda water on the side?"

"No, I'm actually waiting for someone." Emily smiled. "I think he'll be here soon, so I'll just wait, and we'll order together."

For the past six months, Emily regularly worked out of the hotel's co-working space and frequented its little spa. She was working on a novel in her spare time, and she found the hotel to be the perfect combination of quiet people-watching and busy energy to sustain her work. She had a book in her bag, but decided to sit and people-watch instead.

Outside, she saw a young couple sharing a bottle of wine. They were clearly very much in love, their heads were bent closely together, and their feet were entwined under the table. She tried to imagine what they might be saying to each other.

The past six months were shockingly calm compared to the six months before Teddy's death. Emily sold the house she had been living in and found a little loft-style apartment on the edge of the city. It was still quiet, but easy for Emily to get downtown if she wanted to have a night out. Her father begrudgingly understood, and she made it up to him by visiting at least once a week and also by accidentally breaking something in her apartment often enough that he was forced to come by.

Laurie's ribs had healed months ago, and she also became a frequent visitor at Emily's apartment. She started dating the ER doctor who'd treated her injuries, and it was actually going very well. He had the temperament to deal with Laurie's occasional bouts of selfishness and allow it to roll off his back, while also confronting her when she was out of line. What could have been a toxic relationship was actually a well-balanced one, aided by the fact that Laurie was committed to working on her own mental health issues.

Much to Emily's surprise, she ended up in an even better financial state than she'd expected. Teddy had never changed his will, so even though they were divorced, Emily was still listed as the sole beneficiary of his financial and physical assets. It was just as he'd said—he was her husband, and he would always be her husband. Teddy was many things, but he wasn't a man who went back on his word. He believed in his principles, as backward as they were.

Belinda Gaunt didn't even try to fight the inheritance issue. She was an overbearing mother who spoiled her son, but she had also been trapped in an extremely conservative marriage prior to becoming a widow. In her mind, even though she hated Emily with every fiber of her being, her son's opinion always came before her own. Throughout the divorce and Teddy's mental breakdown, he always insisted that Emily was his wife and that relationship needed to be maintained. It was her son's wishes—Belinda didn't have the nerve to go against them. Besides, she had so much money that Teddy's fortune barely made a dent in her own.

For Emily, the money made a massive difference. She didn't *have* to work for Horace anymore, because she didn't have to work at all now, but she continued doing so because she enjoyed it. She was able to pay her father back for the house and set him up for the rest of his life. She sold most of Teddy's assets and donated the proceeds to women's shelters in the area, keeping only one home, which she set up as an office for the local women's shelter.

In six months, she'd completely transformed. Gone was the nervous and agoraphobic woman. In her place was a confident woman who was working on untangling her past. Rather than jump into another relationship, Emily jumped into intensive therapy. She first went to a small rehab center where she could focus on herself, and then graduated to a therapy group for survivors of domestic abuse.

Slowly but surely, Emily was putting her life back together. Old friends from before her marriage reached out to tell her they were sorry for abandoning her. It was understandable—they had no idea Teddy had been the one pulling all the strings. It meant that she was kept busy reuniting with her friends and meeting the little families they'd created in her absence. Occasionally Emily still felt a pang of jealousy—that they'd all had this time to grow with each other and create interesting yet boring lives in the meantime. She knew now that she could have a fresh start, reminding herself of this whenever Teddy's memory popped into her mind.

His memory was impossible to escape. For the first month after his death, Emily had horrible nightmares where she watched him die on the operating table. She had nightmares where she was the one stabbing him, and ones where he was the one stabbing her. To combat these nightmares, she thought back to that night on the boat during their honeymoon. Dr. Wright told her it was only fair that she remember a good memory whenever she was plagued with a bad one.

"But what if I forget? What if I start to replace everything with that good memory, won't that doom me to another horrible relationship?"

"Emily, you don't have to doom yourself. You can have a happy life and still remember your traumatic past. You can learn to recognize the red flags and still move on. If you truly feel like you won't be able to recognize them, you can write it all down in a notebook for yourself to look at in the future. For now, I think it's time you stopped punishing yourself for Teddy's behavior. You don't deserve that, and it's no way to start the next phase of your life."

So that was how Emily ended up sitting at the hotel restaurant, waiting for a date on a Friday night. Months and months went by, and she found she was missing one person from her life. One person who could understand where she was coming from because he'd experienced it himself. One person who was inextricably tied to Teddy's downfall, and therefore also to Emily's renaissance.

"Hi."

Emily looked back from the window and looked up at her date, smiling wildly when she saw him. "Hi," she said.

"What were you looking at?" he asked, sliding into the booth across from her.

"I'm just watching those two on a date. I'm imagining it's a celebration date because the girl just got a promotion, but she thinks it's an unnecessary expense and that they should have gone to Earl's Country Tavern instead."

"A classic choice—that's where all the nurses go to celebrate when someone becomes an RN or starts working in a specialty."

"Exactly, it's the family celebration for us all. Anyway, he thinks her promotion deserves better, but she talks about how Earl's Country Tavern—which you always have to refer to by its full name or by the acronym ECT—made her the woman she is today, so it would be even *more* appropriate for them to celebrate there." She stopped and turned back to her date as she laughed at her silliness. "It's good to see you."

"It's good to see you too. I'm really glad you called. I'd been hoping I'd hear from you."

Emily smiled as William gently took her hand.

"I'm glad I called you too."

THANK YOU FOR READING

Did you enjoy reading *If Only You Knew*? Please consider leaving a review on Amazon. Your review will help other readers to discover the novel.

ABOUT THE AUTHOR

Theo Baxter has followed in the footsteps of his brother, best-selling suspense author Cole Baxter. He enjoys the twists and turns that readers encounter in his stories.

ALSO BY THEO BAXTER

Psychological Thrillers

The Widow's Secret

The Stepfather

Vanished

It's Your Turn Now

The Scorned Wife

Not My Mother

The Lake House

The Honey Trap

If Only You Knew

The Detective Marcy Kendrick Thriller Series

Skin Deep - Book #1

Blood Line - Book #2

Dark Duty - Book #3

Kill Count - Book #4

Made in United States
Orlando, FL
06 September 2024

51228043R00189